WALKING BACK TO HAPPINESS

WALKING BACK TO HAPPINESS

June Francis

Severn House

This first world edition published 2017
in Great Britain and the USA by
SEVERN HOUSE PUBLISHERS LTD of
19 Cedar Road, Sutton, Surrey, England, SM2 5DA

Trade paperback edition first published 2018
In Great Britain and the USA by
SEVERN HOUSE PUBLISHERS LTD
Eardley House, 4 Uxbridge Street, London W8 7SY

British Library Cataloguing in Publication Data
A CIP catalogue record for this title is available from the British Library.

ISBN-13: 978-0-7278-8704-7 (cased)
ISBN-13: 978-1-84751-810-1 (trade paper)
ISBN-13: 978-1-78010-874-2 (e-book)

One

'Lucia, when you finish that job can you make a start decorating the window for Christmas?' called Maggie Colman from the doorway that led into the coffee bar's kitchen, where her husband Josh was in the process of icing a chocolate cake.

'All right,' sang out Lucia, glad to have a change from clearing and setting tables. 'Where are the decorations?'

Blonde-haired Maggie dumped a cardboard box on the table nearest to Lucia and told her where the stepladder was before going back into the kitchen. Lucia fetched the stepladder and set it up at one end of the window before beginning to rummage inside the cardboard box. She dragged out garlands of crêpe paper in a variety of colours and placed them on the table beside the box. Then delved further into the box and found a folded yellow tissue-paper bell, as well as a Father Christmas decoration. As Lucia opened up the Father Christmas and fastened it with the side clip, her thoughts drifted to former Christmases when she and her younger siblings would help their father, David, to decorate the two downstairs rooms in the large Victorian house in Seaforth. Sadly their parents had been killed in a car crash earlier that year, so nineteen-year-old Lucia was going to have her work cut out to make this Christmas an enjoyable one for her younger siblings. Tears pricked her eyes and she forced her thoughts away from her family problems to the job in hand as she hung up one of the garlands before weighing up the merits of the yellow tissue-paper bell against the Father Christmas as the centrepiece for the garland now decorating the window. She looked round for Maggie to ask her opinion, but there was no sign of her; on hearing voices coming from the kitchen, Lucia realized Maggie was deep in conversation with Josh, an experienced chef, who was now the proprietor of the café on Hope Street which had once belonged to his uncle Lenny.

Lucia decided to carry on single-handed. Having fixed on the Santa decoration, she gauged the distance between the stepladder on which she was standing and the centre of the garland. Surely she should be able to manage to pin the Father Christmas in place without falling off? She stretched out and, as she pinned him into place, was forced to slacken her grip on the side of the ladder. The stepladder wobbled and she lost her balance.

At that moment the outer door of the coffee bar opened and a man entered. He paused in the doorway, leaning on a walking stick, watching as the stepladder tipped over. He dropped his walking stick and stepped forward, bracing himself to take her weight on his back, from whence she slid down to the floor.

'You all right, queen?' he asked, turning and reaching down a hand to her.

Lucia looked up into the twinkling blue eyes with eyelashes, the length of which any girl would envy, set in a dimple-cheeked face and with sensuous lips that had a delicious curve to them. She really liked those dimples. Yet there were lines of pain etched on his attractive features due to him having been injured when he had saved a child's life. She recognized him instantly. Maggie's erstwhile boyfriend, ex-jailbird, Tim Murphy. Lucia wondered at him daring to show his face here once more. Surely he must have heard from his brother, Marty, that Maggie was now married and her husband was in charge of the coffee bar?

At the sound of the ladder falling, Josh and Maggie had hurried out of the kitchen.

Lucia watched Maggie's face as recognition dawned in her eyes. Would there be trouble when Josh realized who the man was? Lucia wondered. But Josh, having ascertained that Lucia was unharmed, simply picked up the stepladder and took it away.

'So they let you out then?' said Maggie coldly, folding her arms across her chest and staring at Tim.

'Don't be like that, Maggie. I've done my time and learned my lessons the hard way. I'm on the straight and narrow now; I have to be for my son, Jerry,' responded Tim. 'Actually, I'm looking for lodgings for us both and wondered – what with you coming into contact with so many people here – whether you'd heard of anything, or if you could keep your ear open for a place that might suit us? We're staying at our Marty and Irene's at the moment and, what with Josie there as well, it's a bit crowded.' He paused before adding, 'I need three rooms on the ground floor. Can't do stairs so easily, since I damaged my hip saving that little lad's life when that road hog hit me outside my garage.'

'You've come to the wrong place, Tim,' said Maggie. 'Most of our customers are teenagers.'

Lucia felt a stir of sympathy as well as excitement as she remembered the conversation she'd had only yesterday evening with the old lady who lived next door. Lucia's seventeen-year-old brother Michael had been clearing snow from their neighbour's front step, and Mrs Hudson had told her that her lodgers had moved out and she needed to find someone else to take their place.

'I know someone who is wanting to rent out a few rooms,' said Lucia. 'She lives next door to me in Seaforth. She's an elderly widow who lost her only son in the war and the house is far too big for her. Her previous lodgers, a married couple with three children, have been given a council house.'

She watched Tim's downcast expression brighten and he said, 'Thanks, queen. Give us the address and I'll go and have a butcher's.'

Lucia did so and he thanked her again and left immediately. Josh came out of the kitchen and said, 'Has he gone already? Did the sight of me frighten him off?'

'No, Lucia was able to help him and so there was no need for him to stay.' Maggie smiled at her husband, who looked puzzled until Lucia explained the situation.

Josh said, 'I hope you know what you're doing, kid.'

'Mam and Dad always said we were put on this earth to help each other, and that's what I've done – and Mrs Hudson has the same outlook on life,' said Lucia, who could not wait until it was time for her to finish so she could hurry home and find out if Tim had called on her neighbour.

When Lucia arrived home, she wasted no time in popping next door to speak to Mrs Hudson, who was all of a twitter after Tim's visit and wanted to talk, so she invited Lucia to sit down and have a cup of tea and a slice of homemade ginger cake.

'There is something you should know about him,' said Lucia after an inward struggle.

'If it's about him having been in prison, he told me. He said that it was only fair that I should know before he and his son move in. He's determined to go straight, for the boy's sake. He told me that he is planning to write a book about his experiences, which means he'll be working from home. Apparently, due to some injuries preventing him from continuing as a mechanic, he has to find another source of income.'

Lucia was surprised by the news but pleased that Tim had been honest with her neighbour. Realizing that time was getting on, she left soon after. Her fifteen-year-old sister, Theresa, was seeing to their evening meal, a potentially hazardous situation since it involved having several pans on the stove. She could only hope Michael was keeping his eye on the younger children, Gabrielle, James and Joseph. An unwelcome task if he had homework to do. He would be leaving school next year and good exam results would mean a better chance of a decent job. What she dreaded was him getting interested in girls. She accepted that, sooner or later, he would meet someone and get serious and want to get married and have his own life, but she hoped it would be years off yet.

As the evening progressed, Lucia found her thoughts drifting back to Tim and his son. She wondered when they would move in and wished she had thought to ask Mrs Hudson. Not wanting to appear over-eager or nosey, she waited until the next day to send Theresa to ask Mrs Hudson if there was anything she wanted from the shops, and also to enquire when her new lodgers would be moving in. As Lucia prepared to leave for work, and the children were getting ready for school, she wondered whether Tim Murphy would have in mind a Catholic school for Jerry. If so, it would mean that he could join Gabrielle, James and Joseph at Our Lady, Star of the Sea Primary School. Theresa returned with the news that Mr Murphy and his little boy would be moving in that day. 'Mrs Hudson also wants me to do some shopping for her, seeing the pavements are so frosty. Is there anything you want me to get for our tea?' added Theresa.

Lucia told her to buy some mince, potatoes, carrots and an onion, as well as a loaf. Later, when Lucia arrived at the coffee bar, she had already steeled herself to face a barrage of questions and more warnings from Josh and Maggie concerning Tim. Since her parents' deaths, and despite the fact she had an aunt living not too far away, as well as her uncle, Francis, who was a priest in Liverpool, Josh and Maggie had behaved like surrogate parents to her, even though neither of them was all that much older than she was.

'So did Tim turn up at your neighbour's house?' Maggie asked as soon as Lucia entered the coffee bar.

'Yes, and before you ask, he told her that he'd been in prison.'

'Even so, don't be fooled by him – and tell your neighbour the same,' said Maggie. 'He can be a right charmer when he has a mind to be.'

'From what I've heard, I wouldn't trust him as far as I could throw him,' Josh said before returning to the kitchen.

While Lucia appreciated their concern, she was irritated by their lack of trust in her having enough common sense to be on her guard against such a man. She just hoped they wouldn't go on and on about it. As it was, Lucia need not have worried about what else the couple might say, because the coffee bar was so busy during the next hour or two that the three of them were rushed off their feet and there was no time for discussing Tim. Lucia was relieved when one of the other part-time waitresses, sixth-former Annie Wood, arrived to share the load.

Lucia was glad to arrive home that evening, although there was no opportunity to put her feet up even then. Only once the evening meal was over, dishes washed and the three younger children were in bed, could she relax a little. Theresa settled with a library book in front of the glowing coal fire, while Lucia was letting down the hem of one of Theresa's old dresses for Gabrielle. She stretched out on the sofa after switching on the small black-and-white telly on the sideboard to watch *Coronation Street*.

'Do we have to have this on?' asked Michael, on entering the room.

'What's it to you?' asked Theresa. 'You told me you were going out.'

Lucia stared at her brother. 'You didn't mention going out to me.'

'Do I have to have your permission for everything I do?' said Michael.

'I'm responsible for you,' said Lucia.

'I'm old enough to take care of myself,' he said.

'No, you're not,' she retorted.

At that moment there was a ring of the doorbell and Michael said, 'I'll get it.'

Before Lucia could rise from the chair, he had left the room. She hurried after him, and was a few feet behind him when he opened the front door. On the step stood Tim, and a boy holding his hand, who was as fair-haired as his father, with the same blue eyes. Tim gazed past Michael and smiled at Lucia. 'I hope I'm not disturbing you, but I just wanted to thank you again for your help. Mrs Hudson is a sweetheart. She told me that several of your family go to Our Lady, Star of the Sea. I'm going tomorrow to see if Jerry can be enrolled there and wondered if we could go along with you to school in the morning.'

'Actually it's my brother, Michael, who usually takes the younger ones, but if you don't mind escorting them, it would save him a job,' she said. 'I'd invite you and Jerry in to meet the boys, only they're in bed.'

'Who is this?' asked Michael, regarding Tim suspiciously.

'This is Mr Murphy. He's Mrs Hudson's new lodger. You might have heard Uncle Francis mention him in the past?' said Lucia. 'Mr Murphy used to live in his parish.'

'Right,' said Michael. 'I'd better be on my way or I'll be too late.'

'Where are you going?' asked Lucia, making a grab for him as he forced his way past Tim, throwing him off balance. 'Hey, watch it, Michael,' she added, 'where are your manners?'

'Sorry,' sang out Michael, heading down the step. 'I'll be back by ten.'

'You'd better be,' said Lucia under her breath.

'I can see you have your hands full,' said Tim. 'How old is he?'

'Seventeen.'

'I remember being that age,' he said, thinking back to that period in his life when he had got involved with a gang led by Will Donahue, who one of the girls had called charismatic. Tim had never heard the word before and had looked it up in a dictionary. He'd had to admit at the time that the girl was right in believing there was something about the older lad that attracted one to him. He had enormous self-confidence that he could succeed in anything he tackled, which was inspirational, encouraging younger ones to throw in their lot with him. He also had a way with words that the girls seemed to fall for. Suddenly Tim realized that Lucia was staring at him, as if expecting him to say something more. 'I was struggling to be a man and took a wrong turning. I won't keep you any longer. I'd best get Jerry to bed.'

The following morning, when Jerry met Joseph, it was obvious to Lucia that it was the beginning of a beautiful friendship. They took to each other straightaway. They could have even been taken for brothers, having the same shade of fair hair and similar wiry build.

As the week progressed, Lucia was concerned that Tim might be missing his son's company, because he seemed to be spending a lot of time at their house playing with Joseph, but Tim assured her that he was glad his son had found a friend so swiftly, adding that he hoped Jerry wasn't proving a nuisance. To which she responded that he was a well-behaved lad and she too was glad that the two boys got on so well. Recalling Mrs Hudson telling her that Tim was writing a book, she guessed that Jerry's absence afforded him time to write in peace.

He agreed that he did need several hours of quiet a day, and then he asked after her family. 'Mrs Hudson told me that your parents died earlier this year and that you have three younger brothers and two sisters to care for. That's tough. You really do have your hands full.'

'It isn't easy. At the moment the thing I'm dreading most is Christmas, as it will be our first since Mam and Dad were killed. Still, my aunt and her family don't live too far away, and there's Uncle Francis, who I believe you know. He used to be your parish priest.'

'Father Francis!' exclaimed Tim. 'Fancy him being your uncle. He was a great help to me when I was in prison; visited me regularly, as well as visiting me mam. She still lives in his parish.'

Lucia was pleased that he was prepared to talk openly to her about his having been in prison. She liked his honesty, although she had not forgotten Maggie's warning.

'I don't suppose you get out much in the evenings because of the children,' Tim said, 'but I'm thinking of going to the Cavern this Friday and I wouldn't mind some company if you could fix up someone to stay with the kids? Mrs Hudson said she'd listen out for Jerry.'

'I'd enjoy that,' said Lucia, surprised by the invitation and able to guess what Maggie and Josh would say if she told them of it. Although Tim appeared to be a good few years older than her, she was not going to allow that to bother her. He was an interesting man and she was looking forward to going out with him.

But first she had to see if Michael and Theresa would stay in on Friday evening and look after the younger ones.

'Why?' responded Michael when she asked him. 'Where are you going?'

'I'm going to the Cavern. Mr Murphy asked me to keep him company. Not that it's any of your business,' she replied.

'It's probably his way of saying thank you for putting up with Jerry so much,' said Theresa.

'Maybe,' said Lucia. 'Anyway, I could do with a night out.'

Neither her brother nor her sister disputed that, so she took that as a yes and considered what she should wear for her first night out in ages. She hadn't bought any new clothes for a while, so everything in her wardrobe was fifties-style. Would Tim care that much about how she looked? Hopefully he would understand why her clothes were dated. She took out a straight, dark green skirt with kick pleats, and a pale pink blouse with short sleeves, then rooted in the top drawer of the chest of drawers and found a Waspy belt and an unopened packet of American Tan nylon stockings and a suspender belt. In a Wedgwood powder bowl, which her aunt Babs had bought her last time she was in England, she found a necklace of white plastic pop-it beads and decided they would do for jewellery.

With her outfit settled, Lucia decided there was nothing for her to worry about, but to look forward to her date with Tim. The days passed slowly, but at last Friday dawned. At the coffee bar, Lucia was counting the hours. As soon as her shift finished she was off, praying that everything would be all right at home so she would be able to go out. She need not have worried. Both Theresa and Michael seemed in a good mood, happy to stay in and mind the younger ones, who were happy too, as it was Friday, which meant no school in the morning. They also thought that entitled them to be allowed to stay up an hour later, but Michael wasn't having any of it and insisted they went to bed, although he did say he would let them have their lights on for longer so they could read or play quietly.

Tim called for Lucia at seven thirty and they caught a bus into town. As they left the bus in the centre of Liverpool, she was aware of a bubbling excitement. It seemed an age since she had been in town of an evening and she had forgotten about that air of expectancy in the crowds of people out for a good time after working hard all week.

She was also aware of the extra excitement when it was obvious there were several ships in from foreign parts, proof of which was the number of sailors in unfamiliar uniforms and the buzz of voices speaking broken English or in foreign languages. Lucia hugged Tim's arm, not wanting to get separated from him amongst the bustling crowds. Some were in town to see a play, show or a film, or simply for a drink in one of the many pubs or a meal in a restaurant. At last they managed to break free from the mass of people, and Tim took her, via a short cut, to Mathew Street, where the Cavern was situated in a narrow thoroughfare of tall buildings that had once been warehouses.

There was a queue outside which Tim and Lucia joined. It was not until they were inside and listening to the first act that she noticed her step-cousin, Tony, was there with Nick Walker, whom she had first met in her aunt Nellie's house when Nick had auditioned to replace Jimmy Miller, a sailor who had decided to go back to sea. Lucia had once had a crush on Jimmy and it had almost broken her heart when he had married a friend of his sister, Irene. Lucia told Tim about her step-cousin, Tony, having signed a recording contract a few years ago as a solo artist, and that she hoped he was going to get up on the Cavern's minuscule stage and sing. When he did so the applause was deafening, and Tim commented on the pureness and the range of his voice.

'I must write him up for the *Mersey Beat*,' he said.

Lucia looked at him in surprise. 'That only came out earlier this year – how is it you think they'll accept an article from you?'

'I know a bloke from the Jacaranda Club, who's a photographer now and works for the newspaper. He said he'd put a word in for me as I've always been interested in music and used to write about it years ago.'

'Have you ever sung or played an instrument?'

'No, I was never encouraged to when I was a kid. To be honest my father positively discouraged me. I'd have probably been rubbish anyway.'

'You shouldn't put yourself down,' said Lucia. 'Anyway, would you like me to introduce you to Tony? He's my aunt Nellie's stepson and he has quite a story to tell. He's part-Italian, so you can ask him about his childhood and how he came to Liverpool and got into music.'

'Thanks. You're great.' Tim kissed her cheek and, taking her hand, added, 'Lead the way.'

She drew him through the throng to where Tony and Nick were standing to one side of the stage with a young man and a girl she had never seen before. Lucia introduced Tim to her cousin and his friend and looked questioningly at the latter, who introduced the two strangers to her and Tim as brother and sister, Chris and Grace. 'I stayed with their family after Kenneth, my adoptive father, was murdered,' added Nick. 'Chris and I were at the Liverpool Institute, and now he's a reporter on the *Echo* and Grace and I are going steady.'

Tim surprised Lucia by saying, 'I have a reporter from the *Echo* helping me write my book. In fact it was Isabella who suggested I write about my life.'

'I imagine she wants a warts-and-all story from you,' said Chris. 'She's a tough cookie and has a way of worming any well-kept secrets out of people, especially men – but then she is a looker, and knows how to employ her charms to the best effect.'

'I've no interest in her in that way,' said Tim. 'I discovered some time ago that looks aren't everything. Kindness and having interests in common are more important in a relationship.'

Lucia could not help noticing Tony and Nick glancing down at hers and Tim's interlocked hands. No doubt that information would go back to her aunt Nellie. Tony asked what she was doing on Christmas Eve. She told him that she would be staying home and watching telly after the kids had hung up their stockings and gone to sleep. 'Not that there'll be much in the stockings this year,' she sighed. 'For that reason, I didn't encourage them to send notes to Santa or take the younger ones to the grotto in town.' She smiled at her cousin in a 'what can you do?' kind of way, and Tony looked thoughtful but remained silent.

Shortly after, Lucia asked Tim if they could leave, as she didn't want to be too late getting home. He agreed immediately; it was just as well that they left when they did because once outside they could hear foghorns on the river. Although the fog in the city streets wasn't too dense, there was no knowing if it might turn into a peasouper in the next hour and the buses stop running.

It was only later, as she was getting ready for bed, that she wondered whether it had been a mistake to introduce Tim to Nick. Nick was a policeman, having followed his father, Sam Walker, into the force. Sam had now risen through the ranks and was a detective inspector in Liverpool but, given Tim's past, there was little doubt that he would be known to him.

Two

A few days before Christmas, Lucia called in at her aunt Nellie's on the way home from work. Delighted to see her, Nellie led her upstairs and showed her several parcels. 'These are for you and the kids. Amazing the post got them to us in time, bearing in mind the ships have had terrible trouble docking due to those awful dense fogs in the Irish Sea.'

Lucia looked at the stamps on the parcels and saw that they were American. They must have been sent by her mother's younger sister, Babs, who had married a GI and moved to the States shortly after the war. Her mother had often said that Babs was the flighty one in the family. Lucia had only met her once and had wished her own mother had possessed a small part of Babs's glamour, vivaciousness and generosity of spirit.

Babs had written shortly after Lottie and David's deaths, regretting being unable to fly over for the funeral. Babs was a widow with two sons, her in-laws' only grandchildren, and so the ties between them were strong. After her husband's death, she had decided to stay in America, rather than return to Liverpool to be nearer her sisters and brother, but she wrote regularly to her siblings.

'Do you want to leave them here and open them Christmas Day? You can all come for dinner . . .' said Nellie.

'Could Uncle Michelangelo bring them to ours on Christmas Eve after eight o'clock instead? We'll be staying home on Christmas Day. Mam and Dad always invited Mrs Hudson to have dinner with us, so I'm planning on keeping up the custom.'

'OK, come on Boxing Day instead. But I hope you're not expecting your uncle to dress up as Santa and come on a sleigh?' joked Nellie.

'Now that would be something, but my dreams don't reach that far,' said Lucia. 'Still, seeing these parcels has made my day.'

On her way home, along Bridge Road, Lucia wondered if she had been daft not to open the parcels to see what was inside.

It would have been more sensible knowing what her aunt had sent them. She thought how some relatives would have just sent money, as her great-aunt on her father's side had done before she died. It meant a lot to Lucia that Babs had gone to the trouble of shopping for individual gifts for them, knowing that it would cost her a fair amount to send them to England.

But the surprises for Lucia were not yet over, because the next time Nick came into the coffee bar, he took her aside and said, 'I reminded Dad about your mam and dad having been killed and how tough it was going to be for you and the kids this Christmas, so he said that he would give your particulars to the Police Benevolent Fund; so you'll probably get something from them to help you out and make your Christmas a better one.'

She was thrilled, not only at the thought of getting help from the PBF but also that Nick and his father had taken the trouble to help them; she thanked him fervently.

After Nick left, Maggie came over to Lucia and said, 'What did Nick have to say? If you played your cards right and had nothing to do with that ex-jailbird, he might ask you out.'

'Nick is just a good friend.'

'He told me last time he dropped by that he'd seen you at the Cavern with Tim.'

'So what?'

'You know what. Take heed of what I've told you, Lucia, and have nothing to do with Tim.'

'Asking me out was just his way of saying thanks for having his son round at ours so he can write in peace,' said Lucia, annoyed at herself for making up an excuse. 'Besides Nick is dating his friend Chris' sister, so he's not going to ask me out. Chris works at the *Echo* and knows the woman who is helping Tim write his book.' She wondered what that might entail, recalling what Tim had said to Chris about not considering good looks as important as kindness, but could he remain immune to Isabella's charms when they would be working in close proximity for months? So far, Lucia had not caught sight of any attractive female visitors to her neighbour's house, but maybe Isabella visited Tim to assist with his writing while Lucia was at work. She thought she might casually ask Mrs Hudson whether any 'family or friends' had been to visit her lodger.

Her neighbour's response was immediate and her expression disapproving. 'If you mean that woman reporter, she's been here a few times and had the nerve to tell me that they didn't want to be disturbed by my offering cups of tea or coffee. She made me feel as if she thought I'd make that an excuse to see what they were up to.'

Lucia nodded thoughtfully, curious as to whether theirs was more than just a working relationship. She would like to get a look at Isabella, especially since hearing what Chris had had to say about her. But she was to see someone much closer to Tim before she caught sight of the elusive Isabella. Tim's sister, Peggy, who lived in Bootle with her husband Pete and toddler daughter in his mother's house, paid her a visit.

'I was just after visiting our Tommy and Jerry, so I thought I'd pop by and see how you are getting on,' Peggy said. 'Christmas must be a difficult time for you.'

'It is, but things could be worse,' said Lucia, thinking it seemed strange hearing Tim referred to as Tommy, even though that was the name by which he had been christened. She put on the kettle before shooing the children out to play. 'I've never forgotten Mam being told by Aunt Nellie always to remember that kids have big ears, so don't go talking secrets in front of them,' she said to Peggy before adding, 'Aunt Babs in America has sent presents for us via Aunt Nellie. Tony's dad is going to deliver them here on Christmas Eve.'

'How lovely!' said Peggy. 'That'll make the big day better for you. I suppose you'll be going to Nellie's for your dinner?'

'No,' Lucia explained, 'I plan on inviting Mrs Hudson to Christmas dinner. It's something Mam and Dad always did and I thought I should continue with it. I'm presuming Tim and Jerry will be spending Christmas Day with your family.'

'As it happens, Mam wants us all to have dinner at her house, seeing as how it's years since we've spent it together, what with Tommy having been in prison and before that London and before that Australia. Not that we knew about his being in Australia until a few years ago.' Peggy stared at Lucia. 'Has he told you anything about those years since he moved in next door? I heard on the grapevine that you've been seeing quite a bit of each other.'

Lucia smiled at the fact that the local grapevine was alive and well. 'No, he hasn't spoken about those times, but he is writing a book.'

'So he just told me. Mind you, he's always been secretive – probably with good reason given all the trouble he's got himself into over the years. Wait until I tell Mam and our Lil. I'll mention it to our Marty, too. Although he might already know; he might have kept quiet about it because Tommy wanted to tell us himself as a surprise at Christmas.'

'What does he think of the idea of spending Christmas with the family?' asked Lucia.

'He's not keen. He and our Lil have never got on. She thoroughly disapproves of him and so does her husband, and they live with Mam, of course.'

'So isn't he going to go?'

'He said he'll drop by early morning but not stay to eat. He's decided to call in on his dead wife's family afterwards and then go home. I think he's making a mistake going there because he never got on with his mother-in-law or her youngest son, but he feels he owes it to Jerry that they should visit them. The family live not far from Mam's. He said he's got somewhere else to go in the evening.'

Lucia wondered if he was seeing Isabella later in the day but kept quiet. Perhaps Mrs Hudson had considered inviting Tim and Jerry to share a Christmas meal with her. Lucia decided not to delay speaking to her elderly neighbour about her plans for Christmas. Maybe she should invite all of next door's residents to lunch, so that is what she did.

But the following morning Mrs Hudson told Lucia she had just received a letter from her younger brother down south saying that his wife was seriously ill in hospital and could she possibly come down and stay and help with the children over Christmas.

'Of course, you must go,' said Lucia.

'I knew you'd say that,' said Mrs Hudson. 'He's family so I told him I'd love to see the children. Especially at this time of year.'

'Have you told Tim?'

'Yes, and he says I must go, that I'll regret it if I don't.'

'Then there's your answer,' Lucia responded. 'Tim and Jerry can still come here for dinner.' Even as she spoke, Lucia wondered what Maggie would have to say if she was to hear that Tim and Jerry would be sharing the Brookes' Christmas dinner without Mrs Hudson being present. No doubt Lucia would be warned afresh about falling for his charm. She decided to keep quiet about her plan and not tell anyone.

Three days before Christmas, Jerry told Lucia that his father had said she was not to worry about a bird for Christmas dinner as he would arrange for a turkey to be delivered to her on Christmas Eve. This convinced her that she had done the right thing in inviting Tim and Jerry to share their Christmas meal. She decided that evening to bring the Christmas decorations down from the attic so she and the children could decorate the rooms downstairs, an activity that they all enjoyed and which also involved making their own paper chains. The preparations were not without their sad moments as they remembered their father having always involved himself with the cutting and pasting alongside them at the table. Tears were forced back, and all forbore to mention their last Christmas, when he'd brought home a tree and the lights had blown but he had managed to fix them.

The following evening Tim was gazing up at the lowering sky which had a yellowish tinge to it, hoping it wouldn't snow. Despite knowing that Jerry would be delighted if it did, Tim could only think it would make travelling more difficult. He should never have promised his mother that he and Jerry would visit her on Christmas morning. Public transport was Sunday service and could not always be relied on to turn up on time and, although they could probably cadge a lift from his brother, Marty, who lived a couple of miles away, it would mean it would be a tight squeeze as Irene and their two children would be in the car as well. Besides, he and Jerry would have to make their own way home as they weren't staying for dinner. Perhaps it would be more sensible if he took Jerry to visit his mother on Christmas Eve. Maybe he would even suggest taking her into town, and them having turkey and all the trimmings in a restaurant. He felt certain that would make her happy.

Tim was right. His mother was delighted with the idea and

suggested one of her own. 'Let's take Jerry to Lewis's grotto to see Father Christmas as well. They've got a nice restaurant there, too. I know it'll be crowded in town but the atmosphere will be good.'

Tim agreed, remembering how his father had always been against such visits when he was a boy. William had had no time for the myth of Father Christmas, and had never been the kind of father who spent time playing with his children. Despite not having been round when Jerry had been born and not having known of his existence until a few years ago, Tim was determined that, with God's help, he could be the kind of father he would have liked to have had.

The trip to town was a success and, helped by his mother's advice, Tim was able to buy presents for his nieces and nephews that they would welcome. He left them under the Christmas tree at his mother's house, so they would be able to open them on Christmas Day. He had already bought his son's main present and stowed it upstairs in Mrs Hudson's house. All there was to do now was to look forward to the festivities and think what to take with him to the Brookes' that all the family could share – although he really should buy Lucia something separate. Perhaps that record she had mentioned on their night out. He had bought Isabella the perfume she had said she liked, as he was supposed to be seeing her on Christmas evening. Apparently she was throwing a party at her flat in Everton. He had been depending on Mrs Hudson to look after Jerry, but considered it likely that Lucia would be willing to have him instead.

Later that evening, it felt unreal carrying the parcels next door. A bit like being Father Christmas. It was getting on for eleven o'clock by the time he had completed his task. Lucia offered him a hot drink but he refused, remembering he had Jerry's bicycle to bring down from the attic, which was going to be a struggle. He was tired and his damaged hip was aching, but he told himself it shouldn't be too difficult wheeling the bicycle downstairs once it was out of the attic.

It proved harder than he'd thought, though, because when he moved the handlebars the front wheel twisted, one of his legs got caught up in it, and he and the bike tumbled downstairs. He had a struggle disentangling himself. Fortunately the bike was undamaged, unlike himself. He limped down the next flight of stairs to the ground floor, knowing he was going to need help to get the bicycle to their apartment and into Jerry's bedroom. The only person he could think of was Lucia, but no doubt she would be busy playing Father Christmas and wouldn't want to be disturbed. Then he realized that it was unlikely that she would be alone fulfilling that task. No doubt Michael would be helping her fill stockings for the younger ones. Leaving the front door ajar he went and tapped gently next door. As luck would have it, Michael answered his knock, and did not hesitate to hurry back with him to Mrs Hudson's once he heard of Tim's dilemma.

When Michael returned home, Lucia demanded to know where he had been and what he had been up to. 'What do you think I was doing at this time of night on Christmas Eve?' he asked.

'I don't know, that's why I'm asking. It just seems so odd you disappearing the way you did.'

'It was Mr Murphy from next door. He wanted me to help him.'

'Do what?' asked Lucia suspiciously.

'Carry a bike downstairs. He was doing it himself when he fell and the bike went with him.'

'Was he hurt?'

Michael nodded. 'He was limping more than usual.'

'The poor man. Has he sent for the doctor?'

'I didn't ask him. I wheeled the bike into Jerry's bedroom and then came home. I wouldn't worry. He's a tough nut. Must be with all he's done.'

'What d'you mean by that?' asked Lucia.

'Don't pretend. You know he's been in prison. I don't understand why you've asked him here tomorrow. I must admit I couldn't help wondering where he got the bike from. He doesn't go out to work, so how can he afford it?'

'You're suggesting he stole it?'

'I'm just wondering, that's all.'

'It could be that members of his family all clubbed together to buy it,' Lucia said. 'Although I did hear that he received a big insurance pay-out for the injuries he incurred after saving that boy's life.'

'So he's rich.'

'I don't know about rich. No doubt he has to make the money last until he starts earning from his writing.'

'I bet he buys you a good present. He fancies you.'

'What makes you think that?' asked Lucia, flushing.

'The way he looks at you. Besides, you help him out by having Jerry here. I sometimes think he's using you.'

'I'd rather be useful than just waste my time doing nothing.'

'You sound like Dad. He did more favours for people than proper paid jobs.'

'He had a kind heart.'

'Yeah, but I remember Mam muttering behind his back that doing favours doesn't pay the bills.'

'She loved him, though.'

'Of course she did. He was a loveable person, seldom lost his temper with her.'

'Which was important to her because her father always used to pick on her. Anyway, it's time we were both in bed. The kids will be awake early and tomorrow will be a busy day.'

As Lucia climbed into bed, wishing she had not placed all the hot-water bottles in the kids' beds, she thought of Tim and hoped he was all right after his fall. Should she have gone next door and seen for herself? She chuckled as she imagined what Maggie and Aunt Nellie would have to say if she had done so and ended up spending half the night alone in the house with him. Suddenly she began to ask herself why she worried so much about his welfare and why she enjoyed his company so much. It certainly wasn't that he tried to charm her as Maggie said he would. Although she did love his smile and enjoyed listening to him talk about music. She supposed she would have to get a lot closer to him before he'd tell her more about his past and what his married life had been like. Not that he had spent much of it with his wife, from the snatches of conversation she had overheard at Nellie's music evenings when Peggy, Irene, Maggie, Marty and Pete had been present.

Lucia fell asleep with that thought still on her mind. She was roused from sleep by Gabrielle, James and Joseph telling her that Father Christmas had been. They proceeded to climb into bed with her, dragging bulging stockings with them and placing their freezing feet on her legs. There was a strong aroma of tangerines as they emptied the contents of the stockings on the floral cotton eiderdown. There were several lead soldiers for James, as well as a penny whistle, a packet of coloured pencils and a colouring book, fruit, nuts, a bar of fruit and nut chocolate, a sherbet dab and several pennies. Joseph had some similar items, as did Gabrielle, although she had a small rag doll and a Walt Disney film jigsaw. Joseph had an Airfix aeroplane kit, and a paint box.

'There are more presents for all of us,' Lucia said.

The children's eyes brightened. 'Who are they from? Aunt Nellie?'

She shook her head. 'I think Aunt Nellie will have yours on her Christmas tree at her house and you can have them tomorrow when we visit. The presents I'm talking about are from our other aunt, Babs, who lives in America. They're in the attic waiting to be brought down and opened.'

The three children immediately scrambled from the bed and made for the door. 'Get Michael to go up with you,' ordered Lucia. 'They're to be taken to the kitchen and placed on the sofa. We'll open them all together after breakfast.'

As they hurried out and scampered along the landing, Lucia snuggled beneath the bedcovers for an extra five minutes, remembering Christmases past when her father had produced a stocking of his own, supposedly left by Santa, and removed from it a potato, an onion, a carrot and a turnip. He had pretended to cry and in response the children had kissed him and offered him one of each of their presents. Her mother had gathered the vegetables and said she would cook them for dinner. At the happy memory, she wiped away a tear.

It was only as they were finishing breakfast that Lucia remembered about church. How could she have forgotten to take the children to Midnight Mass on Christmas Eve? The family had attended that service as long as she could remember. She recalled her mother saying that was when Christmas really started. She felt as if she had failed her mother but felt certain that God would understand in the circumstances.

Once the table was cleared, the parcels from America were placed on it and the wrappings were torn off them in haste.

The contents were greeted with oohs and aahhs. There was a Barbie doll for Gabrielle with a couple of sets of clothes. A dirndl skirt in pinks and mauves with a net underskirt and a knitted pink lacy top caused Theresa's brown eyes to glow with delight. Her mother had been inclined to buy more sombre wear than clothes of a bright hue. For Joseph and James there were cowboy outfits and a couple of boys' adventure books; Michael's parcel contained a striped Sloppy Joe and a baseball cap, bat and ball. As for Lucia, there was a vanity case containing Max Factor cosmetics as well as toiletries.

Glancing around the table, Lucia realized how much thought her aunt had put into choosing the presents, although she must have thought James was younger than he was, and said, 'Let's thank God for Auntie Barbara and later we'll write a letter thanking her for these marvellous presents.' The children cheered and then bowed their heads and put their hands together.

Afterwards, the younger ones went into the front room, where Michael had carried a shovelful of the burning coals from the kitchen fire and placed them in the grate in the front room and built on to it, so the parlour soon warmed up.

Lucia and Theresa set about preparing dinner, which would be served around two o'clock. Lucia stuffed the turkey and placed it in the oven while her sister prepared the vegetables. She wondered what time Tim and Jerry would arrive. She hoped Tim had recovered from his fall and wondered if perhaps she should call round and see how he was doing. She would be really disappointed if he did not feel well enough to share Christmas dinner with them.

Three

As Lucia stepped outside the house, she heard the front door of the neighbouring house open. A few moments later her front gate clicked and she watched as Tim held the gate wide with one hand while he guided Jerry, astride his new bicycle, on to Lucia's step.

'You must have read my mind,' said Lucia. 'I was just coming to see if you were all right after your fall.' Her smile faded as he drew closer and she got a good look at his bruised face.

'I look worse than I feel,' he said.

She did not argue with him, only staring intently as he came up to her. His nose appeared to be swollen and was cut in a couple of places.

'Is it OK for Jerry to bring his bike inside?' Tim asked. 'I was going to accompany him round the block so he could have a good ride, but it's far too slippery underfoot.'

'Too right it is. Yes, bring the bike in. I suppose he was reluctant to let it out of his sight?'

Tim nodded as he lifted the bike and Jerry over the threshold with Lucia's help and wished her a Happy Christmas. She wished him the same, kissing him and Jerry. She asked whether Tim had visited Bootle hospital after his accident.

He replied: 'I know my face is a mess but it could have been worse. I don't appear to have broken any bones or damaged any teeth.'

'So they X-rayed you?'

He placed a hand in the region of his heart. 'I cannot tell a lie, I didn't go to the hospital. I had no wish to go on Christmas Eve, and with the weather the way it was! I'm OK, honest.'

'You don't look it.'

'The cuts and bruises are just superficial. They don't hurt much and I want to spend this day with Jerry, not in hospital, so please, don't start fussing.'

She shrugged. 'OK, it's your life. Come through into the

kitchen and I'll make you a hot drink. Jerry can ride his bike up and down the lobby if he's careful. I'll get Michael to keep an eye on him.'

Tim thanked her.

She led the way into the kitchen and found Michael and Gabrielle there. She explained what she wanted Michael to do. He didn't look too pleased.

'I haven't got time for this. I'm meeting someone and I have to leave now if I'm to be back in time for dinner,' he said.

'Who?' asked Lucia.

'Mind your own business,' said Michael. 'You don't have to worry. I'll be back in time for dinner.'

Lucia turned her back on him and went to put the kettle on.

Without another word, Michael lifted his coat from the newel post at the foot of the stairs and left the house, ignoring Tim who was staring at him.

'You are a bit of a fusspot, you know,' said Theresa.

Lucia stared up at her sister, who was leaning over the banister rail upstairs.

'How long have you been listening?'

'Long enough. I wish you could have heard yourself. You sounded just like Mam. It's not just the way you order Michael around. It's the way you spoke to Jerry's dad. He's a grown man, Lucia, and I believe he has a mother. I doubt he's looking for another one.'

'He had a bad fall and thinks he can carry on like it never happened.'

'Well, that's up to him. It's really none of your business.'

'I suppose you think what our Michael does is none of my business either?' said Lucia, unable to conceal her annoyance.

'I didn't say that, but you should try trusting him. He is seventeen.'

'I'm worried he might be seeing a girl,' said Lucia, folding her arms and hugging herself.

'So what if he is? He's more likely to stay out of trouble than if he got involved with a gang that goes looking for a bit of excitement,' said Theresa. 'Anyway, is there anything else you want me to do?'

'You can set the table, use the best cloth, the lace-trimmed one that was Grandma's.'

While Theresa set the table, Lucia brewed a pot of tea and placed several of Maggie's mince pies on a plate. Tim was seated at the table, 'Is everything OK?' he asked. 'Jerry isn't being a nuisance, is he?'

'No, James and Joseph heard the commotion and came to see what was happening. They're admiring the new bike,' replied Lucia, pouring tea.

Theresa entered the kitchen, greeted Tim and sat at the table. 'Has Lucia told you about our aunt that lives in America? She sent us some smashing presents.'

'That was kind of her. Whereabouts does she live?' asked Tim.

'California,' said Theresa. 'Was there a letter with the presents?' She glanced in Lucia's direction.

Lucia nodded. 'I was going to read it out at dinner time.'

'Couldn't I read it now and you can just tell the younger ones what it says?'

'If that's what you want.' Lucia removed the letter from the pocket of her apron and handed it to her sister, who wasted no time in reading it and spouting out what Lucia already knew. 'Aunt Babs is coming over next year and is bringing her mother-in-law with her. I wonder why?'

'Her mother-in-law's never been to Britain before and would like to explore it. It tells you that.'

'They're going to stay with Aunt Nellie.'

'As I'd expect.'

'Do you remember last time Aunt Babs came?'

'Of course! I liked her.'

'Mam was always critical of her.'

'She was jealous. Aunt Babs is so glamorous. I don't think I've ever known two sisters so different,' said Lucia.

'Tell me a bit more about her?' Tim interrupted.

'She's a widow and has two sons. She met her husband over here and went back with him after the war. Both her in-laws are still alive and very fond of the boys, so she's staying there,' said Lucia. 'Her father-in-law owns a canning business.'

'So what about the rest of her family?'

'Shall I have a look at how the turkey is doing, Lucia?' asked Theresa.

'Yes, do,' replied Lucia, turning to Tim. 'I must thank you again. It's a smashing size.'

'My pleasure. Would you excuse me for a short while? I need to make a phone call to Isabella. I was going to a party this evening and was going to ask if you wouldn't mind keeping Jerry here. But what with the weather and my face looking the way it does, I've changed my mind.'

'Sounds sensible,' said Lucia, who was pleased to be having some adult company that evening. Although, by the sound of it, Tim had had some different adult company in mind. He had made his plans for this evening without even consulting her about taking care of Jerry. However much she enjoyed his company, she must not lose sight of what Michael or Maggie had said about Tim using her. Despite his protestations to the contrary, he probably did fancy Isabella if she was the looker Chris suggested she was.

She saw Tim out, wondering if she should have offered him the use of their phone, but maybe he had not wanted anyone listening in on his conversation. She returned to the kitchen and poured herself a small sherry. A few moments later Gabrielle entered the room, clutching the Barbie doll to her flat chest and carrying the sets of clothes in her other hand. It wasn't until she came close up to her eldest sister that Lucia noticed the tearstains on her sister's face.

'What's wrong?' Lucia asked. 'Have the boys been teasing you?'

'Joseph threatened to pull Barbie's legs off. He said dolls are silly.'

'Tell him that dressing up as a cowboy is just as silly,' said Theresa.

'No don't,' said Lucia. 'We want him and James to dress up and go out and play later so we can have some peace.'

'I was thinking of having a walk for some fresh air,' said Theresa. 'Do you want to come with me, Gabrielle?'

The younger girl nodded.

Lucia was about to say that it was freezing outside and slippery underfoot. But remembering Theresa's accusation that she sounded just like their mother, she decided to keep her mouth shut. Theresa had plenty of sense and wouldn't stay out too long; the cold weather and the thought of the turkey would bring her home.

So off the girls went, having changed into their wellies and muffled up to the ears in the scarves that Mrs Hudson had knitted and the pixie hoods that had been in the box from the Police Federation Fund. Gabrielle was clutching her Barbie doll and, not surprisingly, Theresa was telling her she should leave it at home in case she dropped it and it got wet and sandy if they went to the beach. Lucia was just about to close the front door when she heard her name being called. Realizing it was Tim, she waited for him to appear before going inside.

'All sorted out,' he said.

'Was Isabella upset because you couldn't go?' asked Lucia.

'She must have been because she offered to send someone to pick me up. I told her not to bother as I preferred staying where I was in the circumstances; I was in no mood for a noisy party with dancing and games.'

Lucia made no comment, hoping he really meant it when he said he preferred staying where he was and was not just being polite.

Mouth-watering smells weaved about the kitchen and Lucia removed the turkey from the oven. The skin was a lovely crisp golden colour and she couldn't wait to serve the food out and dig in. But there was no sign of Michael or Theresa and Gabrielle. She hoped there hadn't been an accident. The weather had worsened and a fog had descended. She wondered whether to serve the meal immediately or wait for the others to come in. She decided on the latter after explaining the situation to Tim.

An hour later there was the sound of a key in the lock of the front door. Lucia jumped to her feet and hurried into the darkening lobby. She could hear several voices all talking at once and thought she could make out three figures. She reached for the switch and light flooded the lobby; she saw that there were in fact four figures, not three as she had thought at first, one of whom was a stranger, a young woman of about seventeen with flushed cheeks in a delicate, heart-shaped face, framed by blonde hair fluffed out beneath the rim of a black fur hat. Michael stood at her shoulder, holding Gabrielle in his arms.

Immediately he set eyes on Lucia, he held their sister out to her. She took Gabrielle from him and realized the skirt of her coat at the back was sodden. She clung to Lucia and began to cry.

'What happened?' Lucia hissed at Theresa.

'She took no notice of me when I told her not to walk in the gutter where the water had iced over and she began to shatter the ice with the heels of her wellies. Eventually she slipped and landed on her bottom. I dragged her up but she wouldn't stop crying – and that's when our Michael and his girlfriend found us. Of course she cried all the more when she saw him and wanted him to carry her.'

'I wet my knicks,' said Gabrielle through sobs. 'And I dropped Barbie.'

'I did warn you not to take her,' Theresa said, taking the doll from beneath her arm. 'Anyway, she's not as wet as you are.'

'Her dress is dirty.' Gabrielle's tears flowed again.

'Shhh! You're a big girl now and big girls don't cry,' Lucia said. 'You can go upstairs and change your knicks and we can wash Barbie's dress. You haven't hurt yourself, otherwise, have you?' she added, distracted by the presence of her brother's girlfriend. What on earth was he thinking of, springing such a surprise on her today of all days? How long had he been seeing this girl?

'My skirt is wet too!' said Gabrielle, poking Lucia in the chest.

'Well, change it,' responded Lucia. 'And don't poke me.'

'But it's my best Christmas skirt and I want to wear it.'

'Take it off and I'll put it in front of the fire. You can change back into it once it's dry.'

'OK!' Gabrielle struggled to get down and headed for the stairs.

'Don't be long,' Lucia called up. 'I'm about to put the dinner out.' She turned from the stairs and gazed at the girl standing next to Michael. 'So what's your name?' she asked.

'Marjorie Owens.' She proffered a hand. 'Mike's told me all about you. I'm so pleased to meet you.'

Lucia knew she could not express what she was feeling or thinking, aware as she was of her brother's anxious expression, so she took Marjorie's hand and patted it. 'Welcome to our home and Happy Christmas. Have you eaten? We were just about to sit down to dinner.'

'Yes, I have – and Mike's had something as well.'

Lucia bristled slightly at Marjorie's shortening of Michael's name.

'Marjorie's mam insisted I sit down with them,' said Michael hastily. 'But I've still room for some more.'

'And what about Marjorie?' asked Lucia. 'Does she want to come and watch us eat or would she rather sit in front of the fire in the parlour and read a magazine until you've finished?'

'Now there's a choice,' said Marjorie, smiling. 'I'm sure you'd rather I wasn't watching you eat and I'd enjoy a warm and a rest by the fire. Unlike Mike, I couldn't eat another dinner. What magazines do you have? Would you mind if I make myself a cup of tea?'

'Not at all! Although Theresa would happily make you one, I'm sure,' said Lucia, not looking at her sister.

'I'm happy to make my own,' said Marjorie. 'I should think Theresa is tired after her walk.'

Neither sister insisted on making a cuppa for their visitor; after all, she had not been invited and they were both busy, so while Michael led Marjorie into the kitchen, Lucia suggested Theresa set the tureens of vegetables on the table and to ask the rest of the family to sit at table. She then asked Tim to carve the turkey. After they had finished eating, everybody agreed that it was the best turkey they had ever tasted. Not that turkey had ever featured much on the family's Christmas menu in the past, thought Lucia. They had the Christmas pudding that had been in the Police Federation box with custard for afters.

With the meal over, Lucia and Theresa set about dealing with the washing-up. Tim offered to dry and, as for Michael, he was in a hurry to join Marjorie in the parlour. Lucia turned down Tim's offer and suggested that Michael pour Tim a beer.

'Are you worried I might drop the dishes?' asked Tim.

'No, although I couldn't afford to replace them – but you did provide the turkey so I think you've done your share. Why don't you go and relax? Or watch your son at play? Isn't this the first Christmas the pair of you have spent together?'

'Is that what Maggie told you?'

'No, she seldom mentions you, except to—'

'Warn you against me?'

Lucia felt her cheeks warm. 'She told me you were a charmer.'

'That was a warning. It's something I can't help. My mother told me it was a gift from God, that few people are blessed with charm and that I need to be careful how I use it.'

'My auntie Babs has charm.'

'The one who lives in California?'

'Yes.' Lucia put the last of the crockery away in a wall cupboard. 'She's coming over next year to see us. I can't wait. Even on the dullest day she can make you feel as if the sun's about to come out.'

'That's a rare gift. I doubt my family would ever say that about me.'

'I'm sure they care about you, though.'

'Strangely, Marty and Peggy do but not Lil. She hates me.'

'Hates? That's a strong word.'

'It's true, though. She's the reason I didn't want to go and have dinner today at Mam's. Lil's married and has a kid and they all live with Mam. I have no regrets, though. I'm enjoying myself being here with you – and the rest of your family.'

'Not forgetting Jerry, of course!' said Lucia.

'Of course. The last Christmas Jerry and I spent together was in London with his mother. It wasn't the happiest of days. We were living in a basement flat and knew very few people. Bernie was missing her sisters who always spoilt her and waited on her hand and foot. She wasn't much of a cook and wanted me to take her out for a meal, but we didn't have much in the way of money and the only woman I could have asked to babysit was naturally spending the day with her family.'

'So what did you do about a Christmas meal eventually?'

'I fried us a couple of steaks and boiled some spuds and sprouts. It wasn't half bad but she complained it wasn't a proper Christmas dinner like her mother used to make. I resisted reminding her that it was she who had wanted to leave Liverpool to get away from her mother. Eventually I suggested we take Jerry for a walk in the park, but in the end Jerry and I went on our own and kicked a ball around. She said it was too cold for her. I have to admit it was blinking cold but Jerry seemed to enjoy himself.'

'It must have been a terrible shock when she died?'

'Too right it was, but we weren't getting on that well and probably would have broken up eventually. Still, I didn't wish her dead.'

'Jerry never mentions her.'

'It's more than three years ago. If he talked about her to anyone it would be to Josie, my brother Marty's daughter. Jerry's just a year older and they spent a lot of time together when they were toddlers. Then there's Bernie's niece, Monica, who you know. She used to babysit for Bernie when she wanted a night out.'

'I like Monica; she has a great singing voice. I assume you know that she got a recording contract around the same time as Tony?'

'Yer! She's a good kid.'

'She's around my age. You don't regard me as a kid, do you?' asked Lucia.

He stared at her intently and their eyes met and held. She felt her heart beat the quicker. 'No, but I am quite a few years older than you,' he said.

'I know that, but you don't seem much older to me.'

'Maybe that's because you've a lot of responsibility for someone your age and had to grow up quickly.'

Reminded of her responsibilities, Lucia said, 'I suppose we should make a move into the parlour and see what's going on. I'd appreciate your opinion of Michael's girlfriend.'

'I presume you weren't expecting her?'

'No, I didn't even know he had a girlfriend. It's the last thing I wanted and it must be serious because he's met her mother.'

Tim led the way to the door and held it open for her. She thanked him and together they walked down the lobby to the parlour. There was a lot of noise coming from inside the front room but the sound levels dropped as they entered.

Lucia noticed that Michael and Marjorie were seated side by side on the sofa and James and Gabrielle had squashed in either side of them. On the coffee table in front of the sofa were the contents of the Airfix box that had been in James's stocking. Obviously he was wanting his older brother's help to fix the aeroplane together. On Marjorie's lap was Gabrielle's Barbie doll in a state of undress. In her hand she held one of the changes of clothes.

'It would be lovely for Gabrielle to have more sets of clothes for Barbie,' said Marjorie.

'I should imagine they're expensive because she came all the way from America,' said Gabrielle. 'And we don't have much money.'

'Perhaps Auntie Babs will bring you some more dolls' clothes when she comes over here in summer,' said Theresa.

'Mrs Colman at the coffee bar makes dolls' clothes,' said Lucia. 'With her having been a model, she's interested in fashion, and started making costumes for dolls after she gave up modelling and worked in her sister-in-law's tearoom-cum-shop in Whalley in summer time. I could take a set of Barbie's clothing in next time I go to work so she'll have a good idea of the size. I'm sure she wouldn't charge us because I bet she has plenty of scraps of material left over from other things.'

Gabrielle's thin face lit up. 'That would make me happy.'

'Mike told me you work at the coffee bar that was the old Lenny's Place,' said Marjorie. 'I used to go there occasionally with a friend, but I haven't been since she left Liverpool and changed schools.'

Lucia suppressed a wince at the girl's use of the word Mike again. 'So which school do you go to?' asked Lucia.

'Blackburn House. I'll be leaving in summer, which will please Mum. She's a widow. My dad was killed in the war. I'm an only. Hopefully if I get five GCEs, I'll get a job at ICI.'

'Well, good luck,' said Lucia. 'So where do you and your mother live?'

'Near Newsham Park. Do you know it?'

'I can't say I've ever been there.'

'It's not far from where Nick and Bobby live,' said Michael.

'I know Newsham Park,' said Tim. 'You pass right by it on the 27-26 bus route. It was the bus I used to get sometimes when I lived in Liverpool south. It also takes you near Sefton Park.'

'That's where there's a statue of Peter Pan,' chimed in Jerry. 'Dad took me to see it. I stroked a rabbit's head.'

'A real rabbit?' asked Gabrielle.

'No, a bronze one,' said Jerry, a touch scornfully.

Noticing Gabrielle's bottom lip quiver, Lucia said, 'Shall we change the subject and play a game?'

'I'd rather play with my doll,' said Gabrielle.

'You play with your silly ol' doll,' said Joseph. 'I'd like to play Snakes and Ladders.'

'I'd like to as well,' said Jerry. 'What about you, Dad?'

Lucia glanced at Tim to see what he thought of the idea and saw him nod.

'Why not?' he said. 'It's a while since I've played, so you'll have to excuse me if I make mistakes.'

'We can't all play it,' said Theresa. 'I'd rather read my new book.'

'You do that,' Lucia said. 'Otherwise we'd end up with too many round the board.'

'I can't stay much longer,' said Marjorie, glancing at the clock. 'In fact I should be going now.' She looked at Michael, who instantly stood up.

'Don't be home too late,' said Lucia, gazing at the pair.

Michael gave her a look that said, *Don't fuss.*

Lucia watched the door close behind them before giving her attention to Tim and her remaining family. James was still fiddling about with the parts of his Airfix plane. Joseph had the Snakes and Ladders board open on the table ready. A chair had been left vacant for Lucia next to Tim. She sat down, thinking that this time last year her father had been seated where Tim was and her mother had been sitting in Theresa's chair, reading the story of St Francis of Assisi and his love for birds and animals to them. The ready tears sprang to her eyes.

'So what colour counters are you having, Lucia?' asked Tim.

'Green, it's my favourite colour.'

'Why is that?' he asked.

'It reminds me of spring and new growth. My father was a gardener and sometimes he would take me to work with him when I was small. Occasionally he would let me plant some of the cuttings. Seeing them grow was like magic to me.'

'Shush, Lucia! It's time we got started,' said Joseph.

She 'shushed' and gave her attention to the game, but her mind soon wandered to thoughts of Michael and Marjorie and what her mother would have thought of them going out together while they were both still at school. She came to when Joseph let out a yell. Apparently he had won the first game and Jerry looked likely to be second.

'You're last, Lucia,' said Joseph. 'You haven't been concentrating. In fact I thought you'd fallen asleep.'

Lucia roused herself and gazed down at the board. 'Sorry, I was miles away.'

'I beat Dad,' Jerry said proudly.

'Yes, they were both too good for me,' said Tim, looking downcast.

She wondered if he was bored and wishing he was going to the party at Isabella's. Noticing his glass was empty she said, 'Another beer?'

'Thanks, although I don't think it will improve my playing. In fact it could send me to sleep.'

'You can't go to sleep, Dad,' said Jerry. 'It wouldn't be the same playing without you.'

'I'll make sure he stays awake,' Lucia reassured him. 'I want to see if I can beat him too.'

'A challenge!' cried Tim, his blue eyes sparkling. 'Well, let's get started.'

'I'll get the drinks first,' said Lucia. 'Do you boys want a drink too?'

'Cream soda, please,' said Joseph.

'Me too, please,' said Jerry.

'You'll need help to carry that many,' Tim said, pushing back his chair. 'I'll give you a hand.'

'Thanks!' Lucia made for the kitchen, wanting to ask him if he was enjoying himself.

She was glad she didn't because while he was pouring cream soda from a Schofield's bottle, he volunteered the words himself. 'I've really enjoyed today. In fact it's the best Christmas I've had in I don't know how long.'

'I'm glad,' she said simply. 'You've contributed to make it a good day for me and the children; having a man here helped them not to miss Dad so much, I'm sure. He was an only, so they have no uncles from his side of the family, he had an aunt but she was a widow, and it's not quite the same having a priest for a great-uncle, although we do have aunt Nellie's husband, uncle Michelangelo.'

'Father Francis is a good man and I got to know him better when he visited me in prison. I found him easy to talk to – but then he was familiar with the background I came from. He knew how easy it was for a boy to get caught up with the wrong crowd during the war and afterwards. It's something I want to touch on in my book. Isabella is keen for me to write about those days, especially about the leader of the gang and what it was about him that resulted in my being led astray. But what she's really looking forward to reading about is my escape after the robbery and my time in Australia. She thinks the readers will want me to make good there . . . but obviously they're in for a disappointment.'

'But you're going to make good eventually,' Lucia said.

'I hope so, but she keeps saying I'm not to get sloppy on her. That I should be considering how to make the ending exciting, not just going on about a happy ending.'

Tim's constant references to Isabella began to irritate Lucia. 'And I suppose you think she would know, with her being a newspaper reporter? In my opinion one reads so much bad stuff in the papers that it's a treat when we hear about the good stuff, such as when a child is seriously ill and it's going to cost a fortune for a special operation, and those you least expect to send money to help do so.'

'That's not quite the same thing, but I do see what you're getting at,' said Tim. 'My happy ending would be me managing to make enough for me to support Jerry and myself and staying on the straight and narrow.'

'So no time for romance in your happy ending?'

'I suspect Isabella would consider that sloppy – and besides, what woman would want me?' He did not give Lucia the chance to say something positive but added, 'Anyway, hadn't we better get back to those Snakes and Ladders? You know, I actually hate snakes – bloke I knew was bitten by one in Australia. It was horrible.'

'Oh my goodness! What happened?' asked Lucia.

'He died. We were in the bush, miles from help, and the poison took effect incredibly quickly. If I'd realized there were so many poisonous creatures in Australia, I wouldn't have gone there. But I'm back now, so I don't have to worry about snakes or tiny spiders with a deadly bite.'

'Are you sure you want to go back to playing Snakes and Ladders?' she asked, laughing.

'Of course! After all, it's only a game.'

'But if it brings back bad memories . . .?' she teased.

'I can cope,' he said ruefully, pulling a face. 'Besides, I don't want to disappoint Jerry.'

Lucia threw a six, which meant she landed at the bottom of a long ladder, and she took the lead. Tim was not so lucky, but he didn't care because he didn't mind losing to the boys or Lucia. The boys were pleased when she won and wanted another game, but Tim said it was getting late and it was time Jerry was in bed.

'But it's Christmas,' said the boy.

'It's time my lot were in bed too,' said Lucia.

'Couldn't Jerry sleep here?' asked Joseph. 'He can share my bed.'

Tim and Lucia exchanged looks. 'I don't mind,' she said. 'You could stay a bit longer and have a cup of cocoa.'

'I'd like that,' Tim said.

Within the hour the children were all in bed and peace reigned. Lucia made the cocoa and sat on the sofa that had been pulled up closer to the fire. Tim decided it would be sensible not to sit beside her and sat in an armchair. Lucia felt disappointed at him sitting so far away and was surprised because – if nothing else it suggested that he was not going to try and take advantage of her, thus proving Maggie wrong. She sipped her cocoa and wracked her brains for something to say.

'What are your plans for Boxing Day?' she asked.

'Jerry and I are going to Marty and Irene's for lunch. Mam is invited as well. My brother and I will probably take the kids to feed the ducks on the Leeds–Liverpool canal, leaving Irene and Mam to prepare the meal in peace.'

'Will Jerry be riding there on his new bike?'

'He's longing to have a good go on it, but it depends on what the pavements are like in the morning,' said Tim.

'Why don't you have a look and see what the weather is doing now?' suggested Lucia.

He stood up and went over to the window and moved aside a curtain.

'Well?' she asked.

'Come and see for yourself?' he said.

She jumped up and joined him by the window. As they stood

shoulder to shoulder, she was conscious of the warmth of his arm against hers, as well as the chill from the glass on her face as she gazed out. The fog had lifted and she looked up at the silvery half-moon, hanging in an indigo sky scattered with stars, above the glistening slate roofs of the houses on the other side of the street.

'It's going to be a heavy frost in the morning,' she said.

'Which means slippery pavements, so we'll be taking the bus,' said Tim.

'Disappointing for Jerry, but he'll enjoy playing with his cousins, won't he?'

'He's reached that age where he finds girls soppy, prefers boys his own age or a bit older. I remember being the same. I used to follow our Marty around and it drove him crazy. He tried all kinds of ways to get rid of me, but I was crafty and nearly always managed to discover his whereabouts. Eventually I twigged that I was being a nuisance and found mates of my own.'

'Was it because your brother rejected you that you ended up with the wrong crowd?'

'Marty didn't reject me; he often put up with me and got me out of scrapes and even took the blame for things I did. But I was a bit of a rebel and wanted to kick over the traces. I had this cherubic face with dimples and I wanted to prove I wasn't as angelic as I looked. By the time I was twelve, I was wanting to impress the girls.'

'Was there any special girl in your teens? I mean before you met your wife.' Lucia moved away from the window and over to the sofa. She patted the seat next to her and looked up at him. 'It's lovely and warm here in front of the fire.'

He hesitated before joining her on the sofa, and left a good foot of space between them. She wondered if he thought she had been a bit too forward inviting him to sit beside her.

He continued their conversation. 'No one special, but I did date several girls. I wanted to have fun. I loved the flicks and dancing. I had known Bernie for years but I didn't ask her out until I was in my late teens.' He frowned. 'In fact, thinking back, I reckon it was she who suggested we went to the pictures together. The thing was, I couldn't afford to take her out as often as she wanted. I was only earning an apprentice motor mechanic's wages. So I had to find another way to get extra money.' He paused. 'Are you sure you want to hear about this?'

'You're going to write about it, aren't you? So surely it's good practice to think back and put it into words?'

'Well, I think we've had enough about me for one evening. What about you? Has there been any important fella in your life?'

She hesitated before admitting that she'd had a crush on Marty's seafaring brother-in-law, Jimmy, a while back. 'He's married now with twins, so I had no choice but to put him out of my mind and get on with my life. And since Mam and Dad were killed, I've definitely had no time to mope over him. So I can truthfully say I'm cured of my crush.'

'What about that lad Nick you spoke to at the Cavern? He's a good-looking bloke.'

'Yes, and I do like him, but he has a girlfriend, Grace. Her brother is a reporter on the *Liverpool Echo* – don't you remember meeting him at the Cavern?'

'I do, now you mention it. What was his name?'

'It's Chris something. Can't remember his surname, which reminds me – our Michael isn't home yet.'

'He could have missed the last bus. The mother might have suggested he stay the night.'

'You really think she would? They're both so young, I wouldn't have thought she'd want to encourage him.'

'If that were true, she wouldn't have invited him to have Christmas dinner with them.'

'You have a point. What did you think of Marjorie?'

'It doesn't matter what I thought. What did you think of her?'

Lucia pondered, choosing her words carefully. 'She didn't seem a bit shy.'

'No.' Tim smiled slightly. 'Don't you think it a good thing for a girl to have confidence?'

'Yes, my mother lacked confidence when she was that age, according to Aunt Nellie. It turned her into a worrier and filled her with envy. I swore that I would never be like her.'

'You were a daddy's girl?'

'What makes you say that?'

'The way you spoke about him earlier.'

'He did his best to be a good father to us all, but I knew I was his favourite.'

'He didn't spoil you, though.'

'No, he didn't have the money to shell out on gifts, but he spent time with me and told me things. I know the names of lots of flowers and herbs.'

'You must have been a good listener.' Tim glanced at the clock. 'It's getting late. It's time we were both in bed, it's going to be a busy day tomorrow. So if you'll see me out?'

'Of course. I'd got so comfortable and was finding our conversation so interesting that I could have talked all night,' said Lucia, uncurling herself and getting to her feet.

'And that wouldn't do,' said Tim. 'We'd have the tongues wagging and we don't want that.'

He led the way to the front door and paused there before turning to face Lucia.

For a moment she thought he might kiss her and was unsure what to do, only for him to go past her and take hold of Jerry's bicycle. 'I might as well take this next door and put it in his bedroom,' he said. 'I'll see you in the morning.'

'Of course! We'll be heading out in the same direction because we're going to Aunt Nellie's; she lives the other side of the canal. It'll be a nice walk.'

'You're intending to walk all that way?'

'It'll get the fidgets out of the kids' legs and the fresh air will be good for them after so much time spent indoors.' She smiled and opened the front door. 'See you!'

'Yeah, and thanks for everything, Lucia.'

'My pleasure!' She helped him carry the bike down the steps and stood watching him until he went inside the neighbouring house. She wished he could have stayed longer, but it was early days and, in the light of his past, it made sense for them to become better acquainted before their friendship perhaps developed into something deeper.

Four

The following morning privets and laurels in front gardens glistened with frost, as did the ground, but the clear sky had vanished, to be covered by dirty, yellowish ragged clouds.

'D'you think it might snow?' Joseph asked Lucia eagerly.

She thought of Jerry, who had scampered home as soon as he had finished his cornflakes, having politely thanked her for having him. She wondered if Joseph and Jerry had planned on doing something together if it did snow.

'I hope not,' she said, pulling on a dark pink woolly hat.

The children wore coats of a tweed mixture and, on their heads, in Joseph and James's case, hand-knitted navy blue balaclavas from the Police Federation box. Gabrielle wore a red pixie hood.

Theresa placed a multi-coloured tammy on her mousey hair. As for Michael, who had arrived home at nine that morning, wearing an air of defiance even as he apologized for worrying her, was clad in a navy blue duffle coat and had the cashmere scarf Marjorie had bought him for Christmas wrapped around his neck, with the ends dangling outside his coat. Lucia donned an emerald-coloured swagger coat and a pink scarf and gloves.

She insisted that the children wear their wellies, and even Michael and Theresa had put on theirs without being asked, convinced it was going to snow before the day was out. Lucia chose to wear the fleece-lined suede boots that had been the last present her father had given her. She thought how it was a real job getting the whole family prepared for an outing.

'Well, if you're all ready, we'll get going,' she said, opening the front door.

Michael led the way, helping Gabrielle down the steps. As they walked down the path, Lucia heard the neighbouring front door open.

'So you're off,' shouted Tim. 'It's quite a crocodile you've got there.'

'What d'you mean "crocodile", Dad?' asked Jerry, joining him outside.

'It's a name given to school children walking two by two in a line,' Tim replied. 'But don't ask me how it came to be called that.'

'I don't know either,' said Lucia. 'Are you off now, too?'

'Yeah!'

'Couldn't I be part of the "crocodile", Dad?' asked Jerry, grinning and sidling up to Joseph.

Michael opened the gate and Lucia brought up the rear. Tim raised his trilby and wished her a good morning, limping alongside her. She returned the greeting, adding, 'Are you sure you want to do this? People stare at us Brookeses whenever we go out together.'

'You'd rather not have my company?' asked Tim, his dimples coming into play.

'I didn't say that,' responded Lucia. 'I imagine you're only walking as far as the bus stop.'

'No, we're walking all the way. I read in the *Liverpool Express* that the buses aren't running because the roads are too icy. It also said that there were power cuts yesterday in some places.'

'That will have spoiled some people's Christmases,' she said.

At that moment a car came along the road at speed. 'Look at that idiot,' said Michael.

'It looks like it's heading for us,' squealed Gabrielle.

'Scatter, kids,' shouted Tim in alarm.

They all scattered. Tim seized Lucia's hand and, with her help, managed to get out of the way of the car. There came a squeal of brakes and they turned and watched the car skid and go into a spin. It came to a halt against the kerb the other side of the road, facing the way it had come.

'Gosh! They were lucky,' said Tim.

'We were lucky too,' Lucia said. 'They could have run us down if we hadn't got out of the way.'

'I know,' Tim said, his expression grim.

'D'you think we should go and see if they're all right?' asked Lucia.

At that moment the passenger side window was wound down and a man thrust his head out. 'Sorry about that! Tommy boy, is that you?' he asked.

Tim crossed the road. 'I think you're getting me confused with someone else,' he said, a flash of annoyance crossing his face as he gazed down at the man before glancing at the driver who appeared to have knocked himself out.

'Our paths crossed years ago. Your face looks a bit of a mess, so I wasn't sure it was you at first. You been in an accident? If so, you need to start watching your step.'

Tim made no reply but turned away. By then a crowd had gathered and someone said the man from the corner shop had dialled 999, but whether an ambulance would arrive any time soon with the icy condition of the roads was doubtful. Tim carefully crossed the road to where Lucia was waiting with the children.

'Are you all OK?' he asked.

The children nodded.

Lucia said, 'What did that man say to you? I hope he apologized.'

'He said sorry – but there's something odd about what happened.'

'What d'you mean?' she asked.

'He appeared to recognize me, and I have to admit he looked vaguely familiar. Anyway, let's get away from here.' He began to walk away with a swivelling action, careful how he placed his stick on the icy pavement. Lucia walked alongside him. Michael caught up with them and the children swarmed past and went on ahead.

'So was the driver injured?' asked Lucia.

'I wouldn't be surprised if he's concussed,' Tim answered. 'Serves him right because if the driver is who I'm guessing he could be, then it was no accident him aiming the car in our direction. Anyway, let's put it behind us. We don't want it spoiling our day.'

Lucia glanced at him as they carried on walking, trying to catch up with the kids. She doubted any of them would find it that easy to put the experience behind them. It had been too close for comfort. Could it be that Tim had enemies who wanted to frighten him?

It took longer to reach their destinations than Lucia had estimated, and she didn't relish the thought of the walk back, but she said nothing of that to her aunt. The meal they shared with the Gianellis was excellent, and the children enjoyed opening their presents from Nellie and her husband, playing games and singing Christmas songs around the piano. Lucia was assailed by memories of when she was a child and she and her mother Lottie had lived in this house. After her parents had married, and she and her mother had moved to live with her father, David, and his mother in the house in Seaforth where Lucia and her siblings now lived. The house had been left to Lucia on her father's death.

Her paternal grandmother had suffered from a dicky heart and was not used to children, so, what with her health problems and her own mother's health issues, Lucia had been at the beck and call of the two women, and also had to keep the younger children out of her grandmother's way, so she had little time to play out with her school friends or neighbouring children as she grew up. It was Nellie who had seen to it that Lucia was able to mix with other young people besides her siblings by inviting her to the musical evenings held at her house. It was there and at the coffee bar she had developed friendships with Tim's niece by marriage, Monica, and Nick and his step-sister, Roberta, known as Bobby, who had also worked at the coffee bar a few years back.

'You seem to be in a trance,' said Nellie, sitting beside her niece on the sofa.

'I was just thinking of the past,' Lucia responded.

'You mustn't be too sad. It's not what your mam and dad would want for you. They'd want you to enjoy yourself.'

'I wasn't feeling particularly sad. I have lots of happy memories as well as a few not so happy.'

'That's life and it's best to dwell on the good times.' Nellie paused and changed the subject. 'Joseph was telling me that Jerry slept over last night and that he and his father spent most of Christmas Day at yours.'

'Yes, I invited him and Jerry to have dinner with us. Jerry and Joseph get on like a house on fire, so I thought they'd enjoy being together.'

'And Jerry's father – how long did he stay?'

'He left at ten o'clock after a cup of cocoa. He was supposed to be going to a party, but he had a fall on Christmas Eve and his face was bruised and swollen, so he didn't go.'

'Poor man! What does Michael think of him?'

Lucia's face clouded. 'Don't talk to me about our Michael!'

'Why, what's he done?'

'Got himself a girlfriend.'

'Have you met her?'

'Yes, he went out Christmas morning, didn't say where he was going, only that he would be back for dinner – which he was but he wasn't alone. Marjorie came back with him.'

'That's her name?'

'Yes, quite an attractive girl and not the least bit shy.'

'So what else do you know about her?'

'Her mother's a widow. Father killed in the war.'

'Where do they live?'

'Apparently not far from where Nick and Bobby live.'

'Is Marjorie still at school?'

'Blackburn House.'

'That's not far from the school Bobby and her mam, Lynne, went to.'

'Liverpool Girl's College,' murmured Lucia.

'That's it. How did they meet?'

'No idea,' said Lucia. 'But the fact that her mother invited Michael to have some dinner with them yesterday makes me think they have been seeing each other for quite some time. Did I tell you that Tim kindly bought us the turkey?'

'Well, that was something good at least.'

'Mmmm, it was really tasty. But what am I going to do about our Michael and Marjorie?'

'Well, I wouldn't go forbidding him to see her; however much you're tempted to. At least he brought her to meet you, so he's not going behind your back. Forbidden secret meetings can seem more thrilling when one is young. It probably won't last if you don't make a fuss.'

'OK, I'll try,' said Lucia. 'Now tell me whether you've heard anything more from Babs about her intended visit.'

Nellie hesitated. 'Only that they'll be coming in summer so Babs can see more of the children.'

'That'll be nice. We'll be able to have days out together.' Lucia glanced in the direction of the window. 'It looks like it's sleeting. We're going to have to make a move soon with this weather. I hope we do have a good summer.'

'Why don't you stay the night? It's not as if the children are in school tomorrow.'

'I'm in work, though.' Lucia looked out at the weather again. 'Still, I can catch a bus into town from here. If you're sure you don't mind, we will stay, thanks.'

'I wouldn't have offered if I minded. We'll squash you all in somewhere.' Nellie stood up. 'Now, how about a cup of cocoa and a mince pie?'

'Great!' Lucia jumped to her feet and followed her to the kitchen.

It wasn't until she was on her way to work the next morning that Lucia remembered she had made no mention of the incident with the car to her aunt. She thought of Tim and wondered if he would suffer any more of these 'close calls'. And what would Isabella say if he told her about his narrow escape and that the car had been driven by someone he recognized from his past.

Lucia did not have to be in work until eleven, so she had time to pause after getting off the bus in Skelhorne Street and gaze in Lewis's shop windows. Although the sales did not begin until January, and she really didn't have any money to spare to spend on new clothes or household goods, she did enjoy seeing what was on offer. She soon realized she was a bit too early to view the sales goods, as the windows were only just being prepared for dressing and there were huge posters stuck to the glass saying, 'Gigantic Sale starts on 2nd January', which meant she could not see what lay behind them. Her mother had never shopped at Lewis's, saying she could not afford their prices, and instead had patronized TJ Hughes on London Road, where the cost of goods suited her pocket.

Lucia continued on up Renshaw Street, and was just a few feet from the corner where she turned into Leece Street when she saw Tim's brother, Marty, whose workplace was nearby. She greeted him and asked whether Tim was all right.

'He and Jerry stayed at ours last night. We were surprised to see them, thought they'd choose to stay at home. Mam didn't turn up, what with the buses not running. Irene put her foot down and said I wasn't to take the van out to go and pick anyone up. Thank God, the roads have been gritted overnight, so I was able to take Tim and Jerry home before coming to work.'

'Did Tim mention the car accident in our street to you?'

'No, was anyone hurt?'

'Tim seemed to think the driver might be concussed. Someone had phoned 999 so we didn't linger.' Lucia decided not to mention that Tim had recognized the driver, or that the man had appeared to be driving straight at them at one point. Thinking about the incident now, it was possible to believe that he had lost control of the car and had no intention of running anyone down.

'Roll on spring,' said Marty.

Lucia echoed his words, and went on her way, glad that parts of the pavement had been gritted as well as the roads. Even so, it was a relief to arrive at the coffee bar and get inside and have her senses assailed by the smell of freshly brewed coffee, fried bacon and toasted teacakes.

'So you've made it,' said Maggie, who was standing in front of the till, emptying change into the compartments of the drawer. 'Did your Christmas go all right?'

'Yes, thanks! There's something I want to ask you.' Lucia paused to remove her outdoor clothes and hang them up. 'My aunt Babs sent presents from America, and the one for my sister, Gabrielle, was a Barbie doll with an extra couple of sets of clothes. I was wondering if you'd mind making some more for the doll if you have any old scraps of material? If it's too much trouble I'll understand. Especially as I can't afford to pay you.'

'Do you have the doll with you, or even a set of the clothes?' Maggie asked.

'No, we stayed at Aunt Nellie's last night, so I came straight here from there. I'll bring Barbie in tomorrow.'

'That's fine. I'm looking forward to seeing this Barbie. My sister-in-law, Emma, said that my cousin Betty has mentioned the doll. Her little girl has one. Apparently they're all the rage in America.'

'They aren't very big and they're not like the doll I wanted when I was a little girl. You know a doll that you could pretend was a baby and wheel in a pram. I think it's the clothes that are the attraction. Barbie is something of a fashion plate!' Lucia paused and gazed about her. 'Now, what d'you want me to do first?'

'The usual. Wipe the tables and put the cruet sets out.'

'Did you and Josh have a good Christmas?'

'Yes, we went up to Emma's cottage in Whalley. The village looked like a Christmas card because they had snow up there. The kids were made up.'

'So there wasn't just the two of you?'

'No, it was a real family Christmas. Emma and my brother Jared and their two children, my sister Dot and husband Billy and their adopted son, Georgie, were there as well. The cottage was a bit crammed but it was fun.'

'Tim and Jerry came and had Christmas dinner with us and afterwards we played Snakes and Ladders with Jerry and Joseph,' said Lucia. 'Theresa read and Michael went out with his girlfriend.'

'I can't imagine Tim playing Snakes and Ladders,' said Maggie.

'Well, he did and he seemed to enjoy himself, despite not winning a single game. He said it was the best Christmas he'd had since he didn't know when.'

'Compliments are always in plentiful supply with him!'

Lucia slanted Maggie an annoyed glance. 'Are you suggesting he was only saying it to get round me and that he didn't mean it?'

'No, but he's quite sophisticated, so I just can't picture him enjoying Snakes and Ladders.'

'Anyway, that wasn't all we did,' said Lucia, wiping the last table and going to fetch the cruets.

Maggie slammed the drawer of the till shut and stared at Lucia. 'Go on – what else did you do? He didn't snog you, did he?'

'Of course not. We're just friends and I like having some adult company. Besides, can you see him getting serious about me? Not with me being responsible for so many younger brothers and sisters. I mean, marriage isn't on the cards, is it?'

'Men don't have to have marriage in mind to go a step too far,' warned Maggie.

'You don't have to keep telling me. I'm not daft,' Lucia retorted. 'Anyway, he behaved like the perfect gentleman.'

'You need to watch him, he's a crafty one!'

Lucia pressed her lips together to prevent the hot words that were on the tip of her tongue from spilling out. Instead she said, 'You can think what you like, but you might be interested to know that he had an accident on Christmas Eve. He really does need someone to be there for him and Jerry – and before you can say something such as "make sure it's not you", I'll remind you that normally he has his landlady there. She generally has Christmas dinner with us, but she'd gone down south to spend Christmas with her brother and his children.'

'Was Tim badly hurt?' asked Maggie.

'He fell, carrying Jerry's bike down from upstairs. His face is bruised and swollen, but fortunately he doesn't appear to have broken any bones.'

'Did he go to the hospital?'

'No. With the weather the way it was on Christmas Eve, he decided it was unlikely that an ambulance would come out to him. After all, he didn't see it as an emergency and, besides, he couldn't leave Jerry alone in the house.'

'Yes, that's understandable. Poor Tim. He won't like his good looks being spoilt.'

This time Lucia could not prevent herself from saying, 'You really are being bitchy about him. I thought you'd forgiven him for not being honest with you in the past?'

'I have, but the memories still hurt.'

'What memories still hurt?' said a male voice unexpectedly.

Lucia glanced up at Josh standing a few feet away, and then at Maggie who was looking stunned. Lucia said swiftly, 'We were talking about our fathers and how we missed them over Christmas. Some memories make me happy but others make me sad. Maggie feels the same.'

'I know what you mean,' said Josh. 'Anyhow, now isn't the time to feel sad. We've work to do, although I doubt we'll be as busy as during term time.'

Maggie and Lucia agreed.

Even so, as it drew closer to lunchtime, customers began to trickle in. Lucia was pleased to see Nick and his dark-haired, good-looking reporter friend Chris sit at a table, and waited only a few minutes before going over to take their order.

'Hi, Lucia,' said Nick. 'How was your Christmas?'

'Better than I thought it would be. How was yours?'

'Good! Aunt Hester and Uncle Ally phoned all the way from Canada on Christmas Eve, which made Dad happy.'

'The miracles of modern technology,' said Chris. 'It makes one wonder how our ancestors survived without it.'

'They were tougher than us I reckon,' said Lucia. 'I remember Mam and Aunt Nellie talking about their grandfather who was a sailor in Victorian times. When he was younger, apparently his ship had sail and steam.'

'You can understand them covering both options when steam-driven ships were in their infancy,' said Chris.

Lucia agreed, adding, 'Even so, they could be at sea for months, even a year or more. Apparently my great-grandfather arrived home after one such voyage to discover his wife had died while he was away.'

'That must have been terrible,' said Nick. 'And obviously he had children. Who looked after them?'

'He had a sister who never married. Mam and Aunt Nellie both remembered her.'

'The spinster aunt could always be depended on to rally round in the old days,' Chris commented. 'They often get a mention in the novels set in those times. Anyway, Lucia, haven't you anything to say about the accident in your road yesterday morning?'

Lucia's heart seemed to turn over. 'How did you hear about that?'

'Slow news day. I think Mr Murphy must have told Isabella about it.'

'I don't suppose she told you or your colleagues that the car was heading straight for Tim Murphy, me and all the kids – and the driver only managed to avoid running us down because he put on the brakes, went into a skid and spun away across the road?'

'I heard the car went into a skid, but none of the rest,' said Chris, leaning in closer to Lucia. 'It sounds like it could have been a very nasty accident.'

She gazed into his gorgeous brown eyes and let out a sigh. 'I think Tim had his doubts about it being an accident. He recognized the driver from his youth,' Lucia blurted out, without thinking about the effect her words might have on a newspaper reporter and a policeman. 'I can tell you we got away fast. Me and the kids were on our way to Aunt Nellie's and Tim and Jerry were going to his brother Marty's house in Litherland. We had to walk because the buses weren't running. Anyway, that's enough talking from me. I'd better be taking your order,' added Lucia, thinking Tim would probably be annoyed if he knew she had spoken the way she had to these two.

Having taken their order she went into the kitchen and handed it to Josh and told him that the tables were filling up nicely.

'Anyone I know?' he asked.

'Nick, with his friend Chris, the newspaper reporter.'

'I've never met Chris.'

'He's very good-looking and interesting – Nick is going out with his sister. I like Nick. He's a good sort. And they've known each other for years, so they must know they are suited.'

'You've a sensible head on your shoulders, so I'm sure you won't go making any stupid mistakes when it comes to boyfriends,' said Josh.

'Thanks for those kind words. I wish other people believed that and stopped pointing out things to me that I'm completely aware of,' Lucia said hotly.

'You wouldn't mean Maggie, would you?' asked Josh.

Lucia stared at him woodenly. 'Now why should you think that?'

'Because I haven't forgotten her old flame turned up here just before Christmas, and you offering to help him find rooms for himself and his son. Maggie's inclined to consider herself the expert when it comes to Tim Murphy.'

'Does that annoy you?' asked Lucia.

'I'd prefer not to answer that question,' said Josh. 'Now, back to work.'

Lucia did as she was told, not wanting to get on the wrong side of her boss. She liked Josh, and most of the time he was easy to get along with. He was fair and generous and she could never imagine him cheating on Maggie.

She noticed a few more customers had entered while she had been in the kitchen and went over to take their order. 'Two teas, luv, and two Welsh rarebits?' said an elderly woman.

She returned to the kitchen where Nick and Chris's order was waiting for her. She took it over to them with the bill and asked Nick when the group would next be rehearsing at her aunt's house.

'Next Friday,' said Nick, handing over payment for the food. 'Why don't you come and listen and bring Mr Murphy along?'

'I'll ask him. Enjoy your meal.' She headed for the till, hoping that Tim would say yes. After serving the two women their Welsh rarebit, she saw to clearing the tables. Knowing there wouldn't be many customers during the next few hours, Josh told Lucia she could knock off early. Business wouldn't get really busy until the university and college spring terms started. He also handed her half a chocolate cake and several custard tarts. 'For the kids,' he said.

Lucia thanked him and left shortly afterwards. As she walked down to Skelhorne Street bus station, she was thinking of checking whether Tim and Jerry were home so as to invite them round for a cup of tea and to share the goodies Josh had given her.

Five

As luck would have it, Tim was leaning against the doorjamb next door, watching Michael and Jerry sprinkling table salt on the two lots of icy steps.

'Hi, Lucia, can I make you a cuppa?' Tim asked. 'I did offer to help but was turned down. I feel a right lemon standing here, watching the boys working, but Michael said it could be risky for me to help out with the steps being so slippy. Didn't want me having another fall and perhaps breaking my leg this time.'

'And it's not as if this is hard work,' said Michael, 'and you provided the salt, Mr Murphy.'

'I think it's time you took a break,' Lucia said, 'Josh gave me some goodies, so how about if I put the kettle on, and we all have a warm drink and share them?'

'Sounds good to me,' said Michael.

'And me,' piped up Jerry. 'How about it, Dad?'

'I appreciate the offer, but can I bring something to the table? A bottle of milk, say, and I've got some boiled ham that needs eating up?'

'Sounds like this will be a feast,' said Lucia.

Tim went indoors to return a few minutes later with the milk and boiled ham and a packet of biscuits. Jerry hurried over to his father's side. 'You can lean on me, Dad,' he said. 'I want to help.'

'You can carry the biscuits and boiled ham, son,' said Tim.

That settled, it was not long before they were all indoors and Theresa had the kettle on. She laid out cups, saucers and plates in the kitchen, where a glowing fire sent out a welcome warmth. All the children gathered round Lucia as she placed her shopping bag on the table and withdrew from its interior the remains of the chocolate cake and some custard tarts.

'They look delicious,' said Joseph. 'Can we all have a bit of both?'

'Yeah, I'd like to try them both, too,' said Gabrielle.

'Well, if Theresa will line up the plates,' said Lucia.

'You don't have to count me in if there isn't enough,' said Tim. 'See to the kids first.'

'Let me cut the chocolate cake and see how far that goes,' said Lucia.

She counted heads to check that she had the number right, and managed to cut enough pieces so they would all have a taste of Maggie's yummy chocolate cake. Josh's custard tarts were a different proposition altogether. She decided that she and Michael would do without. But when Tim saw the piece on his plate, he placed it on Michael's plate.

'Your wages for all your hard work salting the steps,' he said, winking.

Michael glanced across at Lucia with a questioning look. She nodded, so he put it in his mouth and chomped on the scrummy mixture of melt-in-the-mouth pastry and delicious creamy custard filling, sprinkled with nutmeg. 'You don't know what you're missing, Mr Murphy,' he said.

'If they're that good, I'll give you some money, Lucia, and you can buy some more tomorrow,' said Tim.

'OK,' she said. 'D'you want your tea topped up?'

'Thanks.' He pushed his cup and saucer towards her.

'So have you heard anything from your journalist friend Isabella?' Lucia asked as she refilled his teacup.

'Yeah, she phoned this afternoon to ask how I was after my fall downstairs. I told her about the car accident and she was hell-bent on coming round to see how I was; offered to cook a meal for Jerry and me.'

'Did you tell her that you recognized the men in the car?'

'Not yet.'

'But you plan on doing so?'

'I'm thinking about it. She asked what was I thinking of, going out in such weather when I wasn't fit even to climb stairs safely. I reminded her that I'd told her I was going to visit our Marty and, as you were visiting your aunt and uncle, we had decided to walk along together for safety's sake.'

'So did that shut her up?'

'She said that she'd forgotten and apologized and offered again to cook me a meal.'

'So when is that happening?' Lucia asked, feeling a twinge of jealousy.

'This evening. We'll be working on the book.'

'So if you tell her about the business with the car in more detail, including recognizing the two men, do you think she'll suggest putting it in your book?'

'Maybe! Especially as I've remembered who the passenger was. He was a right bright spark. We knew each other when I was about seventeen and ripe for anything that looked exciting. I remember he was amongst a gang of us who went to watch Bill Haley and His Comets at the pictures. We rocked in the aisles, and when we left the picture house we were still rocking in the street and a fight broke out. Some of us were arrested for disturbing the peace.'

'Perhaps he has learnt you're writing a book and is worried it might affect his chances of promotion if it came to light that he was once in prison.'

'The police let us off with just a caution,' said Tim. 'Isabella could be right and I did let my imagination run away with me in believing the driver was aiming for me. Probably down to when I was hit by that car, after pushing little Johnny to safety.'

'Could be,' said Lucia and, lowering her voice, she added, 'so he was never involved with the gang of crooks you got involved with later?'

'Fred knew them better than I did because he lived in the same street as Will Donahue, the gang leader, so warned me to stay clear of them, but I was a fool and didn't take any notice. I was in need of a few friends as Dad had chucked me out of the house. Now, the driver, I've a feeling he was a cousin of Will Donahue, who was a right bully at times. Fred went out with the cousin's sister.' A shadow crossed his face. 'Let's change the subject? Have you any news about the music group that lad Nick is part of?'

'I saw him today. He and Chris came into the coffee bar. There's a rehearsal at my aunt's house on Friday. You're welcome to come along. Jerry can come too. He'll be able to play with my younger cousins.'

'What about your lot? Who'll look after them?'

'Michael and Theresa, of course,' said Lucia, wondering what her aunt would make of Tim.

'Anyway, I'd best be going,' he said. 'You'll be wanting to take things easy after working all day.'

'I only work part-time,' said Lucia.

'That's useful to know,' he said, smiling.

As she saw him and Jerry out, she wondered what Tim meant by that last remark.

Only after she and Theresa had served out the evening meal did Lucia remember what Michael had said about Tim using her. Could that be what was on Tim's mind? She tried to dismiss the thought but it still lingered. Well, she only had herself to blame if Tim was using her; after all, she had gone out of her way to be of help to him. And if the truth was known, she was only too pleased to do so. It was a way of getting to know him better. Even if he only wanted her or Theresa to keep an eye on Jerry, it was no skin off their noses because Jerry and Joseph got on so well.

It was only later that evening – Lucia heard a car pull up outside as she was drawing the parlour curtains – that she noticed a woman walking up to the neighbouring front door, and questioned whether she should rethink her decision to be there for Tim if he needed her help. It had to be Isabella who was heading up the path. She watched as the older woman patted Tim's cheek as he stepped down on to the step after opening the door to her. You're jealous of her, said a voice in Lucia's head. You've gone and let Tim get under your skin, despite all the warnings Maggie gave you. If you don't step back now, you're going to get really hurt.

Lucia did not sleep well that night, and when morning came and Jerry appeared on their doorstep just after nine o'clock, she didn't have the heart to turn him away. She decided that she would wait until after she and Tim went to her aunt's to listen to the music group before making an attempt to cut Tim out of her life. Nellie and her Italian husband Michelangelo were bound to let Lucia know what they thought of her neighbour. Lucia respected their opinions, so would consider deeply what they had to say about him.

Fortunately there had been a thaw, so they would have no

difficulty getting there by bus. Lucia had made use of the cosmetics that Babs had sent her for Christmas and she thought she looked so different she could only hope she hadn't overdone it. She remembered her mother referring to Babs as 'a painted hussy' once or twice, and thought that her mother would have probably told Lucia to go and wash her face if she had still been alive. But Lucia liked the way the mascara and eye shadow made her eyes look larger, so she was glad to be able to please herself. She only wished she had a new outfit to wear, but just had to make do with the clothes she had worn on Christmas Day.

When she opened the front door to Tim, she was expecting to see Jerry with him, but Tim was alone. Before she could ask after his son, Tim told her that Mrs Hudson was home and had volunteered to listen out for Jerry.

'That's good of her.'

'Yeah, I suggested that she might be too tired, after the journey home from her brother's, but she said that she was glad to rest in front of her own fire in peace and quiet, knowing she was not completely alone but that there was someone else in the house. She doubted Jerry would disturb her.'

'Did she have a good time in the south?' Lucia asked.

'Yes, said it was lovely seeing her brother, nieces and nephews. Anyway, if you're ready, let's be on our way. I told Mrs Hudson I wouldn't be late back.'

Lucia switched off the lobby light and accepted Tim's helping hand down the steps. 'So how is the book coming along?' she asked.

'I had to remove Freddie's name from the manuscript. In fact, Isabella has told me that it's probably best if I delete a lot of the names I've mentioned, otherwise I might end up facing a libel charge.'

'What did you say to that? Surely she should have told you to do that earlier?'

'I said that to her – and also that people have got to have names.'

'Perhaps you should put somewhere that "names have been changed to protect the innocent".'

'She said that too. But honestly, if I change the names they're no longer the people I'm referring to – and why should they be protected? They're no innocents.'

'Maybe because they're trying to turn over a new leaf? Just the same as you are. After all, you've changed your name.' The words were out before she could think what effect they might have on Tim.

'So you still regard me as a criminal?' he said.

'I don't regard you like that at all, but you have to face up to the fact that you were once a criminal and it's something you regret. You've been given a second chance to make good, and perhaps they want the same opportunity and see a need to protect their families.'

'But where does that leave my story if I can't be honest about those involved in the bad times in my life?'

'Couldn't you turn your book into a novel?'

'No! Isabella reckons a true-life story will make more money.'

'I presume she's going to get a percentage of what the book earns?'

'Of course, she's helped me a lot and has already found a publisher.'

'And I suppose they must agree with her? Have they read any of your story yet?'

'The first few chapters, which they wanted me to scrap or work in later in flashback.'

'What's flashback?'

'The character thinking back to an earlier event in his life. They want me to start the book at a more exciting point, just before the robbery. So I'm now actually starting with me just having dropped the gang off. I'm sitting in the car, tense with nerves and excitement, waiting and thinking.'

'Gosh, there's more to this writing game than I realized. Wouldn't it be easier to start at the beginning of your life and carry on from there?'

'Yeah, but apparently that would mean the reader wading through stuff that isn't that exciting to get to the part of my life that is really challenging. Later I can include the things that brought me to that point and made me a person prepared to risk going to jail and bringing disgrace on my family.'

'I see their point and, what with it being a true story, there will be readers who'll want to know what happened next.'

'She's not considering you robbing a bank, is she?' Lucia joked.

'She should know me well enough to know I wouldn't do it.'

'So does she have anything else in mind? Such as what happened with the car on Boxing Day?'

'I asked her about using that near the ending as she was not happy with my suggestion for an uplifting finish. I'd told her it was my story and I wanted a happy ending. I didn't want her thinking of me having a shoot-out with the police or the gang and leaving it on a cliff-hanger with me lying bleeding in the gutter filled with regret for having let so many people down.'

'Surely she wouldn't do that? Although, if she thinks up that kind of stuff, it could be that she should be writing thrillers or scripts for American cops-and-robbers movies.'

'You could have something there. Anyway, enough about Isabella and writing. We're having a night out and I can't wait to hear the music and to do some interviewing.'

Lucia linked her arm through Tim's, slowing her pace to match his as they headed for the bus stop. They huddled together against the chilly wind blowing in from the Mersey and talked music and films. It was a relief when the bus arrived and they could sit down in the warmth. In no time at all they were getting off the bus opposite the library, passing the Red Lion pub and crossing the bridge over the Leeds–Liverpool canal. They turned right past the nursery school where Irene worked and then past the post office on the corner; it was not far from there to Litherland Park, a crescent of large houses with big gardens to the rear.

Lucia paused at a gate with sandstone pillars either side; on one was painted 'The Chestnuts'. 'This is it,' she said, opening the gate.

Tim followed her up the drive and gave a low whistle as the house came into view.

'I know,' said Lucia. 'It's a fair size. I think it was built in Victorian times when lots of people had large families.'

The door was opened to them by Nellie's stepson, Tony. 'Welcome,' he said, bowing and waving them in. He kissed Lucia on both cheeks and shook hands with Tim. 'You're just in time. We're about to start. Lucia, could you see to your coats?'

She nodded, and because they were damp hung them over the banister instead of taking them upstairs. Then she led Tim into the front room, where a welcoming coal fire burned brightly. Several people were sitting facing the five young men, who were arranged with their musical instruments and amplifiers and mike at the far end of the rectangular room.

Lucia waved to her aunt and Irene who were seated together on a huge squashy sofa. They signalled her over so, taking Tim by the hand, she led him across. After introducing Tim to her aunt, they managed to squeeze on to the sofa. As soon as they were seated, the music started with 'Big Bad John'. Then Tony sang Cliff Richard's hit 'When the Girl in Your Arms Is the Girl in Your Heart'. After that came Bobby Vee's 'Take Good Care of My Baby', sung by Nick, who then sang Helen Shapiro's popular bouncy song, 'Walking Back to Happiness'. There was also a rendition of the instrumental, 'Midnight in Moscow', which had been a hit for Kenny Ball and His Jazzmen, which pleased Tim.

Then there was a break for refreshments, during which Lucia offered her help to Nellie and later introduced Tim to a few people and was reacquainted with Nick's girlfriend. A petite young woman with curves in all the right places, blue-eyed with full lips and short black curly hair. She also had a light voice that was pleasant to the ear. Lucia could not help wondering what Nick's stepsister, Bobby, thought of her, because she and Nick had been very close since they had first met in the coffee bar in the mid-fifties. Of course, Nick had already been friends with Chris, so he had known Grace before he met Bobby.

She thought about how many of her acquaintances had been through the mill. Nick had lost both his first adoptive parents early in his teens. Bobby had never known her father as he had died before she was born during the war. Tony had lost his Italian mother as a baby and been put in an orphanage. Fortunately his father had gone in search of him and traced him. Then there was Tim, whose father had hit him so hard in his youth that he had ended up in hospital. How had his mother felt? It must have torn her apart. Lucia hated violence of any sort. She remembered Nellie's father hitting his second wife, an Italian woman, much younger than him, whom he had met just after the war in Italy. Nellie had gone to her defence, only to be threatened by her father. But having to face two angry, defiant women had caused him to back off. Not long after he had died, and not one member of the family had mourned his passing. A sad end to a life.

After refreshments, the second half of the evening began with Tony's rendering of Elvis's 'Wooden Heart'. Lucia had been conscious of Tim having gone over to the group earlier and getting into a huddle in a corner with Nick and Tony. She hoped Tim now had enough information to write a decent article for the *Mersey Beat* newspaper.

She would ask him about it on the bus on the way home, she decided, but before then she'd give Nellie a hand in the kitchen, and find out what she thought of Tim.

'He's pretty well how I expected him to be,' Nellie replied.

'That doesn't help me,' said Lucia. 'Have you been listening to Irene? I know she has no time for him.'

'Can you blame her? He might have saved that little boy's life at the risk of his own, but he was quick enough in the past to dump his son on his brother and Irene.'

'He didn't know that Marty and Irene were together then; he believed his sister Peggy was still sharing a house with Marty – as she had been when Tim left for London with his wife and Jerry.'

'All right, you have a point there,' said Nellie.

'And before you say it, I know he lied to Maggie about who was looking after Jerry for him while he worked at building up his car repair business. She hardly ever stops warning me about him.'

'You obviously haven't taken her words to heart, though.'

'I listened, but decided he needed a second chance to prove he had changed – and he has taken responsibility for Jerry now. But it's not easy for a man on his own to bring up a child.'

'A lot of women are having to do it since the war.'

'I know that – but somehow women seem to cope better – and you have to admit we're glad of someone to relieve us of the responsibility at times.'

'I wouldn't argue, love.'

'I really appreciate knowing you're nearby if I need help,' said Lucia.

'I know you do. But getting back to Tim – where do you see your relationship going?'

'I don't think too far ahead. I have enough to occupy my thoughts with the present. But it is good having a man friend close by who I can talk to and go out with occasionally.'

'That mightn't be enough for him, though.'

'He's not going to want to marry me!' Lucia said, a quiver in her voice.

'But he may want something from you without marriage,' said Nellie hesitantly, in an undertone. 'You're an attractive young woman – and men have needs.'

'You mean sex,' said Lucia, blushing slightly.

'Yes. I see you've thought about it.'

'Not really.'

'What's that supposed to mean? You either have or haven't.'

They both fell silent as Irene entered the kitchen. She stared at the pair of them. 'Am I interrupting something?'

'No, we were just talking,' said Nellie. 'Can I help you, Irene?'

'That's what I was going to ask you,' said Irene. 'Is there anything you want me to do?'

Lucia handed her a tea towel.

Irene said, 'I bet you were talking about Tommy – or Tim, as he calls himself now.'

'If we are, it's none of your business,' Lucia said.

'There's none so blind as those who won't see,' said Irene. 'Open your eyes, Lucia. Falling in love with him will only end in tears.'

'So speaks someone who fell in love with a man she believed to be married at the time,' snapped Lucia.

'Lucia, enough!' said Nellie.

'Why? I'm only speaking the truth.'

'Yes, and it was a very painful journey at the time,' said Irene.

'But it all came right in the end,' Lucia said, folding her arms across her chest. 'I came in here just wanting to know what my aunt thought of Tim once she met him for herself – but obviously she can't help but bring all she's heard about him from those who knew him from the past into the equation. The person she hasn't mentioned is Uncle Francis. He visited Tim in prison and has known him from a boy. He could see some good in him and thinks he deserves a second chance.'

'He's a priest, so he's supposed to think like that,' said Irene.

'So are we,' responded Lucia. 'Judge not, lest you be judged. The same goes for forgiveness.'

'OK, you've made your point,' said Irene. 'I just don't want you getting hurt.'

'I know. But most people don't go through life without getting hurt now and again. I learnt that when I lost my parents in a car crash – and earlier when your brother married someone else.'

'I know, and that was tough. More reason why your friends and family don't want you getting hurt again so soon,' said Irene.

Nellie moved so suddenly that it startled both young women. 'I think it's time to draw this conversation to an end. The music will be starting up again soon.'

They left the kitchen.

'So did you learn plenty of interesting stuff from Nick and Tony?' asked Lucia, pushing the memory of that conversation with her aunt and Irene to the back of her mind. She was glad of the warmth of Tim's arm against hers as they sat next to each other on the front seat of the upper deck of the bus. It had been a bit of a struggle for Tim climbing the stairs, but earlier she had mentioned how much she used to enjoy sitting up front on the top deck when she was a kid and looking down through the window at what lay below on the pavement and ahead. Besides, Tim wanted a ciggie, and was only allowed to smoke on the upper deck.

'I was particularly interested in what they both had to say about their childhood. I wish I'd got to meet Tony's father this evening, but apparently he has his own marble business and was working overtime.'

'Uncle Michelangelo has a lovely tenor voice, although, unlike Tony, he's only half-Italian, his mother was a Liverpudlian who married an Italian before the Great War.'

'So the lad told me. Sadly he scarcely remembers his own mother, but he tells me that your aunt has been like a proper mother to him.'

'Yes, Aunt Nellie loves him like one of her own. She was married before she married Uncle Michelangelo, but her first husband was killed in the desert war and, not long after, she miscarried and lost their baby. To see her now, you wouldn't believe she'd had so much sadness in her life.'

Tim nodded. 'Tony told me that you once lived there with your mother.'

'Yes, it used to be Mam's grandfather's house. Aunt Nellie went to live with him after her mother died. Her mother had been killed in the Blitz; my mam was injured at the same time. So the three sisters all lived there together with the old man for a while. His sister had died years before and their father was away at the war. The old man left the house to Aunt Nellie. He didn't like his son, so he didn't want him to have it, and she had looked after her grandfather even when he started going doolally.'

'Sometimes family members only put up with each other because that's what they're expected to do.'

'Yet more often than not, people turn to family when they're in trouble because they expect they'll get the help they need from them,' said Lucia.

'I can't deny I've done that and received help,' said Tim. 'Despite having let them down.'

'But now you're trying to make up for it,' Lucia said.

'Yeah, which reminds me: I must take Jerry to see Mam sometime during this coming week. I need to wish her a Happy New Year.'

'School will be starting soon.'

'Which means I'll be able to get on with my writing with fewer distractions,' Tim said.

'Do you actually write when that journalist woman comes to help you?'

'No, she looks over what I've written since her last visit and tells me what she thinks. If there's stuff she doesn't like, we discuss it. Sometimes I go along with the alterations she suggests, but if I feel strongly about what she's against, I leave it in. If the publisher were to agree with her, then probably I'd change my mind. After all, they are the ones who have to sell the book, and the whole reason behind me writing it is to make money to support me and Jerry.'

'I'm looking forward to seeing it on the shelves in the shops so when I buy it I can say I know the author.'

'You don't have to buy one. I'll give you a copy,' said Tim, smiling.

'And will you sign it for me?'

'Of course. It'll be a pleasure. But here's hoping I manage to finish it and the publisher likes it.'

'I'm sure they will.'

'Sometimes I feel Isabella is on the side of the gang. She says she can understand if they were mad with me for clearing off the way I did. I asked her what good would it have done if I'd hung around waiting to be arrested by the police? And, as it was, I did end up serving time in prison when I returned to Liverpool, so I didn't get off scot-free.'

'No, you paid for your mistakes and have learnt your lesson.'

'That's what I told her – and also that by writing the book, I want tearaways like me to realize that crime doesn't pay.'

'What did she say to that?'

'That surely most tearaways didn't read, because if they did they wouldn't be out getting into trouble. I was lost for words for a while, wondering if she was right and was I wasting my time putting so much work into writing the book if the people I was writing it for wouldn't read it.'

'But surely your book will encourage them to read? A book written by someone who understands what it's like being them,' Lucia said forcefully.

Tim smiled and thanked Lucia. 'I'll tell her that and then step back while she loses her rag. Isabella is a person who likes her own way and can get really difficult if I go against her.'

'So what will you do?'

'I'm going to write what I want and I'm going to tell her that I don't want her seeing it until I've reached the end. And if she doesn't like it, she's just going to have to lump it.'

'Good for you.'

They both fell silent for a while after that, and did not speak again until they left the bus. The wind was still quite strong and Lucia said, 'I can smell the sea.'

Tim took a deep breath. 'So can I. It's a smell I missed when I was in the bush in Australia.'

'You should have stayed near the coast.'

'I know. But the sea wasn't the only thing I missed, and if I hadn't come back, I wouldn't have discovered I had a son – and I wouldn't have met you and that would have been my loss on two counts.'

Lucia felt as if her heart had flipped over. 'What a nice thing to say,' she murmured.

'I mean it,' he said, taking her hand and swinging it. 'How about us having a walk along the sands?'

She thought how it would be freezing cold on the beach, as well as pitch black, but she kept her thoughts to herself as the idea appealed to her. 'OK, it's not often I get to stroll on the beach at this time of night.'

'There's a first time for everything,' he said. 'And it will be magic. You'll see.'

The moon was hidden by a small puff of cloud but the sky was sprinkled with stars, which meant they could see where they were going; on the other side of the Mersey, the lights of New Brighton reflected prettily on the surface of the river.

It was as cold as she had thought it would be and she shivered. Aware of that shiver, Tim unbuttoned his overcoat and suggested she step inside. She did so and he drew it right round her so she felt snug, pressed against the warmth of his body. They stood still, gazing out over the glistening dark waters, listening to the waves lapping on the shore. She was aware that her heartbeat had quickened, and was half expecting him to kiss her. When he did so, it was with such gentleness that it seemed part of the magical moments they were sharing with the natural world. It did not last long, and soon he was turning and guiding her carefully from the beach. When he escorted her to her front door, she wondered whether he would kiss her goodnight or even suggest that he come in, but he didn't, only thanking her for an enjoyable evening. She told him that it was her pleasure and wished him good night. He walked away and she closed the door and went to see if Michael or Theresa was still up.

Six

Theresa was lying on the sofa reading and Michael was sitting in front of the fire, polishing his shoes. The wireless was on low volume. He looked across at Lucia 'What time is this to be coming in?' he asked.

Lucia glanced at the clock and saw it was only five past ten. 'It's not late and there was no need for you to wait up for me.'

'I couldn't have slept without knowing you were safely home,' Michael said.

'Well, now you know how I feel when you're late,' said Lucia, undoing the buttons of her coat.

Theresa put a bookmark in her book and looked up at her sister. 'Did you have a good time?'

'Yes, the group played well and Tony and Nick sang beautifully. Nick's girlfriend was there, too.'

'What's she like?' asked Theresa.

'Attractive with dark curly hair and nice eyes – lovely long dark eyelashes like her brother Chris. He was there as well. He's a reporter for the *Echo*.'

'How old?' asked Theresa.

'Around my age.'

'Has he got a girlfriend?'

'If he has she wasn't there, and he's never mentioned one. He's very attractive, so it wouldn't surprise me if he was courting.' Lucia stood in front of the slumbering fire, warming herself, hoping her sister wasn't going to start getting interested in boys. It was enough that Michael had started dating. She needed their help with the younger kids for a bit longer. 'Anyway, it's time you were both in bed.'

They didn't argue with her but trailed out of the kitchen. Lucia heard Michael go along the lobby to the front door and bolt it top and bottom before following Theresa upstairs. Lucia checked the back door was bolted too before going to bed. It took her a while to get to sleep because the bedroom was cold and so were the sheets, and when eventually she did warm up, she could not stop thinking of that kiss on the beach and whether it had meant anything to Tim. When she did manage to drift off, she dreamt of a man dressed in a long black coat with several capes enveloping her in the folds of his cloak and carrying her off on a large black horse.

'So what was that all about?' she said aloud to herself, sitting up in bed the following morning and remembering her strange dream.

Sunlight was streaming through a gap in the curtains and she could hear movement downstairs. From outside came the sound of church bells. Time she was up or they were going to be late for Mass. She would give breakfast a miss and make do with just a cup of tea.

Within the hour the whole family was in church, except for Theresa who had said she had a migraine. Lucia bent her head in prayer, aware that Michael's head was bent, and of the fervency of his whispered prayers. Gabrielle was another one whose prayers were whispered in a tone of urgency. Joseph and James, on the other hand, were not even pretending to pray but whispering to each other.

Lucia prayed for their safekeeping and that 1962 would be a happy, healthy and fulfilling year. She was feeling reasonably at peace with herself and the world when she left church, but now her mind was occupied with thoughts of food and she wished she had been up at her normal time so she could have got the Sunday joint in the oven. She need not have worried, though, because when she arrived home and opened the front door, she was greeted by the mouth-watering smell of roasting mutton. She glanced at Theresa with a question in her eyes. Her sister nodded. Lucia mouthed her thanks and hurried to peel the vegetables.

Michael followed her. 'I'm not going to be in for lunch, Lucia. I'm just going to change and then I'm meeting Marjorie.'

'OK, I'll put yours in the oven,' said Lucia. 'Give her my best wishes.'

'I will.' He paused. 'By the way, I've got myself a paper round.'

'Good on you! That should help with the housekeeping.'

The way his jaw dropped was almost comical and then he stood up straight. 'Absolutely not! The money is mine. I'm fed up with hardly having two pennies to rub together. I want to be able to take Marjorie out.'

She heard his feet thundering on the stairs and then the opening of a wardrobe door and a drawer, then silence, before the front door slammed. She could not help but understand his point of view, while at the same time she felt indignant, thinking how she worked her socks off to support the whole family with a little bit of help from various people.

After putting on the vegetables, she asked Gabrielle to set the table. While she did so, Lucia sat down and read a couple of pages of the *News of the World* that Michael had dropped on the sofa, before removing the mutton from the oven, placing the parboiled potatoes in the meat juices and putting them in to roast with the joint.

They were just sitting down to their meal when there was a ring of the doorbell. Gabrielle rushed to answer it, and Lucia rose from her chair and stood in the kitchen doorway listening. Recognizing the voice of the caller as that of Jerry, she called for him to come in. He walked up the lobby, carefully carrying a cardboard tray flat on his widespread hand.

'What have you got there?' asked Lucia.

'Dad asked me to bring them, but told me I wasn't to stay and make a nuisance of myself. He said Joseph could come round and play with me next door. He hasn't seen the other gifts I got for Christmas yet.'

Lucia was taken aback. 'Your dad isn't working on his book?'

'No, he said that it's Sunday, a day of rest.'

'Right,' said Lucia, taking the cardboard tray of iced fairy cakes from him. 'Joseph is just about to have his dinner, so you can either sit and wait for him to finish or go back home and wait for him there.'

'I'll wait here,' said Jerry. 'Dad's doing the dishes.'

'So who made the cakes?' asked Lucia.

'Me and Dad. We used to make them sometimes when we lived in London. Mrs Sinclair, who used to look after me when Mam wasn't well, let me help her. I showed Dad what to do. He said I had a good memory and was a clever boy. Sometimes he would buy a packet of cake mix and we'd just follow the instructions, but we didn't have a packet in our cupboard today, so we made our own.'

'Well, I think that's very clever of both you and your dad.'

'And generous as well to give us so many,' said Theresa.

'Dad said we'd get fat if we ate them all ourselves,' Jerry said.

'You thank him for us,' said Lucia, wondering why Tim had not brought them himself. Could he be feeling awkward after kissing her last night? Perhaps the kiss had meant nothing to him, but he thought she might have taken it seriously? The thought depressed her. She had wanted him to kiss her again, having enjoyed that only too brief contact of their lips. But even more so she had found comfort being held in his arms. Could it possibly be that he still had strong feelings for Maggie? Surely he realized there was no hope for him there and that he had to move on. Or could it simply be that he considered Lucia too young for him, as well as being overly burdened with the responsibility of her brothers and sisters. After all, she had been told he was a man who had avoided responsibility for years, so perhaps he had decided it would be sensible not to get too close to her. At least this latter thought put paid to what her aunt had hinted at when she had said there were men who didn't believe they had to marry a woman to have sex with her.

During the rest of that day and in the days that followed Lucia could not help but ask herself what those moments on the beach had been about if Tim wanted to see less of her. If he did want to see her, then he was going to have to make the first move.

A fortnight later, Lucia was surprised to have a visit from Bobby, Nick and Chris. New Year had come and gone without any fuss. It was early Friday evening and Gabrielle came upstairs to inform her that they had visitors. She went downstairs to discover Theresa playing a recording by one Chubby Checker called 'The Twist'. Apparently a girl at school had been given it by her sailor brother who had bought it in New York; the girl had lent it to Theresa because the other girl now had his latest hit, 'Let's Twist Again'.

'He's in the top twenty in the States and the dance is gaining in popularity,' said Theresa. 'I wondered if you'd heard about him, Nick?'

'Yes, but I'm not sure the Twist will catch on here,' he replied. 'I don't think it is all that exciting.'

'You could be right,' said Theresa, and then turned her head in Chris's direction. 'You're a newspaper man, what do you think?'

'Little as I want to disagree with Nick, I'd say what's all the rage in America more often than not becomes the next fad over here within the year. Play it again and show us how the dance goes?' said Chris.

Theresa did not need asking twice and was soon performing the Twist for their visitors. Bobby and Chris joined her and – not to be outdone – so did Gabrielle and Jerry. Nick exchanged looks with Lucia and soon they were twisting as well. As soon as the music came to an end, Lucia said, 'You'll have to excuse me – we were just about to have our dinner.'

'Sorry to disturb you,' said Nick. 'I thought we'd just pop in and wish you a Happy New Year.'

'That's all right. We don't often get visitors.'

'Except for me and my dad,' said Jerry.

'Your dad?' asked Nick.

'Yes, he's a writer, Tim Murphy,' said Jerry proudly.

'Of course,' said Chris. 'I remember Nick telling me he lived next door to you.'

'That's right,' said Theresa. 'He was with us on Boxing Day when a car nearly ran us down.'

'I remember hearing about that,' said Chris.

'And, don't forget, Chris, Tim also interviewed me and Tony for the *Mersey Beat*,' said Nick. 'I wonder whether he's finished the article yet?'

'Why don't you nip next door and see?' suggested Lucia.

'It's Sunday, he mightn't want to be disturbed,' said Chris.

'Sunday is a rest day, so he won't be working,' said Lucia.

'Then we'll go,' said Nick. 'I wouldn't mind a chat with him. We'll see ourselves out.'

'I'll stay here with Lucia,' said Bobby.

So Nick and Chris went out with Jerry and Joseph next door. The door was ajar so they followed the two youngsters inside. Jerry shouted, 'Dad, visitors!'

A door to the right opened and Tim popped his head round it. 'Oh, it's Nick – and Chris, isn't it?'

'That's right, Mr Murphy,' said Nick. 'I hope you don't mind us dropping in? We called in next door to see Lucia and I thought I'd see how you're getting on with those articles for the *Mersey Beat*.'

'I've done a rough draft,' said Tim. 'Come in. You can read it through and check I haven't made any mistakes. You can check Tony's as well, if you don't mind.'

'No trouble at all,' said Nick.

He and Chris followed Tim into the front room and were waved to a seat. They sat on the sofa pulled up at an angle to the fireplace. Jerry and Joseph had disappeared.

'Would you like a coffee?' asked Tim.

Aware of Tim's disability Nick said, 'We don't want to trouble you. But if you want one just point me in the right direction and I'll make the coffees.'

'That's nice of you, Nick,' said Tim. 'But it's no trouble. I have an electric kettle in here and the doings to save me going backwards and forwards to the kitchen.'

In no time at all the three men were warming their hands on steaming cups of coffee and balancing small plates holding fairy cakes on their knees. Tim apologized for the messy icing. 'Jerry wanted to ice them so I let him. They taste good, though.'

Chris took a bite of the cake, and with his mouth full said, 'You're right. This tastes better than the last lot my sister made.'

'I'll tell Jerry that,' said Tim.

'And I'll keep quiet about it,' Nick said.

'I meant my other sister, not Grace,' murmured Chris.

Tim stood up and fetched the two articles he had written and placed them on the arm of the sofa next to Nick.

Chris glanced across at Tim and said, 'How are you getting on with your book?'

'I've come to a halt because Isabella and I disagree on some things.'

'Is it anything I could help you with?' Chris asked. 'Another man's point of view could be just what you need.'

Tim hesitated and then, leaning forward in his armchair, said, 'Truthfully, she's got me confused. It was her idea that I write this book, and then not so long ago she seems to be hinting that I'm wasting my time and the readership I was aiming for won't read it. She thinks I shouldn't use the real names of the gang, so I asked her if she wanted me to fictionalize my story?'

'What did she say to that?' asked Chris.

'She said no – that real-life stories pay well; and besides, it's what the publisher wants,' said Tim.

'Maybe she's concerned that the gang might seek revenge if you use their real names?' suggested Chris. 'Although their names appeared in the *Echo* when the case went to court.'

Suddenly Nick joined in the conversation, 'I don't suppose you've realized, Mr Murphy, but all of the gang except the leader are due to be released in about a month's time. Dad mentioned it to me when I told him I'd seen you at the Gianellis' house. I don't think you need to worry unless they find out where you live.'

Tim was silent a few moments and then said, 'And what if they do find out where I live and that I'm writing an autobiography?'

'A member of one of their families might have heard about the book,' said Chris. 'It was mentioned in the *Echo*.'

Tim frowned. 'That'll be Isabella wanting advance publicity for it.'

'I presume she's getting a percentage of the royalties,' Chris said quietly.

Tim nodded. 'Which is only fair considering the help she's given me.'

'Have you any reason for thinking a family member of the gang might have discovered where you live?' asked Nick, looking up from the sheet of paper he was reading.

'I recognized the passenger and the driver of the car on Boxing Day,' said Tim.

'I remember now that Isabella said it had to be an accident,' said Chris. 'A colleague had suggested to her that maybe someone had it in for you.'

'Lucia and Michael believed the car was heading straight for us – and I recognized the bloke driving from years back, but he wasn't a member of the gang; he used to go out with the sister of a cousin of the gang leader. The cousin was the one who escaped with me and perished in Australia.'

'I imagine you're including your escape and time spent in Australia?' Nick asked.

'Yeah, I thought readers would be interested. It's a vast country and not without its dangers. Really poisonous snakes, to name but one!' Tim shuddered. 'The bloke who escaped with me was bitten.'

'What did you do?' asked Chris. 'Suck the poison out like you used to see in old Westerns sometimes?'

'You must be joking. He was dead in minutes. Besides, I didn't even think of it. We weren't the best of mates. When I escaped I had no intention of taking any of the gang along with me, but he'd hung about outside the shop and jumped on the running board as soon as I started moving and I couldn't get rid of him. I discovered later why he was so intent on coming with me. He'd sneaked some of the booty from an earlier robbery into the car.'

Nick nudged Chris. 'I think it's time we were making a move. Bobby and Lucia will be wondering what's happened to us.'

'Can you see yourselves out?' asked Tim, wincing as he made to get up. 'I've enjoyed your company. Drop in again sometime.'

'Will do,' said Nick.

Tim struggled to his feet. 'I'd better check up on the boys. See yer!' He raised a hand in a gesture of farewell.

Nick and Chris left the house and went next door.

'About time you showed your faces,' said Bobby. 'We should be getting back. Mam and Dad were talking about going the flicks and they're going to want one of us to babysit.'

'And my mam and the girls will be back from Gran's, and no doubt Grace will be wanting to see Nick,' Chris said. 'I'll babysit with you, Bobby, if you like?'

'Thanks,' she said. 'We can listen to the LP that Nick bought me for Christmas.'

'So had Tim written the piece about you, Nick, for the *Mersey Beat*?' Lucia asked.

'Yes, and there was scarcely anything to pick him up about. Just a couple of spelling mistakes,' said Nick and changed the subject.

Bobby started to make a move. 'So we'll be seeing you, Lucia. Probably see you at the coffee bar soon.'

Lucia saw them out and then settled down with a library

book and tried to immerse herself in the detective story, but her mind kept drifting to a report she had read in the *Echo* about a murder in Knotty Ash, the murderer having taken advantage of the fog to make his escape. When it was real life, it made much scarier reading. Catching sight of the time, she decided to send Theresa next door to fetch Joseph. Even though she was tempted to go herself, she thought it might be better not to seem too keen. She need not have concerned herself because before she could send Theresa to fetch Joseph, there came a ring of the doorbell. James went to see who it was, and came back into the kitchen with the news that it was Joseph, Jerry and his father and should he invite them all in?

Before she could change her mind and be sensible, Lucia said, 'Of course!'

A few minutes later the two boys, followed by Tim, entered the kitchen. When he saw the table was set for a meal, he said, 'I won't stop if you're about to have your tea.'

'You're welcome to share it with us. Regard it as a thank you for putting up with Joseph.'

'You've put up with Jerry often enough,' Tim said. 'But thanks, I accept. I'd enjoy a chat.'

'About Nick and Chris?'

'How did you guess?'

'Easy-peasy! They'd just been to visit you. Let's have tea first, though,' said Lucia. 'Then we can go into the parlour and have a bit of peace for half an hour.'

Tim sat at the table and searched the faces there. 'No Michael?'

'No,' Lucia let out a sigh. 'He's out with Marjorie again. We see very little of him. I'm concerned because he told me he'd be having exams any day now and he seems to have done little revision for them.'

'He might be burning the midnight oil and studying after he comes in,' suggested Tim.

'I'd like to believe that,' said Lucia. 'I don't like to pry, in case he thinks I'm getting at him. He knows how important exams are if he's to get a decent job.'

'Couldn't your uncle have a word with him?'

'You mean Father Francis?'

'I didn't. I meant your Aunt Nellie's husband, but it's true that Father Francis runs a boys' club and has done for years, so he does know something about lads.'

'I know, but I could see Michael resenting his interference. Especially as I have a feeling Marjorie isn't a Catholic.'

'I see. You're probably best leaving things alone. I reckon Michael has a good head on his shoulders and knows what's best for him.'

'I hope you're right,' said Lucia. 'Now help yourself to some sandwiches. There's egg and lettuce as well as cheese and pickle.'

Tim helped himself to one of each and placed a jam tart on his plate as well. As he ate, he listened to the babble of noise about him, thinking about Jerry being an only child and what it meant to his son to be welcomed into this family. Before the Brookes had become part of Jerry's life, he'd only had Marty's daughter, Josie, to play with, apart from the children at the nursery school and primary school he'd attended near Marty's home.

It wasn't long before they were at the jelly and custard stage, and soon after Lucia helped Theresa clear the table and wash the dishes. Then she left Theresa to keep an eye on the younger ones while she and Tim had a coffee in the parlour.

'So how can I help you?' Lucia asked.

'I don't really need help,' said Tim. 'I just thought you might be interested to know that I mentioned to Chris and Nick about recognizing the two men in the car and that I believed it possible they were aiming the car straight at me. Maybe they were only thinking to put the wind up me.' Before Lucia could comment, he added swiftly, 'You might also be interested that Nick told me some of the gang are due to be released from prison next month.'

'Does that worry you?'

'Yes, because those two blokes can tell them where I live, but at least Nick and his father, Detective Inspector Walker, are aware of some of what's going on. Mind you, them finding me and there being a confrontation is probably the kind of ending that Isabella would go for, but she's going to be out of luck,' said Tim. 'What kind of ending do you like, love?'

'Happy ones, or at least ones that leave me feeling satisfied.'

'I'll see what I can do,' said Tim. 'Although I'm not expecting miracles.'

'What kind of miracle would you like to happen?'

'I'd like to be able to walk normally again or, if not that, to be able to drive comfortably.'

'Why is it you can't?'

'I fractured my pelvis. The only reason I can walk at all is because a surgeon pinned it together.'

'So you have bits of metal inside you?'

'Exactly. I'm grateful that the surgeon was able to do that much for me.'

'That would have been unheard of years ago. Our ancestors would have considered it a miracle,' said Lucia.

'True; but enough about me. Have you any news to tell me?'

'Nothing new. I told you my aunt Babs is coming over from America towards the end of June. I can't wait to see her. She's such fun. Although she's bringing her mother-in-law and I don't know what difference it'll make, but I am sure it will be fine.'

'She won't be staying here, though, will she?'

'No, she'll be staying with Aunt Nellie. Mam was the middle of the three sisters.'

'Nellie being the eldest?'

'Yes, Uncle Francis is older than the girls, and there was another brother who was killed during the war.'

'Shame.'

'Yes, but if he had lived, most likely my great-grandfather wouldn't have left the house to Nellie despite her looking after him in his old age. The brother who died was the favourite. I heard he was a bit of a lad but had lots of charm.' Lucia paused. 'Anyway, that's enough about my family. Would you like another coffee?'

'Yeah, thanks.' He handed his cup to her.

'I'll only be a few minutes,' she said. 'Are you warm enough in here?'

He nodded. 'Will you check that Jerry's not being a nuisance?

'He's never a nuisance. He's a well-behaved little lad, as I've told you before.'

'That's thanks to my brother, Marty, and even our Peggy

played her part in looking after him. As did Monica, who used to babysit sometimes, as I think I told you.'

Lucia paused in the doorway. 'Monica comes into the coffee bar whenever she's back in Liverpool. She's gone solo now and travels round the country doing gigs.'

'So I heard. Well, I'm glad she managed to escape her grandmother's house and follow her dream. I'd like to hear her sing live. I do have one of her records.'

'I'll let you know if I hear anything. She keeps in touch with Tony.'

'I'd appreciate that. Perhaps we could go together if she comes and does a gig in Liverpool?'

'I'd like that.' With a song in her heart, Lucia left the parlour and headed for the kitchen, surprised to hear only Theresa's voice coming from there. Only when Lucia pushed open the door did she see the reason for that.

Theresa, James, Joseph, Gabrielle and Jerry were gathered about the table playing Lotto.

'What are you playing for?' she asked Theresa.

'Chocolate drops. We don't have any Smarties,' replied Theresa.

'I'll see if I can afford to get some tomorrow.'

Lucia made the coffee and returned to the parlour.

'So what were they doing?' asked Tim.

'Playing Lotto. We used to play it at Christmas when Mam and Dad were alive. We used to call it Housey-Housey. Do you know it?'

'I know it. I love a game of chance.'

'You mean like gambling?'

'Yes, if you played for money.'

'Mam mustn't have realized. She didn't believe in gambling.'

'Did you play for halfpennies and pennies?'

'No, generally we played for Smarties.'

'Then I wouldn't be worrying. I doubt any of you will turn into serious gamblers from playing at home for sweets.'

'You're teasing me,' said Lucia.

He nodded. 'You're far too serious for a young woman of your age. You need to relax and have some fun. But I suppose that's difficult with your responsibilities.'

'We do have fun times as a family, but the fact that I have to make all the decisions for our wellbeing worries me.'

'But surely Father Francis and your aunt help you?'

'Yes, but it's not as if they're on the spot, and besides, I don't want to bother them.'

'I doubt they'd think you a bother.'

'I know – it's me that worries because they have a lot on their plates as it is.'

'It's time you stopped worrying and accepted that families are there to help each other – I've a feeling we've had this kind of conversation before – and your aunt and uncle having seen more of life will have a load of experience to draw on, so accept that it shows sense to ask for their advice sometimes.'

'You're very wise,' she said, smiling up at him.

'I can only say, as many have before me, that I wish I'd known when I was younger what I know now – but I'd bet my bottom dollar that I've still a lot to learn about life and that I'll make more mistakes.' He was tempted to put an arm around her shoulders and give her a hug, but knew it wouldn't be sensible. 'Enough of this seriousness. Do you know any jokes?'

'None that I can remember. What about you?'

'None suitable for a young lady's ears.'

'Oh, I do like you,' she said with a burst of enthusiasm. 'You make me smile even without telling me a joke.'

He gazed into her sparkling eyes and wanted nothing more than to kiss her, but decided that would be an even more foolish thing to do than giving her a hug. She needed someone younger like Nick – or Chris – who wasn't carrying a load of baggage with him from the past. Although neither of them would probably want to take on the kids.

'I like you too,' he said, recalling having been told by a number of women that they were in love with him, but he couldn't remember any saying they liked him.

He remembered seeing films where a woman had told a man, after he had proposed, that she liked him but did not love him. Which made it sound as if it was easier to like someone than to love someone enough to marry them. Yet it seemed to him now that liking someone was more important in a relationship, because surely with liking came respect, and that was so important in a marriage. There had been times when he had positively disliked Bernie, which was probably why he had been able to leave her behind when fleeing from the police. Yet he had believed he was in love with her. It just went to show that rushing into marriage because you simply lusted after someone was a big mistake.

They were interrupted by Joseph and Jerry, wanting to know if Jerry could stay the night. The two boys had looked to Tim for an answer and he looked at Lucia. She had nodded, thinking that would mean she and Tim could have some more time alone to talk, but she would not make the mistake of inviting him to sit next to her this time. She made two mugs of cocoa and chose to sit in the armchair that had been her father's.

'Has Jerry managed to get out on his bike?' she asked. 'He must be dying to have a proper ride on it.'

'Maybe now the thaw has arrived, he'll be able to get out. Anyway, it won't be too long before spring arrives – he'll have plenty of time then to be out cycling. I'm so glad he's made friends with Joseph.'

'It's not just one-sided. Jerry is good for Joseph. I'd say that brothers and sisters are inclined to want to find their own friends. Perhaps it's a case of familiarity breeding contempt sometimes. They think they know each other inside out but they don't know everything.'

'I'd never have believed our Peggy would have had the guts to leave home without saying where she was going, but she did. As for my other sister, Lil, I've never forgotten her saying that I think I can charm my way out of anything.'

'And can you?' Lucia smiled lopsidedly.

'No, or I wouldn't have landed in jail. I needed pulling up and to think about not only who I was hurting by my actions. Not only was I damaging other people, but that I was also damaging myself.'

'But now you've the chance to start over again and make something of your life,' said Lucia, draining her coffee cup and getting to her feet.

'Yeah, and I don't want to make a mess of things this time.'

'You and Maggie?'

'I mucked up there through not being honest with her. She's

a great girl but obviously not the one for me. I hope she is happy.'

'She is. She and Josh suit each other down to the ground,' said Lucia. 'Would you like another cocoa?'

He hesitated, then shook his head. 'It's getting late. I'd best be going.'

'I've only ever fancied myself in love once before, and that was a few years ago,' Lucia mused aloud. 'I had a real crush on Irene's brother, Jimmy, but it came to nothing and he's married now, which is all well and good, so out of reach.'

'Yeah, that's what's needed if you fancy somebody and you don't want to get hurt or to hurt them. You need to put some distance between the two of you.'

'Hmmm. But it was painful.'

'Our Peg did it, and in the end it all worked out OK.'

'That was because she and Pete still cared for each other and he didn't give up on her but went looking for her,' said Lucia. 'Irene told me all about it.'

'She did?'

'Yes. It was a happy ending and, as I told you earlier, I like a happy ending.'

'Me too! I've enjoyed this evening, Lucia, but I'm going to have to go. I want to get a good night's sleep, so I can get up early and work on the ending of the book before taking Jerry and your lot to school.'

'OK, I'll see you out.'

'Send Jerry home in the morning as soon as you like,' said Tim, shrugging on his overcoat.

'Will do,' Lucia said, wasting no time in opening the front door. 'Good night.'

She did not linger to watch him go into next door, but washed the cocoa cups before going up to her lonely bed, thinking that at least she had her aunt Babs's visit to look forward to. At first Lucia could not get to sleep because their conversation kept going round and round in her head. Eventually she fell asleep, but woke up with Tim still in her thoughts. Was she falling in love with him despite Maggie's warnings?

Her musings were interrupted by a scream which she recognized as coming from Gabrielle, and hurried to see what her sister was making a fuss about. No doubt it wouldn't be earth-shattering. She made her way to Gabrielle's bedroom, where she discovered her youngest sister huddled beneath the bedcovers.

'Why did you scream?' asked Lucia.

'There's a flying thing in the room. It touched my face. I thought it was going to bite me so I hid myself.'

Lucia's eyes scanned the room swiftly and could not see anything. 'I think you've been imagining things.'

'No. I haven't,' cried Gabrielle.

'Did it make a noise?'

'Yes, it snorted.'

'Snorted!' For a moment Lucia was at a loss to think of a flying insect that made such a noise, and then she left the room and went into the boys' bedroom. James appeared to be still fast asleep but Joseph's bed was empty. Of course it was possible that he and Jerry could be in the bathroom, but she suspected they were more likely to be hiding in Gabrielle's bedroom. The pair of scamps! She hurried along the landing and into her sister's bedroom; she looked under the bed but there was no sign of the boys. She flopped on to the bed and there came a giggle. Getting up, she went over to the window and drew back a curtain, and there was Jerry.

Her mouth tightened and she was about to tear a strip off him when a voice said, 'He's not to blame.' She looked about her to see where the voice came from and a movement caught her eye. She saw Joseph peering over the top of the wardrobe. 'Get down from there, you horror,' she bellowed.

'I-I c-can't,' stuttered her brother. 'I-I'm stuck.'

'You got up there, so surely you can get down,' Lucia said.

'I had Jerry's help, I climbed on his back.'

'You could have slipped and both of you got hurt,' she said.

'But we didn't – and the joke worked,' Joseph said, brandishing a fishing rod with feathers tied to the end of the line.

'Your sister didn't find it funny.'

'That's because she's a misery,' said Joseph. 'Will you help me down now, Lucia?'

'No, I won't. You can stay there all day as punishment.'

'But I'll miss school and it's footie today.'

'Tough luck.' She turned her back on him, 'Come on, Gabrielle, get out of bed and dressed.'

'I'm not getting dressed with two boys watching me,' Gabrielle said. 'If I forgive them, can they go?'

Seeing nothing for it but to agree, Lucia said, 'Yes, but don't think that means you'll get off scot-free, Joseph. And as for you, Jerry, I'll be telling your father.'

Jerry groaned.

Lucia told him to go downstairs; once he had left the room, she helped Joseph down from the wardrobe. Taking the fishing rod from him she went into her bedroom and hid it. After breakfast she told Jerry to put on his coat, scarf and cap and went outside with him. She was surprised to see Tim on the neighbouring step talking to a young woman.

He must have heard the door open because he turned and waved. She went with Jerry over to him. 'I need to talk to you, Tim' she said, glancing briefly at the woman with him. 'I wonder if you could spare a few minutes later?'

'Fine, I'll pop over after I've taken the kids to school,' he said, and introduced the two women. Both looked each other up and down.

Lucia said, 'How do you do?' but did not offer her hand to Isabella, wondering what she was doing at the house that early in the day before turning away almost immediately and saying to Tim, 'Leave it until this evening. I've work to go to now.' As she walked away she overheard Isabella say, 'Don't forget, Timmy boy, I'll be here this evening to see to all your needs.' She giggled.

Once at the coffee bar, Lucia could not stop thinking about Isabella, who was more Tim's age and extremely attractive and well-groomed, and also of what she had overheard her say on the doorstep earlier. She was so distracted by her thoughts that she made several mistakes over orders, which caused Josh to ask her if she was all right or was there something worrying her, and if so was it something he and Maggie could help with. She reassured him that she was just thinking about something Joseph had done that morning and she was mulling over what punishment she should dole out.

'Boys,' he said, laughing.

'Yes, boys – not that they're all the same. James and Joseph are completely different.' She pulled herself together and got on with her work.

When she arrived home, she was glad to find Michael at home and that he appeared to be doing homework. Only she would have been more convinced if he didn't keep lifting his head and staring into space. Theresa was another one who didn't appear to have her attention on the job in hand; she was standing at the sink up to her elbows in soapsuds, staring out of the window. But Lucia soon realized that her sister could simply be keeping her eye on the younger ones playing in the garden. The vegetables were on the hob, gently simmering.

Theresa turned on Lucia. 'There was no meat to put on.'

'Sorry, I should have told you I'd buy some sausages on the way home. I'll mash the potatoes and do some onion gravy. You go and have a rest.' Lucia turned her shopping bag upside down, emptying out the sausages and a box of cream buns that Josh had given her. If she cut them in half, there would be enough for all of them.

Tim arrived an hour later. Gabrielle was helping Theresa to clear the table while Lucia was making a pot of tea. Michael had gone upstairs to his room and so Lucia waved Tim to a chair at the side of the fireplace. She handed him a cup of tea and half a cream bun on a plate and settled in a chair the other side of the fireplace.

'So, what is it you want to talk about?' he asked.

Instead of bringing up the topic of Joseph and Jerry's misbehaviour that morning, she found herself saying, 'I'm sorry for interrupting your conversation with Isabella this morning.'

He gave a half-smile. 'I was glad of the interruption. She was going on about my time in Australia with the bloke who escaped with me.'

'The one bitten by the snake?'

'Yeah! She seems to think I'm lying about that and the way the pair of us escaped the police during the robbery. She thinks I forced him to go with me, and that I did so because it was me who had the gun, not the other way around. I asked her why I'd want his company? It wasn't as if we were best mates and, besides, I never had a gun or needed one. I was simply there to drive the car.'

'And what did she say?'

'She seemed lost for words at first, which was unusual. I told her that if she wasn't going to believe me, then I didn't want her help any more.'

'So what did she do then?'

'She tried to sweet-talk me, saying she was sorry and that she enjoyed working with me. She then went on to insist that there must have been a lot of tension between me and Sid in light of him pulling a gun on me. Hadn't I tried to get it off him?'

'I told her I couldn't do that when I was driving the car.'

'She must be a fool not to have realized that,' Lucia said, reaching out a hand to him.

He took it and squeezed it gently. 'Then she apologized and said that she wasn't herself because she had got herself into debt and really needed the book to be a big success. I said that I needed it to be a success as well, to support me and my son. That I couldn't afford to get into debt.'

'I bet that annoyed her,' Lucia said. 'Yet she didn't seem that annoyed when I saw her with you.'

'That's because I agreed to her coming this evening and reading over what I'd written since last we met.'

'You won't allow her to get you to change your mind about anything?'

'Of course not. And I'm determined to see the publisher in her company, so she won't be able to say things about me and my work behind my back,' said Tim. 'Right now all I want is to finish the book. I told her a satisfactory ending for me is my being united with my son. Maybe even opening up the garage again and hiring someone to do what I find difficult.'

'That sounds good to me,' Lucia said.

'She still thinks it isn't exciting enough. I said that there had been enough excitement in my life, and I've described that earlier on in the book.' He drained his teacup and stood up. 'I'd best be going. I need to get Jerry ready for bed and do a bit more writing before she comes. I wish I was back at work fixing cars.'

'So you still have your garage?'

'Yes, there's still a year or so to go on the lease and I haven't been in the mood to get rid of it. I've had my mind on other things and it would have made my life too complicated. I'd have to work out if it was financially viable.'

'You mean it would have to bring in enough money to pay wages and also provide you with an income?'

He smiled. 'Yeah! You have a good business head, Lucia. You're wasted being just a waitress at the coffee bar.'

'It wasn't what I'd planned to do with my life, but I was already working there part-time when my parents were killed, so it was easier for me to continue working there.'

'I can see that,' said Tim. 'Well, I hope life gets better for you.'

'Thanks, but don't go thinking I'm unhappy, I'm not.'

He smiled. 'Thanks for the tea and a share of the cream bun.'

'The bun was courtesy of Josh. He's generous like that. He knows how I'm situated and often gives me something to feed me and the kids.'

'I can understand why Maggie married him.'

'Yes, he's a likable, dependable bloke, and he loves her and she loves him.'

'What more could a woman ask for?' said Tim lightly. He paused on the step. 'I can't believe that you wanted to talk to me this evening just about Isabella.'

'I didn't, but the real reason doesn't seem important now,' she said, realizing she did not want to upset him by complaining about Jerry's misbehaviour. 'Good evening, Tim.'

'It wouldn't have been about Jerry, would it?' Tim asked. 'Because he told me about the trick he and Joseph played on Gabrielle. I told him if he ever did anything like that again, he wouldn't be allowed to play with Joseph any more. Good evening, Lucia. See you around.'

'Yes, see you around,' she said, hoping she had not upset him by using the word *dependable* of Josh. A trait that Maggie had said Tim didn't possess. She could think of no other reason why he would have mentioned what Jerry and Joseph had done that morning. He was letting her know that she could depend on him to discipline Jerry by punishing him in a way that would really hurt. She felt warmth flood her and realized that she was falling for Tim against all the odds.

She called Gabrielle, James and Joseph indoors from where

they had been swinging from a lamp-post with some other children and sent them upstairs to wash and clean their teeth before getting in to bed. She asked Theresa to read a story to Gabrielle while she read one to the boys. Although Lucia knew they could read themselves, she was also aware they still enjoyed being read to. Whilst getting the children to bed, she could not help noticing that Michael was nowhere to be seen, and could only think he had gone out, possibly to meet Marjorie again.

Lucia settled down in front of the fire to sew a button on James's blazer and to watch the television at the same time. She wished *The Avengers* was on, but she was going to have to wait a few days before the next episode was shown. She was still unsure if she liked Cathy Gale, clad in her black leather catsuit, although the way she fought the baddies using judo, she supposed it made sense to wear such an outfit, and possibly some would find it sexy. Even so, her favourite character was Steed, because he was witty and she did enjoy the verbal sparring between him and Cathy Gale.

The minutes ticked by, the hands of the clock reached ten o'clock, and there was no phone call or sign of her brother. Lucia was really annoyed. When eventually she heard his key in the lock, she shot out of her seat and went out into the lobby, ready to blow her top.

'Where d'you think you've been?' Lucia demanded.

Michael adopted an air of bravado. 'To the second house of the flicks, and then I saw Marjorie on to the bus and came home.'

'This isn't on, Michael,' said Lucia. 'Why didn't you tell me you were going out?'

'Because I knew you'd have a moan, despite my having done some homework.'

'A moan! I have a perfect right to moan, as you put it, when you behave so thoughtlessly. I was worried sick, not knowing where you'd gone, and with it getting later and later.'

'I thought you'd have guessed I was with Marjorie,' he said sulkily.

'I did, but that didn't make me feel any better. I'd like to know what her mother feels about her daughter not coming home until after eleven o'clock on a school day.'

'Marjorie told her mam she was going to be in late because I was taking her to the flicks in town.'

Lucia exploded. 'You could have paid me the same courtesy. Get out of my sight! I'm fed up with you. You selfish little sod!' She picked up a cushion and threw it at him.

Michael caught it deftly and threw it back. Lucia stretched up and managed to grip it. She tossed it back at him and he returned it to her. He said, 'This is ridiculous. I'm sorry you were worried about me. But I'm not a kid any more. I can take care of myself.'

'So you say, but accidents can happen and the pubs won't have long let out and you could get caught up in a brawl without intending to and get hurt.'

'Gosh, you don't have much faith in my common sense, do you? Stop worrying and try trusting me.'

'I will if you tell me where you're going and if you're going to be late.'

'OK, I'll try not to forget in future.'

'Never mind trying, you don't forget. Anyway, I'm going to bed. I've work in the morning and you have to be up early for your paper round.' She stomped out and started up the stairs, only remembering halfway up that she needed to be quieter if she didn't want to wake the children.

It was a while before Lucia fell asleep, but at last she drifted off to dream about Tim with a noose around his neck, hanging from a tree and escaping somehow, only to be bitten by a snake. Then Michael was there and hitting the snake on the head with a cushion. She woke up to the sound of a car engine outside, so she slid out of bed to see what was going on. It was still dark, and if it had not been for the street lamp she would not have been able to make out the colour of the car or its licence plate and the face of the man who climbed out and stood looking up at the house. Who was he? She was almost tempted to wake up Michael, only the man got back into the car and drove off. She glanced at the bedside clock and saw that it was two o'clock in the morning. Groaning, she climbed back into bed, hoping she could get asleep quicker this time but without the bad dreams.

The next time she woke, the room was filled with the pearly

light of pre-dawn. She wasted no time getting up and dressed, remembering her peculiar dream. By then the rest of the household was beginning to stir. She went downstairs, then heard Michael thundering down the stairs. He went into the back kitchen and reappeared a few minutes later with a jam butty in one hand and a cup of milk in the other. He drank the milk and left the kitchen, holding the half-eaten jam butty. 'See you later,' he said.

'Ta-ra,' said Lucia, plugging in a small portable electric fire instead of lighting the fire.

The boys and Theresa were on their way downstairs, but there was no sign of Gabrielle, who nearly always had to be dragged out of bed. Lucia left Theresa getting out bowls, spoons and cereal while she went upstairs and woke Gabrielle, throwing back the covers and yanking her upright. 'Rise and shine,' said Lucia.

Her sister groaned. 'I don't want to go to school. I'm not well.'

'Rubbish! You were perfectly all right last night.'

'Why d'you never believe me?' asked Gabrielle. 'I feel sick.'

'You don't look sick. Anyway, if it turns out you are sick, your teacher will send you home.'

'But she knows there's nobody at home.'

'She has Auntie Nellie's phone number and she'll fetch you.'

Gabrielle sighed and rose from the bed. 'You're cruel. Mam wouldn't have made me go to school.'

'Mam was soft with you; besides, she liked the company. I have to go to work.'

'I miss Mam.'

'We all miss Mam . . . and Dad too. Now hurry up and get dressed.'

Lucia lingered no longer but hurried downstairs, pleased to see the boys and Theresa seated at the table eating breakfast. 'You'll still be here for Michael getting back from his paper round? He mightn't have his key with him.'

'Will do. You off now?'

Lucia nodded, thinking of what Tim had told her last evening about his and Isabella's conversation. She'd like to talk to Nick about it, and with a bit of luck he might drop by at the coffee bar.

Her luck was in because Nick entered the coffee bar shortly after the lunchtime rush was over. He was alone and sat at a table by the window. Immediately she went over to take his order and tell him she needed to talk to him. She gave Josh the order of steak and kidney pudding, chips and peas before making Nick a cappuccino and taking it over to him.

'So what is it you want to talk to me about?' Nick asked.

'I want your opinion about Tim,' replied Lucia, glancing about to make certain there was no one in need of her services before sitting in the seat opposite Nick.

Nick's attractive lean features looked taken aback. 'What? Why?'

'Because you've met him, and your father is a detective inspector who was on the scene when the robbery Tim was caught up in took place.'

'He was the driver of the getaway car. Is that what you want to know?'

'No, I know that already. Give me a few minutes to explain.'

Nick gazed at her expectantly from dark blue eyes as she launched into the tale Tim had told her the evening before, about what Isabella had suggested he write and Tim's reaction to her suggestion. 'What do you think, Nick?' she asked when she had finished her story.

'I don't know much about writing, but I don't believe Tim would have had a gun or been able to attempt to disarm the other man while driving a car,' he said. 'Is that it?'

'No, I want you to ask your dad what he knows about the crook who escaped with Tim.'

'OK! I'll do that.' said Nick. 'Now, is there any chance my food is ready?'

'I'll go and get it.' Lucia stood up and left the table. Returning a few minutes later with his plate of food, and leaving him alone to eat in peace, she trusted him not to forget to speak to his father.

That evening, Lucia received a visit from Inspector Sam Walker. Although he mustn't have been far off forty, he was a good-looking man, with few wrinkles, a mop of tawny hair and deep blue eyes. He held himself well and had a good pair of shoulders. She invited him to sit down and offered him coffee and cake. He thanked her, and rested comfortably in an armchair by the window overlooking the back garden.

'You certainly have your hands full,' he said, having turned the chair so he could look more easily into the garden at the children playing. 'I hear one of the children is likely to be Tommy McGrath's.'

'We know him as Tim Murphy,' said Lucia, 'as I'm sure you know. Jerry is the fair-haired lad in the grey shorts and navy blue overcoat. The other fair-haired lad of a similar height and build is my brother, Joseph. They've become great pals.'

'That's good. Jerry being an only will need a good mate to share secrets and problems with.'

'I agree. Jerry spends more time here than he does next door. What with his father writing his book.'

'I've heard about this book and am looking forward to reading it.'

'So am I,' said Lucia. 'I presume you're here because of what I said to Nick?'

Sam's smile was one of singular charm. 'Yes. Sid was the cousin of the leader of the gang, William Donahue. It doesn't surprise me that Donahue would prefer not to believe his cousin would cheat him by hanging back when it came to the robbery and scarpering with the loot from a former robbery, but it surprises me that the journalist doesn't take Tim's word for his version of what happened.' He took a bite out of his slice of cake. 'This is lovely cake. Did you make it?'

'No, my aunt Nellie made it. She often makes two at a time. One for her own family and one for us.'

'It's good that you have her.'

'I know. I have another aunt who's coming over from America this year. It'll be great to see her.'

'There are aunts and aunts,' he said. 'Some are good and others are horrors. My father's aunt, who helped to raise us after my mother died, was a terrible bully.' He glanced out of the window. 'One can't always depend on family to do right by us. But I think in your case, and that of your brothers and sisters, you're blessed. And young Jerry is fortunate to share in that blessing.'

'He's no trouble.' Lucia drained her coffee cup. 'He's been

brought up well – and I hope you're not going to say "no thanks to his father".'

'You know his background?'

'Yes, Tim's told me some of it himself, and Maggie and various other people have warned me against him. My uncle is a priest; he visited Tim in jail and he shares my belief that he deserves a second chance.'

'I agree with your uncle, as well. Father Francis, isn't it? He has a parish Scottie Road way.'

'That's right. I didn't realize you knew that much about him.'

'Our paths have crossed. I believe him to be the best kind of priest. We were both aware when Tommy went off the tracks that his bullying father was partly to blame. He was a bit of a tearaway but there's no evil in him.'

'Thank you,' said Lucia, tears in her eyes.

Sam stood up. 'I'd best be going. Thanks for the coffee and cake.' He held out his hand and she shook it.

'Thank you for coming. I really appreciate it.' She meant that sincerely, as it really helped having a detective inspector saying what she needed to hear.

'I think Nick told you and Tim that the rest of the gang, bar the leader, will be out of prison any day now?'

'Yes, he did.'

'Hopefully they won't give Tim any trouble, but if they do show their faces, tell him to let me know,' said Sam.

It was just getting dark when she saw him out and, while she remained in the doorway waving him off, she heard the neighbouring door open. The next moment she noticed Tim going down the steps towards the car parked at the kerb, then caught sight of him on the pavement and heard the murmur of his and Sam's voices. She wished she could hear their conversation, but unfortunately their voices were not loud enough for her to catch what they were saying, so she went back indoors to dish out dinner and call the children in from the garden, hoping that Tim would not be annoyed with her for discussing his business with the police, if that was what the two men's conversation was about.

Seven

The following morning, thoughts of Tim were thrust to the back of Lucia's mind because Gabrielle complained again that she wasn't feeling well. She looked flushed, and when Lucia felt her sister's forehead, it was burning hot. She knew that she was going to have to keep her from school. 'Well, you do appear to have a temperature. Is there anything going round in school?'

'Patrick McIver was sent home a few days ago and hasn't come back yet.'

'Have you heard what's wrong with him?'

'He's got spots,' Gabrielle said. 'I haven't got spots.'

Lucia swore inwardly. 'That could be because they haven't come out yet. You're staying in bed.'

'Can't I just lie on the sofa by the fire? It's cold upstairs.'

'No, it might be contagious.' Lucia knew she was going to have to make a few phone calls. First she telephoned the school and spoke to the head, who informed her that several children had gone down with measles. She also phoned the coffee bar and told them she was going to be late. She decided that it would be pointless to take Gabrielle to the doctor's surgery when she knew that most likely her sister had caught the measles. Lucia remembered having the ailment herself when she was eight. Michael had caught it, too, so had Theresa. That meant Joseph and James were the only ones who could have already caught it from Gabrielle.

She groaned, thinking she was going to have to keep Joseph and James from school as well. She had better warn Tim that there was a possibility Jerry might have caught the measles too. She would also have to tell Josh and Maggie that she might have to take some time off from work, despite the fact that she couldn't really afford to lose out on wages. It would be far better if Theresa stayed home from school and took care of the children, as that way she could still go to work.

She explained to the children that they were going to stay

home because it was probable that they were already infected and that they were to be good while she went next door to explain the situation to Mr Murphy.

At her knock, Tim came to the door and stood gazing down at Lucia with a frown. 'Jerry's not well, he won't be going to school today.'

'I think he's probably caught the measles. Gabrielle isn't well either, and she told me that one of the lads at school was off with measles. I hope you've had it, Tim, because I've heard it can be even nastier if an adult catches it.'

'Bloody hell,' said Tim. 'I can't remember if I've had it or not.'

'Your mam will remember. Give her a ring. I was going to suggest that Jerry might as well stay with my lot if he is infected.'

'He hasn't got any spots,' Tim said, his face brightening momentarily.

'They don't always come out straightaway,' said Lucia.

'I'd better ring the doctor,' Tim said.

'Do, I'd be interested to hear what he has to say. I'm not bothering. I have a good idea what needs doing. Main thing is to get their temperature down and, in some cases, keep them in a darkened room. I remember that's what Mam did for me, Michael and Theresa when we had it years ago. The spots can be itchy, so calamine lotion can help there. Also it's possible to have spots on the throat which makes swallowing painful, so plenty of fluids.'

'You're going to have your hands full,' said Tim. 'I wish I could help you.'

'You find out if you've had measles first,' Lucia said.

She was dismayed when an hour later Tim knocked on her door and told her that the doctor had confirmed that Jerry most likely did have measles because there was an outbreak in Liverpool that was gaining ground.

'Did you phone your mother?' asked Lucia.

'Yeah. Bad news, I'm afraid. She always kept me away from other children when there was anything going round.'

Lucia groaned. 'If you pass Jerry over to me now, you just might be lucky and miss out on it.'

'I told the doctor I hadn't had it and he looked dismayed and thought it likely I was already infected and suggested Jerry and I both go to bed together.'

'Who's going to nurse you both? I'd do it but—'

'You've your hands full already,' he said. 'I'd suggest me and Jerry staying with your lot so you could go to work, but I don't think I have your nursing skills.'

'Nice of you to think of that, but Theresa is going to stay home from school and take the daytime shift, so we don't lose out on money and I'll do the evening and night shift.'

'You'll be exhausted.'

'I'll survive and it won't last forever. I'd better go now. I've a lot to do. Is there anything you want from the shops?'

'No thanks. Mrs Hudson is doing my shopping.'

Lucia thought it unlikely that the old lady would be doing any nursing. It would be much too much for her, and so she wasted no more time worrying about Tim and Jerry or about Tim's conversation with Detective Inspector Walker last evening out in the street after he had visited her. She felt slightly depressed when she entered the coffee bar and explained her plans to Maggie and Josh. They looked concerned and asked if she was sure that Theresa would be able to cope; they'd be happy to ask Rosie, who helped in the kitchen part-time, to give a hand waiting-on, and they would pay Lucia sick pay so she could have some time off to look after the children.

'That's generous of you,' said Lucia.

'Before you add "but I'm not sick",' Josh said. 'We know that – but you could end up ill working all day and not getting enough sleep at night. We don't want that happening.'

'Thank you,' said Lucia. 'I really appreciate your kindness.'

'You're a good worker and we want to keep you,' said Maggie, hugging Josh's arm. 'Don't we, love?'

'Obviously,' he said.

'Well, I'll stay until Rosie turns up,' Lucia said, her spirits having lifted.

A few minutes later Rosie arrived and the situation was explained to her.

Josh said, 'Why don't you stay and have some lunch, Lucia, before going home? It will put some strength in you, which you're going to need to nurse the kids.'

'Thanks, I will,' she said.

Within moments she was tucking in to bacon, egg and baked beans, washed down with a cappuccino.

'Now you get off home and look after your sister and brothers.'

Lucia thanked him again and left, thanking God for her good fortune in having such a kind employer. It was as she was walking down Renshaw Street that she was hailed by Tim's brother, Marty, who was just coming out of his place of business.

'Hi, Lucia, how are you doing?' he asked. 'I hope that brother of mine isn't causing you any hassle?'

'Not at all,' she replied. 'But I think he could probably do with some help from his family in the next week or so as there's measles in our neck of the woods. Three of my lot have gone down with it, and it looks as though Jerry has it too. Could be that Tim could catch it next, as your mother said that he didn't have it as a child.'

'That's true. She was over-protective with my brother and I don't doubt that she was as much to blame for him going off the rails as my father was. He was jealous of the love she showered on him. It wasn't until I became a parent myself that I realized it's one of the most difficult jobs around. It's absolutely essential that one has a spouse who shares your commitment to bringing up children the right way. I have to admit that I admire you, Lucia, for taking responsibility for your younger brothers and sisters. I hope you don't find it a thankless task.'

'Sometimes I feel like it is, but I love my family and so I carry on fulfilling the role that my parents expected of me if anything happened to them. I'm fortunate in having inherited the family home, mortgage-free.'

'You are fortunate. Good luck with coping with a houseful of sick kids, and I'll tell Irene to be prepared for a possible measles epidemic.'

'Give Irene my love, and perhaps when we're free of the dreaded lurgy we can meet in town and have a cuppa and slice of cake,' said Lucia, remembering the days when she had seen a lot more of Irene when she visited Nellie's house with her brother Jimmy.

Lucia was thinking, not for the first time, how arduous it must be for a parent to bring up their child alone. She remembered how it had been before her parents had married, having been kept apart due to the machinations of her father's snobbish aunt. She had been shocked to the core to discover that the father of the unmarried Lottie's baby was her nephew. A simple soul, Lucia's father had been persuaded to go on a visit to a relative's home, not knowing he had a baby daughter until he returned and managed to see Lottie alone. She had arranged for them to be married by Francis in no time at all. It was then that the newlyweds and Lucia had moved in with David's ailing mother. Lucia had received a lot of love from Lottie when she was a single mother, but there had always been an air of sadness about her, as well as fear, until she and Lucia's father were reunited.

Sadly, due to the war, there were lots of children being reared in one-parent families, and who was to say how this would affect those children in years to come. Would they always feel as if they had missed out on something precious? Or would they realize that there were two-parent families sadly lacking in the love and forbearance that should reign in every family, large or small.

When Lucia arrived home it was to find Theresa reading aloud to the children in the boys' bedroom; Gabrielle was tucked up in bed beside her brothers.

All their faces lit up when they saw Lucia. 'You're home early,' said Theresa. 'Am I glad to see you.'

'Josh let me off early; he's told me to stay home with the kids and he'll give me sick pay.'

'So I'll be going in to school?' said Theresa, sounding relieved.

'You thinking you'll find that easier than helping nurse this lot?' Lucia said, waving an arm in the direction of her younger siblings.

Theresa nodded.

'OK, I'd rather you didn't lose schooling anyway,' said Lucia. 'Can you hold the fort a little longer? I want to nip next door and see how Jerry and his dad are.'

'Oh, Mrs Hudson knocked and said Mr Murphy would like to see you.'

'Thanks for letting me know.' Lucia wasted no time leaving the house and going next door.

Mrs Hudson let her in. 'You're earlier than I thought you'd be.'

'My boss let me off early and I've got the week off too,' Lucia responded. 'How is Jerry?'

'Jerry's not too bad but his dad is real poorly. He can hardly talk. His throat is that sore. The doctor left a prescription but I haven't liked leaving the house in case they needed anything.'

'I could go to the chemist, unless you'd like a breath of fresh air and a break from the house,' said Lucia.

Mrs Hudson's face brightened. 'I would. Thanks, Lucia. Your mum and dad would be proud of you.' She showed Lucia into Tim's apartment and called to him that Lucia was there.

A few minutes later Jerry appeared dressed in pyjamas, and Lucia noticed that a few spots were showing on his face. 'Dad told me to tell you to come through,' he said. 'Follow me. We're sharing a bedroom at the moment with us both being ill.'

She followed the boy into an adjoining room where there were two single beds, a bedside cabinet, a large wardrobe, an ottoman and a chest of drawers. Tim was propped up against a couple of pillows in the bed nearest the window. The curtains were drawn, but as the fabric was pale green and it was still daylight outside, the visibility in the room was good, so she could see clearly how flushed his face was.

'I didn't expect to see you so soon,' said Tim hoarsely. 'Thank you for coming.'

'It's no trouble.' She sat on the side of the bed. 'You sound rough.'

'I feel terrible. It really hurts to talk and the light makes my eyes hurt.'

'Then don't talk,' Lucia said. 'I could get you a pencil and some paper if you tell me where I can find them and you can write down anything you want to say.'

'My desk in the other room,' he said, reaching for the glass on the bedside cabinet.

She left the room and was back in no time with a pencil and note pad.

'I met your Marty while in town, so I told him it was likely that Jerry had caught the measles and possibly you would, too.'

He scribbled on the pad and passed it to her. She read: *If I write a letter to Isabella, will you post it? I don't want her catching it.*

'If you write it now I can post it before I go home,' Lucia said.

Thanks a bunch. You're the tops. Anyway, before I do that — tell me how your day's been?

Lucia smiled and began telling him about her eventful day. He struggled not to laugh several times and, when she finished, he wrote: *You're the right kind of woman to have by any man's side.* She felt herself blushing and said, 'It's nice of you to say so. Is there anything else you want me to do for you?'

I'd like you to stay and keep me company, but that is selfish of me. Your family need you.

She could not deny the truth of those words but, before she stood up, so as to give him more elbow room to write his message to Isabella, she said, 'If you get to feel worse and are worried about Jerry, if he's feeling better, he could come to ours and spend time with Joseph.'

Tim mouthed his thanks.

Ten minutes later Lucia said her farewells and left, clutching the envelope addressed to Isabella. She wondered why he had not phoned the reporter, then remembered he could hardly speak. He could have asked Mrs Hudson to phone, but perhaps he had not thought of it. Maybe it was that he had wanted to send a more personal message? The thought made her feel slightly depressed.

Michael was home when she entered the house after posting the letter. There was a smell of fried bacon and she saw that he was eating a butty.

'You'll spoil your dinner,' she said.

'I'm not wanting you to cook for me,' Michael said. 'I'm going to Marjorie's and eating there.'

'I was hoping you'd do a favour for me.'

'If it's to do with the kids I hope it won't take long.'

'Could you pop into Aunt Nellie's on your way and tell her about the measles and ask her if she could visit Irene. Let them know that Jerry and Tim have definitely caught it, too.'

'Why can't he ring his brother?'

'Tim can hardly speak. He has a really bad sore throat.'

'Couldn't you ring?'

'I have to watch what I spend. It'll be cheaper if you do what I ask.'

Michael agreed, despite looking irritated. He went upstairs to change and was back down in no time at all. As he was on his way out, Lucia called, 'Let me know if you decide to stay overnight at Marjorie's.'

'Will do,' he sang out, slamming the door.

In the silence that followed, Lucia was aware of coughing overhead and then the murmur of voices. She hurried upstairs and into the boys' bedroom. 'Who was coughing?' she asked.

'Me,' said Gabrielle faintly. 'Can I have some lemonade? My throat's sore.'

'So is mine,' James said quickly.

Lucia knew there was no lemonade in the house and decided to buy a bottle. Remembering how Mrs Hudson had been glad to escape the house, Lucia asked Theresa if she would like to go for the lemonade. Her sister agreed immediately and hurried to put on her coat and hat. Lucia asked her to also buy a jar of honey.

While Theresa was out, Lucia asked the children if they were hungry. Only Joseph said he'd like a boiled egg with soldiers. No sooner had he made his request, Gabrielle said she'd love some bread and milk with sugar and nutmeg sprinkled on top. James said that he would like that too. Lucia headed for the kitchen and put eggs on to boil, thinking she and Theresa might as well have the same as Joseph for their evening meal. She heated milk, melting a knob of butter in it, and then cut several slices of bread. She quartered three of the slices and shared them out into two bowls before pouring the warm milk over the bread, sprinkled on demerara sugar and grated nutmeg; after placing the bowls on plates with spoons, she switched off the gas under the pan of eggs. Putting the plates on a tray, she took them upstairs, not forgetting to fling several tea towels over her shoulder.

'Now don't spill anything on the bedclothes,' she warned Gabrielle and James, handing them each a tea towel before passing them the bowls.

'Where's my egg and soldiers?' asked Joseph.

'Coming up shortly,' Lucia replied. 'I've just got to toast the bread.'

She left the bedroom and went downstairs, removed the eggs from the water and put them in egg cups, before lifting the toasting fork from a hook beside the fireplace and forking one of the slices of bread. It was relaxing, kneeling in front of the fire, holding the bread out to the red glow of the slumbering coals. Once all three slices were toasted, she buttered them and cut them into soldiers.

Then she placed some on a plate with one of the eggs and a teaspoon and carried it upstairs and handed it to Joseph. She noticed that Gabrielle had finished her bread and milk and was running a finger around the bowl and sucking the sugar and nutmeg from the finger.

'You enjoying that?' Lucia asked.

'Hmmm! It made my throat feel nice and warm. Now where's my lemonade?'

'Theresa's not back with it yet. Be patient.'

'I've finished,' said James, holding out his empty bowl to Lucia. 'Thank you.'

'Good lad,' she said, 'Now be good, all of you, and when the lemonade arrives, I'll bring it up, and you can all have a drink with some honey and a tablet to make you start feeling better.'

'Can I have my Barbie doll?' asked Gabrielle.

Lucia fetched it from the top of the chest of drawers in the bedroom next door and remembered to take some outfits as well. She thought the clothes that Maggie had made were as good as the ones Babs had sent. Maggie – having been a model, and also having spent some time as a personal dresser to Liverpool actress, Dorothy Wilson – really knew something about style.

When Lucia arrived back in the bedroom, James was reading the *Wizard* comic and Joseph was mopping up spilt yolk with the end of a soldier. He looked up at Lucia and said, 'Did you say hello to Jerry for me when you went next door?'

'No, but I told his dad that as soon as Jerry is feeling a bit better, he can come round here and spend time with you.'

Joseph smiled and handed his plate to her. 'Thanks, that was smashin'!'

She kissed the top of his head and went downstairs; She was eating her egg and toast when Theresa came in. 'You've been a while,' said Lucia.

'I got talking,' Theresa said, placing the bottle of Schofield's lemonade on the table, along with a pot of Gale's honey and a McVitie's ginger cake.

'What's with the cake?' asked Lucia.

'I saw it and fancied it. I know you like it, and I thought we deserved a treat.'

'OK, I won't give you a lecture on how we can't afford to buy everything we fancy, because I think you're right and we do deserve a treat,' Lucia said. 'Now you sit down and get warm and I'll bring your egg and make us a cuppa before doing the kids' drinks.'

'You've done them something to eat?'

'Yes.' Lucia handed a plate to Theresa.

When Lucia came back with the teapot, she asked her sister who she had been talking to.

Theresa hesitated. 'A girl from school who was doing shopping for her mother. Her little brother has measles as well.' She looked about her. 'Where's our Michael?'

'He's seeing Marjorie.'

'He should be staying in and helping with the kids. Boys – they get away with everything.'

'He's doing a job for me.'

'What kind of job?'

Lucia told her.

Theresa made a snorting sound. 'He's not actually straining himself, is he?'

'Let's change the subject.'

'So Jerry's dad has got the measles bad?'

'Yes,' replied Lucia. 'He could do with someone there full time to keep an eye on him; that's why I asked Michael to pass the message on to his brother.'

'I'm glad you didn't volunteer for the job,' said Theresa. 'I know how fond of him you are.'

'He's interesting company.'

'He's an ex-jailbird.'

'Uncle Francis believes he deserves a second chance. Anyway, hopefully his mother will come and visit him.'

'Have you ever met his mother?'

'No, but I suppose I'll get to see her if she does come to see Tim and Jerry. I did offer to have Jerry, so Tim doesn't have to worry about him.'

'You're a right glutton for punishment,' said Theresa. 'As if we didn't have enough invalids to look after.'

'I thought he'd be company for Joseph once they're on the mend.'

'I suppose you've got a point,' said Theresa. 'Anyway, the burden will be on you because I'll be at school.'

'You can do the shopping; I'll have to stay in.'

'OK.' Theresa lifted the teapot and filled two teacups. 'I suppose things could have been worse.'

'Yes, I suppose they could.'

Theresa fetched a knife and cut two slices of ginger cake. 'This would be lovely with custard.'

'We haven't enough milk to make custard, more's the pity,' Lucia sighed. 'Enjoy what you've got.'

'I will. Shall I get some cups for the kids' lemonade?'

'Yes, I'm going to heat it up slightly and put a spoonful of honey in each cup – and they can have some Junior Disprin with their drinks,' Lucia said. 'I hope the doctor prescribed something to bring Tim's temperature down. His face was really flushed.'

'Oh, stop worrying about him. You sound like a mother hen,' Theresa said.

'I can't help it. I'd feel sorry for anyone suffering in such a way.'

Theresa pressed her lips together and went and fetched the lemonade.

Lucia said no more about Tim, but ate her ginger cake and washed it down with tea before preparing the children's drinks and taking them upstairs. She made them all go to the toilet before having their drinks and tablets and then read to them from Enid Blyton's *Adventures of the Wishing-Chair*. Then she went downstairs and settled down to watch *Z-Cars*.

The following morning Theresa was already up and had lit the fire when Lucia went downstairs. She watched silently as Lucia entered the kitchen and said, 'Do you mind if I go out this evening? That girl I met in the corner shop mentioned that a film is showing that I'd like to see. I thought of going first house.'

Lucia wanted to remind her that she needed some time off, but remembered her sister complaining about Michael, so decided fair was fair. 'All right, but make sure you come straight home afterwards because I'll be ready to drop by then.'

Eight

Lucia put two bowls on the table and placed Weetabix in them, sprinkled the cereal with sugar and poured on milk, thinking hard as she did so and eventually asked Theresa, 'Where did you get the money from for the pictures?'

'I saved the last two shillings Aunt Nellie gave me for pocket money.'

'I see.'

Lucia remembered the days when her aunt had given her a weekly shilling, and added to the shilling her father had given her, she had felt quite rich. Happy days! Now she was fortunate if she balanced her budget, knowing she would have to go without keeping any money back for herself. She guessed it was the same for many single women with a family to care for – it was different for men, though. On the whole it was accepted that they'd continue to be the breadwinner, while women would volunteer to take on the unpaid task of caring for the children. Of course some single carers remarried. She wondered if Tim were to remarry how Jerry would feel about sharing his daddy. Relationships were fraught with difficulties if one made the wrong choice.

Having similar interests didn't always mean life would go smoothly. Neither did being the same kind of people. It made sense if one partner was practical and good with their hands, and that wasn't always the man. She knew wives who were wizard with a paintbrush and at wallpapering due to having to do those jobs when they had no man around to fit into the role expected of them. Then there were the men who always took care of the finances, even though they were hopeless with money, but were not prepared to hand the job over to their wives despite them never overspending on the housekeeping their husbands doled out.

Thank goodness, times were changing now, as more wives were determined to go out to work, having become accustomed to earning money of their own during the war, and not having to depend upon their menfolk for every penny. Although she supposed there would always be women like her mother, who believed it was right that husbands should support their wives and children as it was a wife's role to look after the children and their husband and the house.

Thinking back, Lucia could seldom remember seeing her mother read a book. A newspaper or magazine, yes! Sometimes she had wondered whether she had only looked at the pictures because she couldn't read very well. Her father, though, had enjoyed reading Edgar Wallace detective novels. She was glad to be living in an era when it was considered right that all girls should be educated, as well as boys, from an early age.

She went upstairs and discovered James and Joseph were awake but Gabrielle was still snuggled beneath the bedcovers, so Lucia decided not to disturb her. She told the boys to dress and go downstairs for breakfast. They seemed happy to do so, despite their faces still being covered in spots, as were their necks and hands and arms.

After they finished breakfast, she cleared the table and spread it with newspaper and produced paper and pencils, colouring books and paint-boxes.

'Now if anyone starts feeling tired, then you must say so and you can have a rest,' she said.

'Down here?' asked James.

She nodded, thinking: anything to save her running up and down stairs.

The morning passed slowly but peacefully, except for one incident when a paste jar of water was knocked over and soaked into a page that James was painting. Tempers were short and James slapped Joseph, who burst out crying. Obviously the boys were still not themselves.

Lucia declared there was to be a break for lemonade and biscuits, which calmed everyone down. She took the opportunity to go upstairs and check on Gabrielle. Her sister was awake and said that the light hurt her eyes, so Lucia closed the curtains.

'Would you like a drink and some cereal?' she asked.

'Just a drink, please,' said Gabrielle huskily. 'How are the others?'

'Not too bad. Do you want to go to the lavatory? I'll help you there if you feel weak.'

'I'd like that.' Gabrielle threw back the bedcovers and shuffled to the edge of the bed on her bottom.

Lucia helped her up and kept an arm about her as they made their way out of the bedroom. She could feel the heat emanating from her sister through her nightdress and decided to get a couple of Junior Disprin down her as soon as possible; if she was still burning hot at lunchtime, she would sponge her down with cold water, and if she still did not improve then she would phone the doctor. There was always one in a family who was worse than the rest, and in their family it always seemed to be Gabrielle. Lucia remembered when her sister had the vaccination for diphtheria: she was the only one who had a reaction. Her mother had immediately thrown a wobbler, as she had not been keen on having any of the children injected, but had been persuaded by Nellie, who had reminded her that diphtheria was a really nasty disease and could be deadly. Several children had died of it when Nellie and Lottie were children.

Lucia escorted Gabrielle back to bed and then hurried downstairs. James offered to go up and read to his sister, seeing that her eyes were hurting. Pleased by his thoughtfulness, Lucia said he should do that while she made a drink of lemonade and honey and dissolved two Disprin tablets in it for Gabrielle.

When she arrived upstairs, she found James reading the Hardy Boys adventure story that Babs had sent at Christmas to Gabrielle, who told Lucia that she was feeling a bit better. Lucia stayed until her sister had emptied the cup and then she went downstairs, having been aware that the noise level below had sunk. It was as she reached the bottom of the stairs that there came a knock on the door. Responding to its summons, she found Jerry standing on the step.

'Hello, Jerry. What are you doing here?' she asked.

'Dad said I was to ask nicely could I come and keep Joseph company? I'm much better and it is so boring at home.'

'How is your dad?'

'The doctor's coming out to see him again.' Jerry paused for breath. 'Mrs Hudson is going to listen out for him – and Marty is bringing Granny to see him.'

'Well, I'm sure your dad will soon be feeling better – and it's good that your granny is coming to visit, isn't it? You'll be wanting to see her.'

He agreed. 'Dad will tell her where to find me. Can I come in?' he asked, looking slightly anxious.

'Of course! What am I thinking of, keeping you on the step?' She ushered him indoors, telling him to go into the kitchen, and watched as he and Joseph greeted each other like long-lost brothers. Within moments they were comparing spots, each trying to count how many the other had.

Lucia made herself a drinking chocolate and went into the parlour with a library book. She sat in an armchair by the window so she could keep an eye out for comings and goings next door. She had not been there long when she saw a car draw up at the kerb. Marty stepped out and went round to the passenger side and opened the door and helped out an elderly woman. She was dressed in a russet-coloured coat with a fur collar and a brown hat with a brim trimmed with beige ribbon and a cream flower. They crossed the pavement and walked up the neighbouring step.

Lucia wondered if she should immediately tell Jerry that his grandmother and uncle had arrived, or wait until one of them came for him. She decided on the latter, thinking that most likely they would want to talk to Tim undisturbed. She had to admit that she felt slightly concerned that he had felt the need to summon the doctor again.

She attempted to lose herself in the library book, but found herself re-reading two pages without taking in much of the story, so she gave up and went into the kitchen to see how the boys were getting on. She also loaded the washer of the twin-tub. Then she settled herself in the armchair by the window in the parlour again and soon saw another car parking out at the front and the doctor stepping out. No doubt Marty or his mother would be knocking on her front door very soon.

When the knocker sounded, Lucia opened the door to the elderly woman she had seen earlier. She introduced herself as Mrs McGrath, Tim's mother, and asked if Jerry was there. Lucia invited her inside and led her into the kitchen, saying, 'Jerry, your grandmother is here.'

Instantly he jumped to his feet and ran over to the elderly lady and flung his arms about her waist. 'And how is my little cherub feeling?' she asked.

'I've got hundreds of spots, Gran, but I feel lots better than yesterday.'

'Well, one thing is for sure, you look a lot better than your poor dad. So are you coming to say hello to your uncle Marty?'

'Has he brought Fang with him?'

'No, your dad has enough to cope with at the moment. He can't be caring for a dog as well, when he's ill.'

Jerry nodded and then looked at Lucia. 'Can I come back later, please?'

'Of course you can, if that's all right with your dad and gran.'

Mrs McGrath looked at Lucia. 'My son has told me a lot about you, Lucia. I hope you don't mind me calling you by your Christian name, only he's never mentioned your surname.'

'It's Brookes but I don't mind at all you calling me Lucia.'

'I believe Father Francis, my parish priest, is your uncle.'

'Yes.'

'He's a lovely man,' said Mrs McGrath.

Lucia agreed that he was, and wondered if it was via her uncle that she could worm herself into Tim's mother's good graces, although why she was thinking such a thing she did not know. It wasn't as if she expected to have much to do with her.

'I do appreciate all the help you've given my son in taking care of Jerry.'

'Jerry isn't any trouble,' Lucia said. 'But how is Tim this morning?'

'His temperature is still high but the doctor has prescribed a stronger medicine that should bring it down. He's always been a delicate boy.'

Lucia found that hard to believe but kept her thoughts to herself.

'I'd better go,' said Mrs McGrath. 'It's been very nice meeting you, Lucia.'

'Likewise,' murmured Lucia. 'I'll see you out.'

She stood at the door, watching until Mrs McGrath and Jerry disappeared inside next door. Then she went upstairs to see how Gabrielle was doing. When she reached the landing, she expected to hear James reading to his sister, but all was quiet. Opening the bedroom door she found James lying on the bed, reading to himself.

'She's asleep,' he said, glancing at Lucia.

'Good! Best thing for her.' Lucia felt Gabrielle's forehead and was relieved to find it cooler. 'I think she's turned the corner.' She looked at James. 'You can go downstairs now if you like.'

'It's OK. I'm comfortable here and it's quieter – better for reading. I can also keep my eye on Gabby.'

'Don't call her that. Mam always insisted on us being given our full names.'

'But Gabrielle is a mouthful.'

'I know, but Gabby isn't very complimentary, is it?'

'I've called her it before and she doesn't mind.'

'Well, just don't call her it in my company.'

'It's all right for you. Your name's short. Mam's dead, so what does it matter if we shorten our names? Besides which, Mam's name was Charlotte but nobody called her that – she was always just Lottie.'

'Maybe that's why she insisted on us being called by our full names,' Lucia said. 'Now I'm going down.'

'Who was at the door?'

'Jerry's grandmother. She came to visit him and his dad, so Jerry's gone back next door.'

'Good. He's always here. You're not going to marry his dad, are you?'

Lucia's heart did a peculiar little jump. 'Why should you think that?'

'Because you obviously like him and he likes you. I can tell by the way he looks at you.'

'How would you feel if I did marry him?'

'I'd hate it. He'd be telling me what to do, and besides, we don't need another man in the house. We've got our Michael.'

'Only when he's here,' Lucia said. 'Anyway, I doubt Tim would ask me to marry him when it means taking you lot on as well.'

James gave a satisfied smile. 'Yes, but you're forgetting he's no Tarzan. He can't even walk properly. I bet he can't dance and you like dancing – and he's an ex-jailbird.'

Lucia turned and left the bedroom, controlling her temper and closing the door gently behind her. Brothers! They think they have everything sussed out. Yet she could not deny the truth of his words.

All was reasonably peaceful downstairs, so she put the washing in the spin drier and then prepared lunch.

Joseph asked if he could go next door and ask to play with Jerry.

'No,' she said.

'Why not?' he asked. 'I'm fed up all on my own painting a silly ol' picture.'

'Because Jerry and his dad have visitors, so they won't want to be bothered with you.'

'I wouldn't be a bother – and I bet Jerry would rather play with me than talk to visitors.'

'Just do as you're told,' Lucia said. 'I'm making lunch anyway.'

'Can I go after lunch?'

'No!'

'Why not? The visitors might have gone by then.'

'And they mightn't have. Why don't you just do as you're told?'

'Because I want to play with Jerry. If we didn't have the measles we could be out, taking turns riding his bike.'

'You wouldn't – you'd be at school. Now stop bothering me and be a good boy. It could be that Jerry will come here as soon as the visitors have gone,' she said.

Those words were enough to satisfy Joseph for the moment, and he returned to the kitchen and his colouring in. Lucia picked up the washing basket and went out into the garden, glad to have some fresh air. She hung out the washing as it was windy and dry and she hated having it drying inside unless absolutely necessary – she loved it smelling of fresh air – then it was back indoors.

Joseph must have heard her come in because a few minutes later he was back trying to persuade her to let him go next door. She said, 'You have to understand, love, that you can't always have your own way. If Aunt Nellie was coming to visit, she'd want to see you and have your whole attention, not have you playing with the boy next door.'

'She wouldn't want to talk to me for long. Grown-ups don't. She'll want to get all the gossip from you.'

Lucia could not deny the truth of that. 'Even so, Jerry's dad is very poorly and won't be able to cope with having you there. Be patient and let's see if Jerry comes back this afternoon. In the meantime you can help me make gingerbread men after I've made some soup.'

'OK,' said Joseph cheerfully. 'Can I cut them out?'

Lucia nodded.

It didn't take her long to make a pan of lentil soup, and then she collected all the ingredients together for the gingerbread. When she had mixed it and rolled it out, she passed the cutter to Joseph and watched him press it in to the pastry. Several times she wanted to take over from him, but managed to restrain herself until she could gather the leftover pastry into a ball, then rolled it out and cut out four more little men. She emptied currants into a small bowl and, between them, they gave the gingerbread men eyes and a nose and buttons down their fronts before placing them on a baking tray and putting that in the oven.

'They won't burn, will they?' Joseph asked anxiously.

'No, they'll bake and come out nice and crunchy.' Lucia cleared up the mess before getting out bowls, spoons and a loaf of bread; the crust crackled when she sliced it. She set the table and then went to tell the sleeping beauties that lunch was ready. Then she went to check the gingerbread men and, with Joseph hovering beside her, took them out of the oven.

'They smell lovely,' said Joseph. 'I can't wait to taste one. I'm sure Jerry would love one.'

'We'll save one each for him and his dad,' said Lucia, thinking if Jerry did not come knocking that afternoon, once Theresa came in from school, she would pop next door with Joseph and take two gingerbread men and see how Tim was.

They did not hear from Jerry, so when Theresa turned up at a quarter to five, Lucia called to Joseph so they could nip next door while Theresa kept her eye on the two upstairs, and got things ready for supper. Lucia had noticed that Marty's car had gone, so presumed that Tim and Jerry were now alone.

'Is Michael home?' asked Theresa.

'Not yet.'

'I bet he's with Marjorie.'

'I wouldn't think so this early,' said Lucia. 'Anyway, I haven't time for this right now. I'm off.'

She and Joseph hurried to the neighbouring house. To her surprise the front door was slightly ajar, so she walked inside and knocked on the door of Tim's apartment.

The door was opened by Jerry. His face lit up when he saw Joseph and he dragged him inside. 'Come and see the Meccano set that Grandma brought me from my mam's sisters.'

It was the first time that Joseph had heard that Jerry's dead mother had sisters, but he made no comment and just let himself be dragged by Jerry to his bedroom, but not before he had asked Lucia for his friend's gingerbread man. She kept hold of the one for Tim and asked Jerry if his dad was in bed.

'Yeah,' said Jerry. 'Uncle Marty moved my bed back into my room so I wouldn't be disturbing Dad too much.'

Within a few minutes, Lucia was seated on a chair at Tim's bedside, thinking he didn't look or sound any better. 'I thought your mother might have stayed to look after you.'

Tim reached for pencil and pad and wrote: *She had promised our Lil to babysit as she and her husband have an engagement party to go to, so Mam has to stay home this evening.*

Lucia felt indignant on his behalf, thinking, what was a party compared to her son's health?

He answered her unspoken question by writing: *Mam would never hear the end of it if she put me before our Lil's needs. Lil thinks the rest of the family should cut me off.*

'That's sad.'

Not really, wrote Tim, *I have no time for our Lil so I don't care if I never see her again. She's a hypocrite, and not in the least like our Marty and Peggy, who've never let me down.*

'I suppose your Peggy hasn't visited you because she doesn't want her little girl catching measles and she'd have to bring her with her?'

I told Marty to tell her not to come, Peg has enough on her plate.

'It can't be easy living with a mother-in-law,' Lucia said.

He wrote, *No, but it's better than being homeless like so many were after the Blitz.*

'That's very true. Anyway, how are you feeling? What did the doctor have to say?'

That I must stay in bed, no getting up and trying to write. I have to rest, plenty of drinks, and I must make sure and not miss taking any of the tablets he's prescribed.

'How are you going to manage all that on your own? And with all those drinks you're going to need to get up to go to the loo. He must have thought your mother was staying because she was here when he visited.'

'Yeah!' croaked Tim. 'And Mam seems to think Mrs Hudson could help me out.'

'But she's an old woman; older than your mother, I'd say,' murmured Lucia.

Tim nodded.

'Anyway, while I'm here I can give you a helping hand,' said Lucia. 'What would you like me to do first? Help you to the loo?'

'You're all right there,' said Tim huskily. 'Marty did that and helped me shave. I'd better take a tablet, so if you could get me a drink?'

'Sure. What would you like?'

'Lemon barley water. Mam brought it. The bottle's by the electric kettle which Marty filled,' Tim whispered.

Lucia wasted no time bringing him a drink. 'Joseph and I baked some gingerbread men and I brought you one, but you might find it painful to eat.'

'I could dunk it if you don't mind making me a coffee before you have to go?'

Lucia brought her head closer to his in order to hear him properly. She took the opportunity to feel his forehead and came to a decision.

'How do you feel about me sponging your face with a cold flannel?'

'It sounds lovely,' he whispered. 'A cold bath would be better. But that's out of the question. Fortunately I have a sink in here, though, and a flannel.'

She went over to the sink and filled it with cold water, soaking the flannel before wringing out the surplus water and then going over to Tim's bedside. She placed the flannel on his brow and held it there.

'That's lovely,' he croaked.

She smiled down at him. 'I was wondering if you have any ice in your fridge?'

'I seldom use ice, but there just might be some in the ice-cube tray in the freezer compartment that's been there for ages.'

'I'll have a look later,' she said, removing the flannel and sponging the rest of his face with it.

He seized her wrist and lifted her hand to his lips and kissed it. 'I don't know why you're so kind to me.'

Lucia was deeply moved. 'I told you, I like you, and when you like people you want to help them.'

'But why d'you like me when I've done so many selfish and wrong things?'

'I admire you. You're sorry for what you did and I think you are trying really hard to put the past behind you and forge out a new life for you and Jerry. I believe you need all the help you can get and I want to encourage you. We all need lots of encouragement when we go through a bad patch.'

'But you've got so much on your plate with the kids having measles.'

'It's only Gabrielle who's got it bad, and Theresa's back from school so she is holding the fort right now.'

'She's a good kid, is Theresa. What about Michael, is he helping out?'

'Not so as you'd notice. All he seems able to think about is Marjorie.'

'Love's young dream, hey?' he said huskily.

'You can say that again.'

'We've all been there,' he said.

'Yes, and a lot of good it did me, I don't think.'

'Same here. But I wouldn't have Jerry if I hadn't married Bernie.'

Lucia said, 'He's a good lad. I believe some people are just meant to be born against the odds.'

'You mean because God has a purpose for them in life?' His voice sounded strained.

Lucia had forgotten her task and now got up and went over to the sink, dipping the flannel, which was warm with the heat from Tim's face, in the water.

Time was getting on and Tim was starting to feel sleepy. He stifled a yawn.

'You're tired,' Lucia said. 'I'll go in a few minutes so you can get some sleep.'

He caught her hand again. 'You'll come back tomorrow and see me?'

'If that's what you want.'

'I want it to be what you want as well,' he whispered.

Nine

Flushed with excitement, Lucia returned home, wondering if she should have lingered longer. Was it possible that Tim might have gone on to tell her that he was growing fond of her, and maybe even that he was falling in love with her? Her knees went weak at the thought. Too shy to make the next move, she'd hurried away to the kitchen to replace the flannel in the freezer before he could say anything else.

As soon as she entered the kitchen, Theresa said, 'You've been ages . . . and our Michael is still not home.'

Lucia could not conceal her annoyance. 'His behaviour is beyond the limit. I'll have something to say to him when he finally arrives.'

Exhausted, Lucia nodded off in front of the fire, and did not wake when Michael crept in and headed straight to his room. It was Theresa who notified her of his arrival, coming downstairs and shaking Lucia awake.

'He's in,' she said. 'Came straight upstairs. Are you going to tear a strip off him?'

'Let me wake up first,' said Lucia, gazing blurry-eyed into Theresa's determined face. 'Did he have anything to say to you?'

'Only asked how the kids were – as if he cared.'

'I don't know what's got in to him. He didn't used to be like this.'

'No, it's like living with a stranger.'

Lucia pushed herself up out of the chair. 'I'm going to rinse my face. Tell him I want to see him down here. I'm not going to have a row upstairs. I don't want to wake the kids.'

'Our Joseph is playing up and Gabrielle is tossing and turning.'

'Has she complained about anything?'

'Her throat being sore.'

'So nothing new. Give her a spoonful of honey in lemonade.'

'The lemonade has all gone.'

'Then just give her the honey in warm water with a Junior

Disprin. As for Joseph, tell him he'll be staying in bed all day tomorrow if he doesn't go to sleep right now.'

'OK!' Theresa left the room and Lucia went and rinsed her face in cold water to wake herself up fully. Then she braced herself to confront her brother.

'So what's up?' she asked as soon as Michael entered the kitchen. 'Why haven't you been coming home?'

'I've been with Marjorie. She needs me and I'd rather be with her than in this mad house.'

'That's a nice thing to say about your home and family,' said Lucia, trying to hold on to her temper.

'Don't be pretending that you haven't felt like that about it,' said Michael, taking up a defiant stance.

'I suppose it's nice and peaceful at Marjorie's mother's house?'

'Not always; although her mother is, usually, very easy-going.'

'So what's happened to change her mood?' asked Lucia, aware of a sudden sense of dread.

Michael threw back his head and met his sister's gaze with a hint of arrogance in his expression. 'Marjorie's having my baby. We're going to get married.'

Lucia felt as if the room was spinning and the floor was coming up to meet her. 'I always thought you had some sense,' she muttered. 'But now I see that I was wrong and that you're stupid and selfish.'

'We love each other and want to be together,' he retorted, a flush in his cheeks. 'You've never been in love, so you don't know how powerful a feeling it is.'

Lucia would have smacked his face if she hadn't felt so weak, so instead she simply sank into a chair and placed her head in her hands and gave way to tears.

'Don't cry,' pleaded Michael, getting down on his knees in front of her. 'I was dreading telling you. I knew you'd be upset, but it's not the end of the world.'

'No, but it's the end of any chance you have of getting a good job. I'm presuming from what you've said that Marjorie's mother knows her daughter is pregnant.'

'Yes, and she was annoyed at first but she's accepted the situation now and says we can live with her until we can get our own place. She's looking forward to having a grandchild.

She loves children and says she would have had more if her husband hadn't been killed in the war.'

'I see. So how are you going to support a wife and child while you're still at school and the only money you have coming in is from your paper round.'

'I'll leave school straightaway and see if I can get myself an apprenticeship.'

'Just like that!' Lucia said, snapping her fingers wearily.

'Well, I don't suppose it'll be that easy, but there are jobs around.'

'But not the kind of well-paid job you could have had if you'd stayed on at school and got some more qualifications.'

'Dad managed without qualifications.'

'Just managed, by not only working hard physically, but with hand-outs from the family. I hope you don't think I'll be able to help you with money?'

'No. I know you've got enough on your plate as it is. I'm sorry, Lucia, but we love each other and got carried away. Forgive me for spoiling your plans for me. I don't want us to fall out.'

'All right, I don't want us to fall out either. You're still my brother. So when is this wedding to be?'

'Next week at St Mary's, West Derby,' Michael added hesitantly. 'It's a Proddy church that Marjorie and her mother attend.'

For a moment Lucia's breath was taken away and she couldn't speak. When she was finally able to do so, she said, 'How could you desert the faith?'

'I'm not deserting the faith. Marjorie's a Christian. We'd already discussed getting married before she fell pregnant. We knew we'd have to make choices sooner or later. She's not insisting I stop being Catholic or attending my own church. There are a lot of things the two churches agree on.'

'That's as maybe, but I don't know what Uncle Francis is going to say, or Aunt Nellie.'

'It's got nothing to do with them.'

'Mam would turn over in her grave,' said Lucia.

'Dad wouldn't. He'd just want me to be happy.'

Lucia knew Michael was right, but even so she was tempted

to say that she hoped he didn't live to regret leaving school early and marrying Marjorie. She managed to bite back the words, though.

'I presume this won't be a big white wedding?'

'Marjorie is wearing the ivory satin and lace gown that her mother wore when she got married.'

'That'll save money but you'll need a new suit,' Lucia said, wondering where she was going to get the money from.

'That's not your worry,' said Michael. 'Besides, it doesn't have to be new. I mentioned to Tony I was in need of a suit if he was thinking of buying a new one because of all these meetings he was going to in London to do with his singing career. So he passed down his old one to me. There's hardly any wear in it.'

'That was very kind of him. What did he say when you told him why you needed it?'

'I didn't have to tell him, but I did, and I didn't swear him to secrecy because I thought he could tell his dad who will mention it to Aunt Nellie, and that way I wouldn't have to tell Uncle Francis because she will. Unfortunately, Tony's going to be in London for the wedding.'

'I didn't realize you were so devious.'

'I thought it would save you embarrassment — although, I don't kid myself I'll escape a lecture from Uncle Francis,' Michael said, pulling a face. 'The vicar did mention asking Francis whether he'd like to take part in the service. Apparently St Mary's is high church, so some of their ritual is similar to ours and there are meetings going on at a certain level in the wider Church about the different denominations coming together.'

'I hope it happens but I can't see it,' said Lucia.

'Why not? All it needs is goodwill on both sides and lots of prayer.'

Lucia was in no mood to discuss the subject. She'd had quite a day and was tired and needed her bed, and said as much to Michael. He shrugged broad shoulders and wished her a good night. But when she settled to sleep her thoughts were far too busy to allow her to relax. She decided what she needed was to check Gabrielle was all right, and then she would go downstairs and make herself a cup of cocoa and read her library book.

To her relief Gabrielle was fast asleep, and the other children all seemed to be out for the count, so Lucia went downstairs and, instead of returning to her cold bed, she sat in front of the slumbering fire with a cocoa and her library book. Unfortunately she could not lose herself in the story because her own problems kept coming between her and those of the characters. Perhaps because she was not far enough into the story to have got to care about them enough, but most likely because her own troubles loomed so large that she could not see an easy way out of them.

She had just come to the conclusion that she needed to discuss them with someone when Michael came into the room. 'What are you doing down here?' he asked.

'I couldn't sleep.'

'Neither can I,' he said. 'But it's pointless you worrying, Lucia. It's my problem and you have to trust me to deal with it. The only way you can help me is by accepting Marjorie into the family and not judging her.'

'You think she'll want to be one of us?' asked Lucia, her voice uneven.

'I know she does. There's only ever been her and her mam and she loves the idea of being part of a bigger family.'

'And what does her mother think of that?'

'Her mother's only too pleased to be having a man about the house.'

'Won't it be a shock to her after not having one around for years?'

'I'm pretty sure she's looking at the positive side of things. Of course, she doesn't like the thought of the neighbours gossiping about Marjorie "having to get married". But she's going to put a proud face on it and looks forward to seeing her only daughter walking down the aisle of the church where she herself got married.'

'She's not bothered about you being a Catholic?'

'I wouldn't say she's completely happy about it, but she says we believe in the same God and Christ's crucifixion and that's what's important.'

'I suppose that's something,' Lucia said, closing her book. 'I take it she's not Orange?'

'No, she has no time for "this sectarian nonsense", as she puts it. She feels the same about those on the Green side who go looking for a fight on Orange Day.'

'Then we should get on all right,' stated Lucia, getting to her feet. 'I think I'll go to bed now. I'll see you in the morning.'

Saying her prayer, she fell asleep almost as soon as her head touched the pillow, and when she woke it was to find it was daylight and the clock stood at half past seven. She loved it when the days began to draw out. She lay there, listening to the sparrows chirping beneath the eaves. She became aware of James ordering Joseph to be quiet, and then she heard Theresa telling them both to shut up or they'd disturb Lucia.

She slid out of bed and went over to the window and drew back the curtain slightly, gazing down at the garden where the daffodils were growing apace. Before she knew it, Easter would be here. Valentine's Day had slipped by without her even noticing it. If there had been a card for Michael from Marjorie, he must have picked it up before she came downstairs. She turned away from the window, thinking she would check on Gabrielle. She was not going to worry about Michael and Marjorie right now. She padded in her bare feet across the cool linoleum, dressed only in her flannelette flower-sprigged nightdress, along the landing to the girls' room and pushed open the door.

'So how are you two this bright March morning?' she asked.

'We're fine, aren't we, Gabrielle?' replied Theresa, nudging her younger sister.

'Yes, I'm feeling much better,' said Gabrielle.

'I feel great because I was able to sleep the whole night through,' said Theresa.

'I got myself a drink,' said Gabrielle proudly. 'I've been wondering if I could have a bath. I know it's not Saturday but I smell with sweating so much.'

'All right,' said Lucia, hoping she had a couple of spare shillings for the electric meter, as the water might not be hot enough in the back boiler behind the fireplace. 'Don't pull the plug out; James and Joseph can have the water after you.'

As she dressed, Lucia thought that if it had not been for Michael's news and wondering how Tim had got through the night, all would have felt right with her world. The kids were on the mend and spring was on its way. Easter Day was late this year on 22 April, so Mothering Sunday, which was about halfway through Lent, was the first of April. She must visit her parents' grave in Ford cemetery and place fresh flowers in the urn and encourage the kids to come with her. They could drop in at Nellie's afterwards. Right now, though, she needed to clear out the grate and get a fire lit before preparing breakfast.

To her delight, when she reached the kitchen, it was to discover that Michael had got the fire going and set the table for breakfast. He was wearing his school uniform and poured tea into two cups as she entered.

'You're going to school?' She could not disguise her surprise.

'I have to explain to the Head what's happened and that I'll be leaving school straightaway because I need to find a job,' he said. 'I know you're disappointed in me and I'm sorry, but these things happen.'

She knew there was no point in doing anything other than encouraging him to take responsibility for his actions. 'You're doing the right thing,' she said. 'Would you do me a favour before you go – help Theresa here while I nip next door and see how Jerry and his dad are doing?'

'OK,' he said. 'But don't be there for hours.'

She gave him a look as if to say 'don't push it', put her coat on and went next door. She felt certain that Jerry would be up and about and so would Mrs Hudson. She had no need to ring the bell; she saw the curtain twitch in the window to her left and caught sight of Jerry's face. He waved to her and then disappeared.

'I was coming to yours in a minute. Dad wants to see you,' Jerry said.

'How is he?'

'His voice is getting better.' Jerry led her into the apartment and asked would she like a cup of coffee.

'I'll make it,' she volunteered.

'I can make it,' he said. 'Dad showed me how. I've already made him one. You go through and I'll bring it to you,' he said.

Not wanting to discourage him from being his father's little helper, Lucia did as she was told and went through into the bedroom. She was delighted to see Tim sitting up against a couple of pillows.

'It was good of you to come so soon,' he said. 'I only managed to prevent Jerry going round to yours as soon as he got out of bed by asking him to make me a coffee.'

'He's making me a cup now. I was a bit worried in case he scalded himself.'

'He's very careful, and truthfully his hands are more steady than mine at the moment due to this stupid measles.'

'You sound better, although your voice is a bit strained.'

'My throat is still sore but it's more bearable.'

'A touch of sherry might help. Uncle Michelangelo recommended it as a lubricant for the throat to his son, Tony.'

'Well if it's good enough for a talented singer like Tony, then I'll take up your recommendation. I'd ask Mrs Hudson to get me a bottle from the off-licence, only I don't think she'd like going in the off-licence. Would you mind going for me if you're able to leave the kids?'

'I would, only Michael is back, so I'm sure he'd go for you.'

'Great! And how is Michael?'

Lucia told herself later that if Tim had not asked, she would not have unburdened herself on him. As it was, all that her brother had told her, coupled with her concern for the young couple and the expected baby, poured from her. When her voice tailed off she could not look at Tim, so horrified was she for having given way. When she felt able to lift her tear-drenched countenance, it was to see a thoughtful expression on his face.

'What are you thinking?' she asked.

'Young fool! But at least he's faced up to telling you, as well as accepting his responsibilities. I'm glad you told me for, as they say, a trouble shared is a trouble halved. If Michael will fetch that bottle of sherry, ask him to bring it to me himself.'

She said that she would, but it wasn't until she was on her way into her house that she realized that Michael was not yet eighteen so was under-age for buying alcohol. She would have to go herself; only then she remembered how keen Tim had appeared to want to see Michael, so she decided to leave things as they were. After all, it was not as if her brother was going to drink the sherry, and he looked older than his seventeen years. Although his birthday being in October meant he was nearer to eighteen.

Michael was more than willing to fetch a bottle of sherry for Tim when Lucia told him what it was for and how bad Tim had sounded yesterday. She handed him a pound note. 'But I'll have to come home first and change out of my school uniform,' he added.

That showed sense, she thought, as she made her breakfast of cereal and toast.

All the children were up, dressed and had eaten breakfast. Gabrielle was playing with her Barbie doll, James was reading one of Willard Price's Adventure series books to Joseph, and Theresa was placing a couple of exercise books in her satchel.

'Well, I'm glad you all seem well enough to amuse yourselves,' said Lucia.

'Will Jerry be able to come here today?' asked Joseph.

'I don't see why not, if his dad agrees,' replied Lucia.

'Shall I knock on my way to school and say Jerry's welcome if he wants to come and play with Joseph?' asked Theresa.

'Yes, why not?' Lucia said, thinking she was going to have to tell Theresa soon about Michael and Marjorie getting married. She wasn't looking forward to it, but she couldn't put it off because the wedding was next week.

The rest of the morning passed with the only annoyance being Gabrielle knocking over a glass of milk. As she watched the liquid spread over the tablecloth and drip on to the floor, Lucia could have cried over the waste of nourishment and money. But she could not scold her when she saw her bottom lip tremble, and she was quick to say sorry.

Later, just as the children had settled down in front of the television for 'Watch with Mother', there came a ring on the doorbell. Lucia rushed to answer it and found Nellie on the front step.

'So how are you all?' Nellie asked brightly.

'The kids are getting better – but I presume Tony has mentioned Michael's news to you?' said Lucia awkwardly.

'What news is that?' Nellie asked.

'Marjorie is having a baby, so she and Michael are getting married next week.'

'Well, worse things happen,' said Nellie. 'At least he'll have a roof over his head because they'll be living with her mother.'

'So Tony did tell you.'

'He mentioned it to his father, who told him to tell me.'

'So that's why you're here.'

'Not entirely. I did want to see for myself how the children were getting along, and to invite you all for Sunday lunch if the children are fit. You and Theresa could do with a break. Michelangelo said he'll come and pick you up.'

'He won't fit us all in the car.'

'Then he'll make two journeys,' said Nellie.

'Did Tony tell you that Marjorie's a Proddy?'

'Yes, and I hope you aren't going to hold that against the girl?' Nellie said strongly. 'I don't know if your mother ever mentioned to you that I was a widow when I married Tony's father?'

'Yes, she did!'

'But I don't suppose she told you that my first husband was a Proddy. My parents wanted nothing to do with us. When I wrote to your mother and Babs, my mother intercepted my letters so they would believe I didn't want anything to do with them. It wasn't until Mother was killed and your mother was in hospital that Francis found one of my letters. He wrote to me in the Lake District, telling me the news, and also that Granddad needed someone to keep house for him. So I left my job and came to live with him and Babs – and eventually Lottie, as well, when she was discharged from hospital.'

'What about your husband?'

'Teddy was in the desert with the army. I was pregnant with our baby when the news came that he had been killed. I fainted and miscarried.' Her voice trembled. 'When my father came home from sea, he said it was my punishment for marrying a Proddy.'

'What a terrible thing to say,' murmured Lucia, tears in her eyes.

'He wasn't a nice man, and he treated your mother abominably. Babs was always his favourite; she was pretty and had a lovely way with her. She still does.'

'I wonder why Mam never told me about . . .' Lucia stopped abruptly.

'I think you can work that out for yourself,' Nellie said.

Lucia nodded, remembering her mother constantly attending Mass, even if she'd been the day before. 'I've no intention of cutting Michael and Marjorie from our lives. I love him too much for that.'

'I didn't believe you would, but I thought if you hadn't heard about my having married a Proddy, it would interest you. Anyway, enough said about sad, far-off times. At least you won't have to do any of the arranging for the wedding. Presumably Marjorie's mother will do most of that.'

'Michael sounds to me as if he likes her,' said Lucia.

'That's a good start,' Nellie said. 'Now, is there anything you'd like me to do for you?'

'Your company's enough,' Lucia said, going over and hugging her aunt. 'But if you could stay with the kids while I nip next door, I'd appreciate it?'

'You're visiting Jerry's father?'

'Yes, and take that tone out of your voice. I'm just being neighbourly. He's been very ill and Jerry doesn't want to lose another parent.'

Nellie nodded. 'I'm sorry. I know you are a good girl. It's not as though Michelangelo and I didn't encounter some prejudice. Lots of people in Liverpool had no time for Eyeties when Mussolini entered the war on Hitler's side, and even later when Italy came over to the side of the Allies.'

'You've never regretted marrying him, though, have you? You always appear so happy in each other's company.'

'It's true I have no regrets. We've been blessed.' Nellie changed the subject. 'Now you go off next door and see if all is right with Jerry and his father. Did any of his family visit him, by the way?'

'Marty brought his mother in the car yesterday, but she had to go back home because she was babysitting for the daughter and the husband who live with her.'

'That would be Lily. According to Irene, there's no love lost between her and Tim.'

'So I've heard.'

Lucia left her aunt. No sooner had she pressed her neighbour's doorbell than the door opened and Tim stood there, smiling down at her.

'You're up and dressed!' she exclaimed.

'Our Peg phoned to say she and Pete would be coming to visit me this evening. I didn't want to welcome them from my bed, so I made an enormous effort, and with Jerry's help you can see I'm fit for company once more.'

'I'm pleased to see it,' Lucia said, 'but don't go overdoing it. You still sound hoarse and you don't want a relapse.'

'Yes, nurse,' he said. 'Are you coming in?'

'Only briefly. My aunt's here, so I said I wouldn't be long. I thought I'd let you know Michael is getting your sherry and will bring it to you. I also wanted to ask if you'd mind if Jerry came round to ours to play with Joseph?'

'As long as he's back for tea because Peg is bound to want to see him.'

'I'll make sure of it,' she promised. 'Where is he now?'

'Plaguing Mrs Hudson who's making jam tarts. Since we tasted your gingerbread men he's been wanting to have a go at baking again. She said she didn't have any cutters for gingerbread men, so he agreed that jam tarts would be fine.'

'She's a lovely lady.'

Tim agreed. 'I can never thank you enough for telling me about this place and preparing the way for me with her.'

'It was my pleasure,' said Lucia, blushing. 'When Jerry's finished helping Mrs Hudson, tell him he can come round when he's ready?'

'Will do,' said Tim, twinkling down at her. 'I'll see you out.'

'No, you won't. You'll stay in the warmth and rest,' she said firmly.

'I hear and obey,' he said, saluting.

She giggled. 'I'm glad you're up to making jokes. You worried me when you sounded so rough.'

'You mustn't worry about me,' Tim said. 'You have enough on your plate right now without that.'

'Oh, stop it,' said Lucia. 'If I want to worry about you, I will. Although, I don't think I need to now. When you're completely better, maybe we can go to the flicks, or go somewhere to listen to music? Get away from the house. It would be lovely to get out into the countryside, but that's out of the question.'

He nodded his fair head, a lock of which curled on his

forehead. 'Sounds good to me. I'll sit and read last night's *Echo* and see what's on next week.' Even as he was speaking, Tim was thinking, if only he still had his car and was able to drive, he could have taken her out into the countryside. They could have gone through the Mersey tunnel to Eastham Woods or to Chester Zoo – although that was an outing that Jerry would like to be part of – and then there was the lovely North Wales coast to visit, not to mention Snowdonia National Park. Just thinking of all that scenic beauty lifted his spirits. It also gave him ideas which he prayed he could put into action. He looked forward to Michael's visit, as well as that of his sister, Peggy, and her husband, Pete Marshall.

Michael turned up at five o'clock, holding Jerry by the hand, and was soon seated across from Tim in front of a glowing fire with a cup of coffee. 'You look better than I thought you would,' said Michael. 'Although, you do sound croaky.'

'I'm a lot better, thanks to your sister and the tablets the doctor prescribed,' said Tim. 'I don't know what he'd make of your uncle's recommendation of sherry to lubricate the throat, though.'

'Lucia swears by honey for the kids. I find it a bit sweet for my taste, although she does generally give it to them in warm water.'

'She's a sensible young lady.'

'Lucia's nineteen,' said Michael. 'How old are you Mr Murphy?'

'I'll be thirty next birthday, so ten years older,' Tim replied, not avoiding the direct question. 'How old are you, Michael?'

'Eighteen next birthday.'

'Lucia told me that you'll be leaving school any day now and looking for work. I'd like to put a proposition before you.'

Michael gave him a suspicious look. 'What kind of proposition?'

'It's above board,' Tim said dryly. 'You can't believe that I'd betray your sister's trust by involving you in anything criminal?'

'Does Lucia know about this then?' asked Michael, flushing.

'No!' He paused. 'You might have heard that I used to have a garage in Lark Lane, near Sefton Park on the south side of Liverpool?'

'Yes, Lucia told me.'

'I served an apprenticeship as a motor mechanic, and eventually was able to go into the motor repair business for myself. Everything fell apart when I was badly injured. Anyway, I still have the garage and the ground lease still has a few years to run. My brother has been on at me to get rid of it, but I just couldn't let it go. All my dreams of going straight had been tied up in that garage business. But my injuries meant I couldn't do the work I once could. My proposition is this – would you like to be my hands and legs and, under my direction, learn a trade? You wouldn't only be learning to be a motor mechanic, but how to run a business as well, because I'd teach you the organization side too.'

Different emotions flitted across Michael's face, and he took a deep breath. 'Can I think about it before giving you my answer?'

'Of course, it's an important decision. You might want to talk it over with your young lady.'

'I will,' said Michael. 'Did Lucia tell you Marjorie and I are getting married?'

'She did. I hope you'll both be very happy.'

'Thanks, Mr Murphy. I'd better go now. I have an important phone call to make.'

'You've forgotten one thing, Michael.'

Michael glanced over his shoulder. 'How much will you pay me?'

'You do know that apprentices don't earn much while they're training?' said Tim.

'I am aware of that – but I consider our situation a little out of the ordinary,' said Michael.

'Yeah, so how does ten pounds a week to start with sound to you?'

'I have no idea of the going rate, but it sounds good to me.'

'If I told you that when I started my apprenticeship fifteen years ago I was paid two pounds fifteen shillings, does that help to put it into perspective?'

Michael nodded. 'I'll drop in to see you tomorrow, Mr Murphy.'

Tim lowered himself into the chair he had vacated and wondered what he was doing offering to pay Michael so much.

He reached for the sherry bottle. It occurred to him that there was something else he should have mentioned to Michael. Should he call him back or wait until tomorrow? He decided on the former and, getting to his feet, went after him.

'There's something else I should tell you before you make your decision. I have enemies, and now some of the crooks are out they might show their faces. So I've been thinking that we should alter the name of the garage from "Tim Murphy" to yours – or better still, your father's.'

'My dad's dead.'

'He doesn't need to be alive. It's just so that if anyone asks, you can tell them that I've sold the garage to your father and he's put you in charge. If they ask you for my address you say you don't know it; that your father only ever met me in a pub in town, and on the paperwork the address I gave was the garage's.'

'But what if you're around if they turn up?'

'I have every intention of staying in the background . . . and there's a back entrance to the property, as well as an office and upstairs rooms. Besides, you can put up a notice saying nobody is allowed in the actual indoor work area for safety reasons. If you agree to accept the job, all I need to know is what name to put on the yard gates and invoice headings.'

'Brookes – Davy Brookes was my dad's name,' said Michael hesitantly, aware of excitement and apprehension churning inside him. 'I'll tell Marjorie and Lucia that I've a job but won't mention your name just yet. By the way, I think you need to know I can't drive.'

'Well, we can remedy that – I'll buy a second-hand car. We're going to need a works van at some point, too; not only will I teach you how to drive, but you can learn all about the anatomy of the automobile at the same time,' said Tim. 'You can also do a course at one of the technical schools in town. We can discuss all this in detail at a later date.'

'Right,' said Michael, squaring his shoulders. 'I'd better get going. I've a date with Marjorie.'

Tim felt all of a tremble as he made his way into his sitting room and lowered himself into the chair in front of the fire. He hoped he was doing the right thing, but he was convinced the way would have been blocked by Michael turning his plan down if he had erred by trying to help Michael in this way. Hopefully none of the gang would get wind of what he was doing and cause trouble. He sat there, watching the flames dancing, half-expecting Lucia to call if the lad had not been able to keep Tim's plan to himself. But there was no ring of the door bell or knock on the window, and gradually Tim relaxed, his eyelids drooping. He drifted off into that half-conscious state when one can hear but is not disturbed by sounds until they are loud enough to demand attention.

Which is what happened an hour later when Mrs Hudson came into the room and told him that Isabella had been knocking on the window but had failed to rouse him.

'I thought you were dead,' Isabella said, from a position three feet away. 'You look dreadful. No more good looks. I thought the spots would have gone by now – but they're still there and your face has gone puffy for some reason, so your lovely dimples are barely noticeable.'

'Thanks for making me feel so much better,' Tim rasped. 'You'd best not stay if you can't stand the sight of me.'

'No, you've given me an idea for an article. How adults can suffer when they succumb to childhood complaints. We'd need a picture, of course, to stress the point. You wouldn't object, would you?'

'Yes, I bloody would. Where are your brains, woman? You've just told me how terrible I look, so how can you believe I'd want this face staring back at people throughout Merseyside?'

'I'd make it a very sympathetic article.'

'I don't care. Besides, you haven't uttered a word of sympathy to me since you came in.'

'I'd offer to kiss you better but you don't sound as if you'd welcome my kisses.'

'I didn't think you'd want to kiss me – unless you've already had measles?'

'I wouldn't have mentioned kisses if I hadn't.' She came alongside him and slid an arm about his neck and snuggled up, pressing her lips against his cheek before drawing back, 'Gosh, you're hot stuff.'

'Is that a compliment or a complaint?'

'I'm not complaining about anything, sweetie. It'll be more fun, though, when you're A1.'

'That shouldn't be too long – and once I'm back to normal I've plans for if the book doesn't make my fortune.'

'Our fortune, sweetie,' she cooed, kissing his ear. 'Tell me your plans? Is it a bigger and better book? After all, we are in this together.'

'I doubt you'd want to be part of what I have in mind to help young Michael next door. He's having to get married and needs a job, so I've offered him the chance of earning some money by taking over the garage. I'll teach him all I know and I can see him doing well.'

She was silent a moment before saying slowly, 'Is this your proposed ending for the book? Haven't you listened to anything I've said about the need for an exciting finish?'

'This is for real,' said Tim, his voice breaking. He eased her away from him and reached for the sherry bottle. 'What can be more exciting than helping the younger generation?'

She stood, gazing down at him as he took a swig of sherry from the bottle. 'I never saw you as a philanthropist,' she said.

'There's still a lot you don't know about me,' Tim said, offering her the bottle. 'Like a swig?'

She shook her head.

'You don't have to look so disgusted, I have it on excellent authority it's good for the throat.'

'Maybe, but it's time I was going. It's obvious you're still not yourself.'

He admitted he was feeling exhausted and that it was probably best she left.

Placing a hand on his cheek, she said, 'Nightie-nightie,' and sashayed out of the room.

After she left, Tim mulled over the scene until Jerry joined him in the sitting room. As he listened to his son chatting away, Tim told himself that his relationship with Jerry and Lucia and the opportunity to get his business back on its feet again was more important than getting his manuscript published; although surely his having a contract for the book with a publisher meant he could still see it in print one day as long as he finished it? Having come to that conclusion, he put the matter out of his mind and opened a tin of Baxter's Scotch Broth, heated it up in a saucepan, and cut several slices from the fresh Vienna loaf Mrs Hudson had fetched for him from the corner shop. He then served out the soup in two bowls, placed them on the table and bade Jerry sit and eat.

It was as they sat across from each other and heard a dog barking outside that Tim was reminded of Fang, the stray mongrel, who had wandered into the garage not long after Tim had started up in business. While he had been in prison, Marty had taken the dog in. Tim had intended taking control of Fang once he had his own place, but had not considered it right to bring him to Mrs Hudson's house. He recalled that his original plan when he had adopted the dog had been to keep him at the garage as a watchdog. Tim had slept in a room over the office at the time: it had not been suitable for Jerry to live with him there, so Jerry had lived with Marty and Irene for a while.

After they finished the first course, Tim opened a packet of chocolate marshmallows: they ended their meal with half an orange each. Then, after a coffee and a drink of milk, Tim read one of Enid Blyton's Secret Seven stories to Jerry in front of the fire before seeing him to bed. Then he switched on the wireless and made himself a coffee, ate another chocolate marshmallow and listened to some music, trying to remember the name of the sign writer who had done a job for him several years back. He could only hope that his plan would work and there would be no trouble for either him or Michael.

Ten

Michael stood in the yard, gazing at the sign, leaning against a wall, on which was painted in black and red, DAVY BROOKES & SON, SERVICES & REPAIRS, BODYWORK & TYRES. He thought how proud his father would have been to see his name with that '& Son', if he had still been alive, although instead of 'Services', etc., his father would have inscribed, 'Garden Tidying, Weeding, Tree Felling, Bed Planting, No Job Too Small'. The board would be put up outside as soon as they were ready for business.

Michael walked up the yard to the brick building where he had left his employer in the office. Tim was sitting at a desk with a large ledger open in front of him. On the wooden floor at the side of the desk in a patch of sunlight a dog sprawled.

Michael bent and patted its head. 'Hello, boy,' he said.

Fang twisted his head and licked his hand.

'He likes you,' said Tim.

'Just as well if I'm going to be working here.' Michael yawned and stretched. 'Which reminds me, when do I get started?'

'Well, I don't think we should wait until the customers start knocking on the gate. I'll show you some tools and explain the kind of jobs they're used for, and also you can read some car-maker's manuals. We'll also have to do some advertising to bring the customers in, so you can help me design a flyer.'

'You mean to go in the *Echo* and the like?'

'Yeah! Also to put through letterboxes. I've seen a second-hand car advertised in the *Echo* which I think I'll go after. I'll give it a good going over and hopefully get the price down. Then we'll do a service when we get it back here,' said Tim. 'You can come with me. We've still some way to go before we can open for business but we're getting there.'

Michael nodded, thinking he was going to be extremely busy over the next few weeks, but felt certain Marjorie would understand when he told her the news.

'I presume you're home this late because you've been at Marjorie's?' asked Lucia later that day.

Michael shrugged off his jacket and, without looking at his sister, said, 'It's true I've been to Marjorie's, but I've also been working. I have an apprenticeship.'

'That's quick! Doing what?'

'Working in a garage. Eventually I'll be a qualified motor mechanic.'

'Getting your hands dirty?'

'What's wrong with getting my hands dirty as long as it's honest work? Dad got his hands dirty and he loved his job. You're so snobby, our Lucia.'

'No, I'm not. I just want you to have life easier than Dad.'

'You sound like Mam, who always thought working in an office was best for me. From what I've heard, office work can be boring.'

'You have the brains to be a teacher.'

'Working with kids. No thanks! I've had enough helping with our lot. Besides, I'd have to go to teacher training college. I've got a job and so far I'm enjoying it.'

'Where is this job?'

'The other side of Liverpool.'

'So near Marjorie's mother's.

'I can't say it's just round the corner, but it's closer to hers than here.'

'So you'll save on bus fares, which is all to the good, because you'll need every penny once the baby arrives.'

'Why don't you try cheering me up?' Michael said sullenly.

'Fact of life, little brother,' said Lucia.

'You could do a better job than you are,' Michael pointed out.

'It suits me,' she said.

'Exactly. And the one I've got suits me.'

'OK, you've made your point. Your dinner's in the oven. And, by the way, what time is the wedding on Saturday?'

'Three o'clock. It'll be a small affair and we'll be going back to Marjorie's mother's after the ceremony. Can't afford to hire a hall or any of that stuff.'

'Fine. Ask her is there anything she'd like me to bring to help share the expense?'

'I'll mention it. But I suspect she'll turn your offer down. She knows our family isn't well off.'

'We're not paupers. Besides, she can't be that well off if she's a widow.'

'She's been saving for Marjorie's wedding for a while. I think she's got quite a responsible job and earns good money. She's been in her job since the war.'

'So she must be disappointed she can't make a big splash for the wedding.'

'She said the money will go to the baby.'

'She sounds a very reasonable woman.'

'I reckon, as mothers-in-law go, I could have done a lot worse,' Michael said, leaving the room to take his dinner out of the oven.

Lucia wondered if he would still think that once he was living under Marjorie's mother's roof.

The wedding came round only too quickly for Lucia, but she supposed it couldn't come soon enough for Marjorie and her mother. The day dawned bright and clear and Lucia hoped the good weather would last the rest of the day as she set the table for breakfast. She had decided to give the bridal couple some money in an envelope, with a wedding card from the whole family, rather than try and choose a suitable gift.

She planned to set out at least an hour and a half before three o'clock, as she and the children would be travelling by bus to the church. Michael had been secretive about who was to be his best man and how he would get to the church. No doubt Tony would have been best man if he had been home, but he'd had to return to London.

Lucia entered St Mary's Church, West Derby, with a certain amount of trepidation; she had never set foot in a Protestant church before and did not know what to expect. She need not have worried though because, as the service was in English, she was able to follow it without any difficulty. The surroundings felt familiar too, as there were candles and a faint smell of incense, just as there was in her own church.

What did come as a big surprise was to see Tim standing beside Michael in front of the sanctuary. Suddenly it occurred

to her that he might have something to do with her brother
deciding to be a motor mechanic. Later she was to discover that
they had arrived in a car driven by Michael, under Tim's tuition,
and which apparently belonged to his garage business where
Michael worked. Michael was a quick learner. She didn't know
whether to be pleased that Tim was helping Michael or annoyed
that they had both kept the fact secret. She decided not to get
worked up about it because, after all, what was of more importance
at that moment was the wedding; she found it moving because it
was obvious to all those there that the young couple loved each
other and meant every word of the vows they were making.

Marjorie had just one bridesmaid and unusually her mother
gave her away. Everything went off without a hitch. Only the
immediate families were attending the wedding breakfast.

Lucia found herself liking Adele, Marjorie's mother, on sight.
She was of medium height and build, but her dyed blonde hair
was fashioned in a bouffant style that made her appear taller;
she also wore very high heels of burgundy-coloured patent
leather that went well with a tan linen suit and a pink floral
blouse. Her eyes were slate grey and her wide mouth was outlined
in a cherry red lipstick. Her eyes and mouth were what Lucia's
father would have called smiley.

'It's lovely to meet you,' said Lucia. 'May I introduce Michael's
younger brothers and sisters?'

Adele lowered her head and beamed at the children. 'What
a good-looking bunch you are,' she said. 'You're a credit to your
sister.'

'Say how do you do to Mrs Blake.' Lucia tapped each child
on the head and named them and they did as she bid them.

Next Adele introduced them to her sister Phyllis and fourteen-
year-old niece, Janice, who had been the bridesmaid. With
introductions over, the party headed off to Adele's house, which
was situated in West Derby village, not far from the main entrance
to Croxteth Park. A buffet was set out and drinks were served
in a rear room with French windows opening on to a garden.
After collecting a plate of food and a drink, they were directed
to the comfortable front room, where a coal fire burned in a
cast-iron fireplace surrounded by tiles.

Soon Theresa and Janice had their heads together as they

discussed schools, films, music, pop stars, boys and fashion, scarcely touching the food on their plates until they were reminded to eat by mother and sister. Lucia was pleased that her sister had made a new friend of Marjorie's cousin. She also felt easier in her mind about her brother's marriage and him living in this house. She admired Adele for putting on such a good spread for the young couple at such short notice. Her thoughts were also on Tim; she was determined to have a few words with him at the earliest opportunity about him having provided Michael with a job. She soon realized she was going to have to wait because, soon after having a short conversation with Michael, Marjorie and her mother, Tim left in company with Michael.

Michael was not away for long, and Lucia decided that now was not the time to have it out with her brother as to why he had not told her that it was Tim who was employing him. By half past six, she felt it was time to leave. She could tell that James and Joseph were starting to get fed up, and Gabrielle was beginning to droop, not really having recovered completely from her bout of measles. So Lucia made their excuses, gave their thanks, kissed the bride and groom and said their farewells, and went to catch a bus into town, intending to go to Nellie's and tell her all about the wedding. Only she changed her mind because it was such a lovely evening and so, having caught a bus from West Derby that terminated at the Pierhead, Lucia walked with the children down to the landing stage so they could watch the ships on the Mersey for a short while. It was something they hadn't done for a long time.

The children enjoyed it as much as she had thought they would, and Lucia remembered how it had been a favourite place of her father's. She had been ten when he had taken her on the ferry to Seacombe and walked along the front to the retirement home for old sailors where his uncle had lived. She had never forgotten that the old tar with the white beard had not only given her an Uncle Joe's mint ball, but also a sixpence.

She watched Joseph as he stalked a gull, only for it to take flight as he crept closer and closer. As for Gabrielle and James, they were standing shoulder to shoulder, gazing at the Isle of Man ferry as people embarked.

'I'd love to go sailing in a big ship,' said James, his eyes shining. 'It would be a real adventure.'

'I'd like to do that as well,' said Gabrielle. 'I'd like to go all the way to America to visit Aunt Babs.'

'You don't have to do that to see Aunt Babs,' said Lucia, thinking how well the two got on. 'She's coming to visit us soon.'

'Goody-goody gumdrops,' said Gabrielle, jumping up and down. 'I can't wait to see her. Perhaps she'll bring me a new outfit for Barbie.'

'Perhaps she will,' Lucia said. 'But you don't go asking.'

'As if I would,' said Gabrielle.

'Well, you just make sure you don't,' warned Lucia. 'Anyway, I think it's time we were leaving. It's getting late and I want to go to Aunt Nellie's before going home.' She called Joseph and Theresa who had been watching a couple of sailors tying up a ferry boat.

When they arrived at Nellie's, it was to find that she had a couple of visitors in the shape of Chris and Nick, who were wanting to get in touch with Tony but did not have his address in London. As it was, the two young men said they were glad to see Lucia and would accompany her and the kids home because they'd quite like a talk with Tim.

But before they could all go off, Nellie wanted to hear all about the wedding and Lucia's impression of Marjorie's mother. She was as surprised as Lucia had been when she heard that Tim had been Michael's best man, and was even more taken aback to hear that Tim was employing him as an apprentice motor mechanic. Lucia changed the subject, not wanting to hear her aunt cast doubt on the wisdom of Michael working for Tim, and picked up the conversation from before she had mentioned Tim.

'I liked Adele, and what's more important is that she and Michael get on well,' said Lucia. 'Anyway, I thought I'd invite her to tea one Sunday, and you can come as well, so you can get to know each other. She's nearer your age than mine, so you'll probably have lots to talk about.'

'I'd like that,' said Nellie. 'And, while I remember – am I right in thinking you're back in work on Monday?'

'Yes, the kids will be going to school.'

Nellie said. 'That must be a relief. Now you'd better be off.'

Lucia hugged her aunt and thanked her. 'I don't know what I'd do without you.'

'Families are supposed to help each other,' was all Nellie said.

Lucia and Theresa had just finished tucking the children into bed, having read them stories, when there came a hammering on the front door. Theresa hurried downstairs, and there was Chris and Nick standing on the doorstep, back from visiting Tim. She invited them in and went to put the kettle on just as Lucia entered the kitchen.

'So did you have a good talk with Mr Murphy?' she asked.

'Yes,' said Nick, producing a copy of *Mersey Beat* and holding it out to her. 'The article he wrote about Tony and me is inside.'

'Well done,' she said, adding, 'by the way, has your father anything to say about the gang who were being released from prison?'

'No,' said Nick.

'But Mr Murphy was telling me that he and Isabella are getting on well with the book, although they're still not in agreement about the ending,' said Chris. 'Also, he wasn't too pleased about another idea she had.'

'What was that?' asked Lucia.

'She wanted to do a piece about what can happen when adults succumb to childhood complaints. It wasn't that he was against her doing that, but apparently she had said that he looked terrible and wanted a photograph taken to go with the article. He said no and they argued.'

'He did look terrible when he was really bad with the measles,' said Lucia, her heart singing at the thought of Tim not falling in with Isabella's wishes. She wished that the book was finished and she was no longer on the scene. 'But what's going to happen about his book?'

'He doesn't seem to care that much, but he does have a contract so he's going to have a go at finishing it as he can't afford to pay back the advance. I offered to give him some editorial advice and help him with the ending,' Chris said. 'He's back in the garage business, so he was hoping that might be a good enough ending. I'm not as certain as him.'

'A bit dull, do you think?' asked Lucia.

Chris shrugged. 'Anyway, I'll be popping next door now and again,' he said.

'Call in and see us when you do,' Lucia said, thinking that she could probably learn from Chris what Tim's plans were regarding Michael and the garage, which she thought preferable to confronting Tim and her brother herself. She didn't want Tim thinking she didn't trust him when it came to Michael's wellbeing, and she didn't want her brother thinking she was fussing like a mother duck with her ducklings when they took their first swim. Maybe she could also make Tim jealous by making something out of Chris popping in to see her when he called at Tim's.

It did feel strange those first few weeks after the wedding, not having Michael around, but eventually all of the family, except Gabrielle, grew accustomed to his absence, and even she was beginning to come to terms with it because Lucia reminded her constantly of the forthcoming visit of their aunt in the summer.

The weeks passed slowly, despite being back in work, and Lucia looked forward to having a break. At last Easter came and, although the weather was not brilliant, it was dry. After the services on Good Friday and Easter Sunday, Lucia decided to take the children to Seaforth Sands on the Bank Holiday Monday, and she suggested to Jerry that he ask his father if he could go with them. To her delight, Jerry returned with the information that his dad would like to go as well if that was all right with Lucia.

'It's a free country,' replied Lucia, thinking she might discover more of his plans for the garage if he did so. She had seen Michael only a couple of times since the wedding, and the second time he had told her that he was enjoying married life and working for Tim; he was content with the responsibility that Tim had laid on his young, inexperienced shoulders, as it made him feel more mature and that Tim trusted him. Lucia decided that perhaps it was time she stopped feeling responsible for her brother and accepted that he could take care of himself. After all, come Christmas, he would be a father, all being well. She remembered to hand him a note for his mother-in-law, inviting her to afternoon tea in a fortnight.

On Easter Monday there was the outing to Seaforth Sands, so she needed to prepare a picnic. She made some sandwiches and packed them in greaseproof paper, and placed the fairy cakes she had baked in a tin. She prepared a couple of bottles of watered-down orange juice and also a flask of coffee. She packed them in brown paper bags and placed them in a knapsack. She told the children that they would have to carry their own towels, bathing costumes, buckets, spades and bat and ball. Then she sent Jerry to tell Tim that they were ready to go and that they would meet him on the front step.

He was ready and waiting by the time she had hustled the children outside, and she thought he looked a sight for sore eyes and that it was brave of him to be prepared to be seen in public, walking with so many children. They could almost be mistaken for a Sunday School outing.

'Well, you all look fighting fit after the measles,' Tim said, smiling down at them.

'And you look heaps better,' said Lucia. 'How's the book getting on?'

'I've a touch of what is called in the trade "writer's block". That's why I was glad of your suggestion of an outing. Considering how close we live to the beach, we don't go there often.'

Lucia could not help remembering the evening the two of them had walked along the sands and kissed. She wondered if he ever thought about it as she did.

'Most likely that's because the sands get crowded, and I don't know about you, but I prefer it quieter. I've never forgotten getting lost once and not being able to find Mam and Dad when I came out of the sea after having a paddle. I was frightened and thought I'd never find them.'

'But surely they would have been watching out for you?'

'Yes, but it's surprising how far one can go when splashing along through the shallows parallel with the beach, and what with so many children and people, it's difficult to distinguish one from another.'

'But they found you eventually?'

'A friend of Mam's spotted me and took me by the hand and gave me a biscuit and helped me to find them. Now I worry about losing sight of the younger ones when there are crowds.'

'Surely Joseph, James and Gabrielle are old enough to be wary of the sea. They're also likely to stay together and run for help if one of them gets into difficulty. Anyway, we can take turns keeping an eye on them.'

She nodded. 'That way I'll be able to relax a bit.'

They had come to the main road and had to wait a few minutes before being able to cross in company with about twenty other people heading for the sands. To their left was Gladstone Dock, and beyond that was a line of dockyards all the way to Liverpool, as well as the largest tobacco warehouse in the country, dating back to Victorian times. A number of the docks were named after famous mariners and battles, such as Nelson and Trafalgar. After passing through a grassy area, they came to the sands. The children ran on ahead; the older ones looking for a space large enough for them all to sit down to eat their picnic when the time came.

Having laid claim to an area of firm sand halfway down the beach, with room to make a sandcastle, the older children stood waiting for Lucia and Tim to reach them, but Jerry and Joseph were already resting on their haunches and making use of their spades to fill their buckets.

Lucia removed an old army blanket from a bag and spread it on the flat sand, and then laid a towel over it before sitting down. For a while she watched Joseph and Jerry building a sandcastle, and then her gaze wandered to Theresa, James and Gabrielle, who had undressed down to their bathing suits and were heading for the water. She glanced in Tim's direction to see that he had wrapped a towel around him like a sarong and was obviously changing into bathing trunks. She averted her gaze, thinking how much easier for the opposite sex it was in so many ways. She would only put on her bathing costume if the clouds cleared and there was a good large patch of blue sky. Then she would have Theresa hold her towel up for her while she undressed beneath it and dragged up her costume; otherwise she would make do with sitting in her frock and forgo a swim.

As soon as Joseph and Jerry were clad just in bathing trunks, they were off down the beach to the water to join the others, and in no time at all they had launched themselves into the waves and were splashing about.

'Damn!' muttered Tim, scrambling to his feet.

'What's wrong?' Lucia asked, shading her eyes from a sudden shaft of sunlight as she looked up at him.

'I don't think Jerry can swim.'

'You don't know?'

'I've never taken him swimming. I'd better go and make sure he's all right.'

Lucia watched Tim limp down to the water's edge and then, knee-deep in the waves, bend over Jerry and speak to him. The boy hit the surface with the curve of his hand, splashing water over his father. The sun glistened on the water droplets that landed on Tim's shoulders and chest. As he turned and looked back at her, she caught her breath, admiring his muscular physique. Then she realized she could make the best of the opportunity, now the sun had come out, and change into her bathing costume while Tim was out of the way.

She wasted no time in doing so, although she had to manage without Theresa's help and had her bathing costume half up when she heard Tim's voice nearby asking whether she needed a helping hand to hold the towel. She blushed and turned down his offer, saying that she was nearly finished, and dropped the towel on the blanket.

'That's a snazzy cossie,' he said, his sparkling blue gaze washing over her.

'Thanks, it's the first time I've worn it.' She had bought it from a Littlewoods catalogue, won over by the combination of maroon, lime and white diamond-shaped patterns and a double frill at the top.

'It suits you. You've got a good figure.'

'You don't look bad yourself,' she retorted.

'I could do with a tan. When I lived in Australia I was a great colour.'

'I can imagine,' said Lucia. 'I had a tan when I went to Italy.'

'I've always fancied going to Italy. What did you think of it?' he asked, lowering himself on to his towel so their eyes were almost on a level.

'A lot of the buildings are crumbling but the countryside is beautiful and I liked the food and the people.' Lucia flicked some sand off her thigh. 'An artist friend who used to work at the coffee bar told me that I'm a Philistine. Actually, she's Maggie's cousin.'

'Betty,' said Tim. 'I remember her being mentioned. She lives in America. Irene visited her the other year.'

'That's right. My aunt Babs has visited her, too, the one who is coming over at the end of June.'

'I remember she sent you all presents at Christmas.'

'That's right. She's lovely. I'm blessed in having two generous aunts.'

'I haven't any aunts that I know of.'

'Poor you.'

'Life could be worse. At the moment I count myself lucky. The sun's shining and I'm here on the beach with a lovely girl.'

'You're teasing me. I'm not lovely.'

His eyes met hers. 'You're lovely inside and out. I don't think I've ever met anyone as unselfish as you.'

'I'm no angel,' she said gruffly.

'I'm not on the lookout for an angel,' Tim said. 'Just someone to spend the rest of my life with.'

Lucia's heart felt as if it stopped for a moment. 'What are you—' Before she could finish, there came Gabrielle's voice demanding attention from a few feet away.

'Can I have a drink, please? I swallowed some sea-water and it tasted horrible.'

Just behind her was James, who picked up a bucket from near the sandcastle. 'I thought I'd make a moat for the sandcastle and fill it with water.'

'Do Jerry and Joseph know you're going to do that?' asked Tim. 'It is their castle, after all.'

'But they've left it so they can't really care about it,' James said.

'I'm not sure I agree with you there, young man,' said Tim, standing up and appearing to loom over the boy. 'I'll go and see how they feel about it – and I'll take a couple of buckets so they can bring water if they're in favour of your plan.'

As soon as Tim was out of earshot, James said sulkily, 'Why did he have to interfere? I wasn't doing any harm.'

'You should have mentioned what you planned to them when you were in the water.'

'I wanted to do it without them interfering and also to give them a nice surprise.'

'They mightn't consider it a nice surprise but think you're muscling in on their territory.'

'You're taking his side,' snapped James. 'I hope you're not going to marry him.'

'I'm not taking sides. Why don't you build your own castle?'

'Maybe I will – and it'll be better than theirs,' James said with a sniff, picking up a spade and moving several feet away from her to a clear area of sand.

Lucia sighed with relief and hoped that was the end of the subject. She watched Tim approaching with Joseph and Jerry carrying buckets of sea-water.

'We're going to need more water than this,' said Tim as the two boys dumped the buckets on the sand close to their castle. The three gazed at James.

Lucia said, 'James decided he would build his own castle.'

'Now that's what I call a sensible decision,' said Tim.

A few minutes later, Gabrielle appeared on the scene and immediately offered to help James. He gave her the task of fetching water for the moat. She made no protest but went and did what he asked. Jerry and Joseph set about building a moat for their castle. Tim volunteered to collect some shells to decorate the castle. Lucia said that she would go with him. He handed her a bucket with a smile and they sauntered off, shoulders touching every now and again.

'What did the boys say when you told them James was going to build a moat for their castle?'

'They decided that a moat was a good idea and wasted no time in getting back to their castle. I felt a bit of a fool when I saw James building his own.'

'All's well that ends well,' Lucia said. 'I think, though, that we're going to have to share the shells and any decent pebbles we find between both castles.'

Tim slanted her a smile. 'You know exactly how to be tactful, Lucia. It's something I need to learn.'

'I'm sure you'll get there,' she said, wondering how she could guide their conversation back to the earlier one that Gabrielle had interrupted, without it being too obvious. She settled on a plan of attack. 'How do you think Jerry would react if you were to marry again?' she said, only to realize that she was speaking to thin air because Tim had darted ahead and was in the act of picking something up from the sand. She swore inwardly and then asked, 'What have you got there?'

He straightened up and held out a shell that reminded her of a miniature ice-cream cone. 'I think Jerry and Joseph will like this, don't you?' he asked.

She agreed. 'We're going to need to find a lot more, though.'

'We'll have to keep our eyes on the ground then,' he sighed. 'When I'd much rather be looking at you. I'm not surprised Chris pops in to see you whenever he visits me. He told me how much he enjoys his visits to your house.'

Lucia could feel herself blushing. 'Are you flirting with me, Tim?'

'Yes and no. I have it in mind to court you, Lucia – and that isn't only because I'm sure Jerry would love to have you as a mother.'

Instantly Lucia's emotions were in a whirl of confusion. She liked the idea of being courted, it had such romantic connotations, but his mention of her being a mother to Jerry reminded her of what Irene had said about Tim shirking his responsibility for his son and leaving it to her and Marty to care for him. Neither had she forgotten what Michael had said about Tim using her, despite her being willing to help him out by having Jerry play at her house with Joseph. Yet even having thought about these things, she could not help but understand the sense in his wanting to provide his son with a new mother.

'Forgive me, Lucia, for springing this on you,' Tim said. 'I can see it's come as a shock. Yet you must have realized I think a lot of you and enjoy your company, especially when we manage to get some time together, just the two of us? Of course, you might not consider me good husband material with my history, and definitely not the right man to help you ensure the well-being of your brothers and sisters, when I don't appear to have taken on enough responsibility for my own son until recently.'

'I admit you've taken me by surprise,' Lucia said. 'I thought you had something going between you and Isabella.'

'Only a working relationship and, besides, I don't think she cares for kids. She never asks after Jerry.'

'I love the idea of being courted by you. I guess it means we'll make time to be just the two of us for a while before we talk seriously of our relationship going further.'

'Naturally courtship should lead to marriage, and my intention is for us to be husband and wife and have children of our own one day. I was hoping it's what you'd like too. Being older than you I wouldn't want a long courtship, although I don't want to put pressure on you if you need longer to think about my proposal.'

She turned over in her mind what he said and came up with the words, 'Shall we wait and see how we go for a couple of months before we mention this to anyone else?'

He nodded. 'If that's what you want. I can name a few people who would immediately try and persuade you not to take such a step as marriage with me.'

'I know, but I make my own decisions, so you don't have to worry about them. If we love each other and are determined to make a go of things, I'm sure it will work out. Don't you agree?'

'Yes, although I question whether you could ever love me,' he said in a low voice.

She wondered if he was trying to get her to admit that she did love him. Surely he must realize that she had already committed herself to him, otherwise she would not have helped him so much with Jerry, or had them both for Christmas last, or visited him when he had measles.

'I've told you already that I like you, so surely that's a good start on the path to loving someone?' she said.

'Of course, so we take things from here,' he said, taking her hand and lifting it to his lips. 'Shall we walk on a bit further so I can tell you how I love the way you try not to laugh after telling the boys off for being naughty because you've found what they've done amusing. Your lovely mouth twitches at the corners and there's a gleam in your eyes that belies the sternness you're trying to show.'

'You must be watching me very carefully.'

'You're worth watching. You're a feast for the eyes. Especially in what you're wearing now. I'd like nothing more than to make love to you.' His gaze washed over her in a way that made her want to throw herself at him, but she continued to walk sedately at his side, now with her eyes downcast, looking for shells and pebbles.

'I think we'd need to find somewhere quieter,' she murmured. 'We wouldn't want to shock people – we especially don't want to shock the children.'

'Do you think they'd all be shocked if I kissed you?'

'That would depend on the manner of your kisses. Little affectionate ones or one big passionate kiss.'

He was still holding her hand, so he tugged on it and she turned to face him. He placed a hand on the back of her head and brought her close and kissed her in a fashion that sent warmth coursing through her veins as his lips gently explored hers. The kiss did not last long, but its effect lasted the length of their walk; she was aware of the weakness in her knees every time she bent to pick up a cockle or razor shell or an usually coloured pebble and placed them in the painted metal bucket

When they approached the children, hand in hand, Lucia was aware that James and Theresa were the only two who gazed down at their clasped hands. The other three were more interested in what shells or pebbles they had found, and in getting their hands on them and decorating their sandcastles.

While they were so occupied, Tim suggested that he and Lucia go and have a swim. She agreed, and raced Tim down to the water's edge. It wasn't until she was up to her thighs in the sea that she remembered his injury and that the race had not been a fair one. She turned and watched him limping along and cursed herself for her thoughtlessness. Especially after his having said she was the most unselfish person he had ever met.

'I'm sorry,' she said, as soon as he drew alongside her. 'I forgot you couldn't run.'

'I'm sorry too,' Tim said, linking hands with her. 'I wanted to catch you.'

'Are you able to swim?' she asked.

'I don't know. I haven't tried since I came out of prison. Perhaps if I had done, Jerry would be a better swimmer than he appears to be. He tells me that Marty took him to the swimming baths with Jessie a few times but he would have had to divide his time between the two of them. After the accident I had years of really severe pain and discomfort to get through, as well as withdrawal symptoms when getting off the painkilling drugs.'

'Maybe you should start going to the swimming baths. There's one in Crosby with a trainer pool right by the beach. See your doctor and ask his advice. Water helps to support the body, so the exercise shouldn't be too difficult.'

'If the doctor were to give me the go-ahead, would you come with me?'

'Yes, if we go during school time, I can fit it in with the hours I'm not working, once we know the opening hours.'

'Right, all being well, it's a date,' Tim said.

Tim had difficulty getting to see the doctor, so decided not to bother. Surely swimming wouldn't put any more strain on his hip than walking did? Yet when Lucia asked him what the doctor had said, he lied, instead of admitting he had been unable to get an appointment. He felt uncomfortable about not being honest with her but unable to backtrack.

They fixed an afternoon to go swimming and, except for having a slight difficulty getting into the pool, to his relief he was able to swim a length of the pool using a slow, careful breaststroke. Lucia swam alongside him, murmuring words of encouragement. After a few words with the lifeguard, Tim took up his suggestion of simply walking the length of the pool, and he found that comfortable despite having to forge against the water. He was slightly concerned about slipping but found Lucia's presence reassuring. He decided to seek out a physiotherapist who could advise him about exercising in the pool and about any other exercises he could recommend at this stage of his recovery.

The physiotherapist was in favour of Tim swimming and walking in the pool, and also suggested some treatment and other exercises; ones that Tim remembered the prison hospital physio advising him to do, but that Tim had not kept up for long. Now he was determined to gain a better state of fitness and so he suggested to Lucia that they go swimming regularly.

She agreed, but told him that when her aunt came over from America, she would have to give it up for a while.

Despite his disappointment, Tim accepted that he could not expect Lucia always to fall in with his wishes. After his first marriage being a failure, he wanted to make certain that he got it right this time – and not just for himself.

A few weeks into his new regime of swimming and treatment, he had another visit from Isabella wanting to see if he had made any progress with his manuscript, reminding him that he had a deadline to meet.

'I haven't forgotten,' Tim said.

'Glad to hear it,' said Isabella. 'So how far off the end are you?'

'A chapter and a half I reckon,' he said.

'Then you'll have to go back to the beginning and check it through,' she reminded him. 'You don't want to be leaving in stuff that shouldn't be there. Perhaps you'd like me to copyedit it for you now?'

'No, thanks. I'm feeling much better and I've actually had a friend giving me some help with it. I would rather finish it before you see it. I only wish I knew what you were thinking when you suggested I had a gun and forced Sid to escape with me. Who put the idea into your head?'

Isabella ignored the question, only asking, 'What friend?'

'None of your business.'

Her lips tightened. 'I hope you haven't forgotten we have a contract and I'm entitled to a share of the profits from the book?'

'I haven't forgotten.'

'Good! So the ending – how have you decided to finish it?'

'Hopeful that I have a happy future ahead of me. Isn't that how most books should end?'

'I presume you'll need to carry on writing if you want to make a living.'

'There are other ways of making a living, as I think I remember mentioning to you not so long ago.'

Isabella looked taken aback. 'I wouldn't have thought there was much going for you. Unless you planned on turning to crime again.'

'Now there's a thought,' Tim said, a pensive gleam in his eyes. 'Time for you to leave, Isabella. I have somewhere to go.'

'Sounds like you want to get rid of me.'

'I don't deny it, but I have somewhere I need to be.' He gave her a nudge in the direction of the door.

She had no choice but to leave, but she did not go far. Hiding behind a privet hedge, where she could keep an eye on the house, she didn't have long to wait before she saw Tim walking in the direction of the bus stop. As soon as she saw him climb on to a bus she followed him. Seeing no sign of him on the lower deck she went inside, thinking he must have gone upstairs for a smoke. She would keep her eyes open for when he came downstairs and tail him, convinced that he had something up his sleeve that he didn't want her to know about.

The bus drew up at the stop nearest Marty's house but Isabella noticed Tim did not leave the vehicle, and she soon realized that he must be going into town. She hoped her instincts were leading her aright when Tim left the bus in Lime Street. She followed suit and tailed him along Lime Street, past the Adelphi Hotel and into Renshaw Street, where he stood at a stop waiting for a bus that would take him to south Liverpool.

It was then that she began to get an inkling where he could be going as she ran over again in her mind their conversation in his apartment and what he had said about there being other ways of making a living.

She decided not to follow him any further, and instead to go and have a cup of tea and a cake in Lewis's café. After that refreshment she went and caught a bus that would take her to Walton. There was a man she needed to see. He would decide what to do with the information she had. One thing was for certain, he wouldn't want Tim's dream of his garage business thriving coming true. Besides, the writer in Isabella rejected such a tame ending. She wanted drama and excitement and felt certain her contact could arrange both.

Eleven

A month later Michael was working late, finishing a service on a pale green Morris Oxford, when he heard a rumbling growl coming from Fang.

'What is it, boy?' he asked, glancing in the dog's direction where it lay on a remnant of old blanket.

Naturally Fang's only way of answering was by stretching and moving towards the double doors.

'A late customer, the boss, or trouble,' wondered Michael aloud, making no move to open the Judas gate, remembering the men who had asked him to do a paint job and change some licence plates not so long ago. They had offered him money to rush the job and keep it quiet from Tim. He had been tempted, but he had told them he wasn't interested.

He placed a hand on the dog's head and hushed him. Michael remained motionless in that position, listening to the slightest of scraping noises while watching the gate from behind a car. Then there came a snap and the gate swung open. A man came through and then another. Instantly Michael recognized them and knew he could be in trouble. They were the men who'd asked for the paint job and a change of licence plates on a Sunbeam saloon.

Lucia and Marjorie would have thoroughly disapproved of him breaking the law. Besides, his father's name was written on the doors and there was no way he would bring disgrace to that. He really should have mentioned the incident to Tim.

As they moved further into the yard, he was certain that the men had not yet noticed him or Fang, although he could hear the rumble deep in the dog's throat still. He wished he could reach the telephone in the office, but knew if he made a move he'd be spotted. He noticed that the men carried what appeared to be short sticks and they were heading for the working space under cover. Michael wished he had a spanner to hand. At that moment he felt Fang move beneath his hand

and then he bounded in the direction of the men, barking fiercely.

Michael drew in his breath with a hiss as one of them raised what the young man now realized was a cosh and brought it down on the dog. Fang yelped and collapsed on to the concrete floor. The man raised his weapon again. The action was enough to bring Michael from his hiding place, and he picked up a spanner that was lying on a bench a few feet away. He charged at the man but, before he could reach him, Michael caught a flash of movement out of the corner of his eye. Then there came pain in his head and he felt himself falling and all went black.

When he regained consciousness he could not think where he was for a moment, and then he came aware of a headache and the hardness of the floor. He lifted his head carefully and glanced about him. He could make out shapes moving about in the light of a single light bulb and suddenly he heard a whimper. Fang! Slowly he managed to drag himself in the direction of the sound and, as he did so, realized that there were tins on the floor; at one point he felt his hand land in a pool of liquid. By the feel and smell of it, he guessed it was lubricating oil. Suddenly it struck him that his attackers had broken in with the intention of wrecking the place. Most likely they had not expected anyone to be here.

Could he be right in believing they were Tim's enemies? What should he do first if he managed to escape? Phone Marjorie or Tim, or race to the police station along the lane in the hope of reaching it before the crooks caught him. He decided to get in touch with Marjorie first, as most likely she would be worrying about him being late and worry was not good for her. He thought about the car he had been working on and of Tim being on his way to check the service he had done. Fortunately it had been tucked away in a corner at the back of the workshop after he had finished with it, so they might not have noticed it in the shadows. All the time he had been thinking, he had still been on the move, and had managed to skirt a pool of petrol. He pushed himself upright and got his bearings and stealthily headed for the office, which was in darkness. Once inside, he could see through the window overlooking the workspace the damage that the men had done. Tins of paint as well as cans of oil had been spilt all over the place and shelves had been smashed; as for the car he had serviced, they had sprayed obscenities over the paintwork. He could also make out Fang huddled on the floor. He could see no sign of the men, so presumed they had left, and so he left the office and went over to Fang and lowered himself on to his haunches and stroked the dog's head and spoke soothingly to him as he took in the bleeding wound on Fang's shoulder. Then he returned to the office.

Relieved that the telephone was still working, he dialled his mother-in-law's number. He was glad that the bang on his head hadn't appeared to have damaged his memory. Fortunately Marjorie picked up the receiver; he explained he was finishing a job so wouldn't be home for an hour or so. He was just about to phone Tim to check whether he had left home when he heard footsteps outside and a loud voice called, 'Is there anyone there?'

He put down the receiver and left the office to find a bobby gazing about at the mess. Michael recognized him as one he had seen before; presumably this was part of his beat.

'What's been going on here?' asked the bobby.

'Two men broke in. One knocked me out and hurt our dog and they've been wrecking the place while I was out of it,' said Michael. 'I was just about to dial my boss.'

The bobby took a notebook and pencil out of a pocket. 'Did you recognize them?'

'No! At least I have seen them before, but I don't know them.'

'Pity! Any idea what time this happened?'

Michael said, 'Must have been shortly after seven. Normally I knock off at six but I was doing a service and I'd just finished and checked my watch.'

'You haven't been unconscious long then; perhaps they heard me coming and I frightened them off.'

Michael glanced at his watch and saw that it was only twenty-five to eight. 'They must have worked at lightning speed to do all this damage,' he said.

The constable nodded. 'They wouldn't have wanted to hang about. How's your head feeling?'

'It aches but I'll survive.'

'You need to go to the hospital and have it X-rayed.'

'I will but I need to phone my boss first.' Michael lifted the receiver.

'Well, while you're at it, phone for an ambulance.'

Michael nodded, then wished he hadn't, because it hurt. He was glad when the constable left the office and began to wander around the workspace. Swiftly Michael dialled for an ambulance and then called Tim's home number.

As soon as Michael recognized Tim's voice on the other end of the line, he said, 'You'd better prepare yourself. We've had a break-in and it's a mess here. They've injured Fang and hit me over the head. There's a bobby here. He's insisted on my ringing for an ambulance so they can check me out.'

'I'm on my way,' said Tim, managing to get a word in. 'You look after yourself.'

'Don't tell our Lucia. I haven't told Marjorie yet and I don't want Lucia phoning her and asking after me and putting the wind up my wife.'

As soon as he put down the receiver, Tim shrugged on his overcoat and clapped a trilby on his tawny hair. Then he went to ask Mrs Hudson if she would listen out for Jerry as he'd had an important phone call and had to go out. Only then did he decide to phone for a taxi instead of summoning his brother, Marty.

As he waited for the taxi to arrive, he seriously thought of having a go at driving again. In cases like this, and even in general, it made sense for him to have the use of a vehicle. Even having the use of the works van would be better than nothing. Why he had hesitated from taking such a step earlier was because he had lost his confidence; besides which, he had been in no state physically to start driving again. Now he felt so much fitter since visiting the swimming pool with Lucia and having physio.

Having come to a decision, he concentrated his thoughts on Michael and what he faced at the garage. He had no doubts about the identity of the men who had attacked Michael and Fang and wrecked his business premises, although he was puzzled as to how they had found out he was involved in Davy Brookes & Son. He supposed it was possible one of them or a member of their families could have kept an eye on the garage and spotted him. He gazed out of the taxi window and recognized a couple of shops on Scottie Road. Hopefully he would reach his destination in approximately three-quarters of an hour, depending on the traffic.

The taxi drew up behind the ambulance parked outside Davy Brookes & Son. Tim paid off the driver. The ambulance driver wasn't in his cab, so he went through the entrance into the yard and there he found Michael, two bobbies and a couple of ambulance men. There was an overwhelming smell of petrol and oil fumes.

Michael's face lit up when he caught sight of Tim, who heard him say, 'Here's Mr Murphy now.'

'So can we get you off to hospital straightaway?' asked a red-haired ambulance man.

'Yes, if Mr Murphy can come with me,' said Michael.

The ambulance man cocked an eye in the direction of the policemen.

'We do need to talk to you, Mr Murphy,' said the sergeant, standing beside the constable who had first discovered the crime.

'All right,' Tim said, and then turned to face the ambulance man. 'Which hospital are you taking Michael to?'

'Smithdown Road,' he replied. 'The lad doesn't appear too seriously injured to us, but it's always wise to check head injuries out with an X-ray.'

Tim saw Michael into the ambulance and listened keenly to what the lad had to say. He wished Michael had told him about the men's proposition at the time. 'With Marjorie having the baby, I confess for a moment I was tempted by their offer,' said Michael.

'Now you know how easy it is to be led astray,' said Tim in a low voice. 'Anyway, I'll visit Marjorie and reassure her about you.' Then he returned to the garage and had a closer look at the damage, and at poor Fang.

'I reckon they intended to set fire to the place,' said the police sergeant. Tim agreed, wondering how he was going to sort the mess out, and saying as much. 'We've phoned the fire brigade,' continued the sergeant. 'It's not safe with all these fumes. One spark and it could all could go up in flames. Even switching on the light could have been tricky. Anyway, the fire brigade will be able to dampen everything down. I can't see you being able to use these premises in a month of Sundays.'

Tim thought the same and felt depressed. His dreams were in ashes and he was at a loss to know what the future held for him now. As well as that, he was concerned about Michael who, with a baby on the way, was now out of a job. Tim had wanted to help him, but instead he had almost got the lad killed. He looked about him and thought that at least the business premises were detached from any of the surrounding buildings. Even so he'd like to get his hands on those who had ruined his business and injured Michael and Fang in the process.

'Do you have any idea, Mr Brookes, who could have done this?' asked the sergeant.

The question caused Tim to realize that the two policemen had no idea of his true identity, or his criminal record. 'Yes, but I'd like to speak to Inspector Sam Walker at Dale Street, if I may, please?'

'You're acquainted with the inspector?' said the sergeant.

Tim nodded.

'Well, let's get along to the local station and we'll get in touch with him,' the sergeant said.

Tim asked whether he could fetch a few things from the office first, as well as bring Fang along. He collected a whole bundle of paperwork, including the insurance policy; having handed them to the sergeant to hold for the moment, he wrapped Fang in the remnant of blanket. In the distance he could hear the clanging of a fire engine and, remembering what Michael had said about the car he had just serviced, he looked for it. He had just decided to drive it out of the gates, having dumped Fang on the back seat, when he remembered that even a spark could set the fumes alight. He wasted no time lifting Fang out of the car and hurried as fast as he could after the two policemen who had gone outside to greet the firemen.

Tim stayed until the firemen had done what they thought fit to prevent a fire occurring, and then he locked up and went along to the police station on Lark Lane with Fang still wrapped in the piece of blanket in his arms. He was glad to hear that the sergeant had spoken to Detective Inspector Sam Walker and that he was on his way. Tim didn't have long to wait, and he pounced on Sam as soon as he came through the door.

'I never thought the day would come, Tommy, when you'd be glad to see me,' said Sam, a teasing smile lighting his attractive features.

'The name's Tim now,' said Tim.

'Of course, sorry. I should have remembered. So what's this all about?' Sam asked.

Tim repeated what Michael had said to him but kept quiet about to the constable. 'I'm just glad that a bobby arrived when he did. Otherwise Michael and Fang could have perished if the place had gone up in smoke.' A cold shiver went down Tim's spine just thinking how he would have had to face Lucia with the tragic news that her brother was dead. She most likely would have blamed him and it was something that he could never have put right. Thank God, it hadn't come to that – but it had been a close shave for Michael and Fang.

'Who is this Michael, and how did he come to be working for you?' asked Sam.

Tim explained, adding, 'I'm sure you've sussed out why I wanted to speak to you. Nick told me you'd mentioned that some of the gang were out of prison, so I thought a watch might be kept on them so that you might have some idea where they were and what they were up to. Of course, I might be doing them an injustice; they might have just returned to their old neighbourhood and families and be set on living the simple life. It might not be them at all who are responsible for this mess, but somehow I doubt it.'

'I'll look into it,' Sam said. 'Although the ringleader is still in prison, so he's out of the frame . . . I'll visit our prime suspects right away, before they use their brains and decide to get rid of the evidence.'

'Their clothes will stink of fuel,' said Tim.

'Exactly! And it's possible their womenfolk might have already persuaded them to strip off and get rid of what they were wearing.' Sam frowned. 'I'm off.'

'Keep me posted,' Tim shouted after Sam as he went through a doorway, calling out a few orders.

Tim was aware of a sense of anti-climax, then he remembered

he needed to take care of Fang as well as go to the hospital. Even if he was not allowed to see Michael, he could ask after him before going on to visit Marjorie. It was at this point that Tim wished anew he had the use of a vehicle. Was it possible the works van was parked round the back, or even in the next street? He expressed his thanks to the sergeant and constable for their assistance and then left to look for the works van, glad that it had not been parked in the garage.

He found the van parked round the back and was relieved that he had ordered a spare set of keys, which he had kept himself in case Michael happened to misplace his set. He opened the door on the driver's side and managed to climb up into the van without too much difficulty, having placed Fang in the well of the van on the passenger side first. He sat unmoving for a few moments just gazing at the steering wheel, gearstick, and the instrument panel, before doing what had once been almost as natural as breathing to him, and drove off in the direction of Smithdown Road. Fortunately he had renewed his driving licence as soon as he had decided to teach Michael to drive.

It was as he had thought – he was not allowed to see Michael – but he had left a note for Tim, which was passed over to him. He did not read it until he was back in the van; when he did so there were tears in his eyes, because Michael's thoughts were not for himself at all but for his wife and his siblings and even for Fang.

As Tim parked outside Marjorie's mother's house, he felt a mixture of satisfaction and apprehension. Fang whined as he climbed out of the van so Tim walked round to the other side, opened the passenger door and patted the dog on the head. 'I'll be back soon,' he said.

Then he walked up the path, aware that a curtain twitched in the front window. The door opened before he could knock and Marjorie stood in the doorway, an anxious expression on her comely face. 'What's happened?' she asked, her voice choking.

'Can I come in?' asked Tim.

'Of course,' she held the door wide and stood to one side.

Tim stepped over the threshold and followed her into a back room.

Adele got up from the sofa. 'Is Michael all right?'

'He'll be all right. There was a break-in at the garage. Michael was hit over the head but he'd already regained consciousness before I got there. It was Michael who phoned me to tell me what had happened.'

'Where is Michael?' asked Marjorie, sitting down.

Her mother put an arm around her shoulders and invited Tim to be seated.

He did so and briefly told them the gist of what had happened.

Marjorie wept quietly and her mother patted her shoulder. 'There, there, duck. He's all right. He'll be sitting with you here tomorrow evening.'

'I know,' said Marjorie. 'But he's going to be out of a job. What will we do for money? What with the baby, we need every penny.'

'Don't you be worrying about money for the baby. I've a little nest egg tucked away,' said Adele.

Tim groaned inwardly, thinking that he could not see Michael being happy to be dependent on his mother-in-law for financial support for his little family. He had been so proud of having a job and being able to do that himself. But Marjorie was right about him being out of a job. There was no way the garage could be used as a motor repair business as things stood. He could not chance putting Michael's life at risk. He was going to lose money as it was and, although there could be some insurance money, it would take time to sort matters out.

He would also have to replace the customer's car that had been damaged, and he wanted to do what he could for the young couple. He proposed paying Michael sick money until he was completely well again. He would also try and help Michael get a job in another garage if that was what Michael wanted until he felt it was safe to start up in business again. For now he would reassure Marjorie that Michael would be paid for at least a month.

Tim aimed to discuss matters with the lad as soon as possible. For now he needed to be on his way. Hopefully Jerry was still in the Land of Nod, unaware that Tim was absent. He said his farewells to Marjorie and her mother and made his way to the van, only remembering when he climbed into the driving seat that he still had to see to Fang. He would have to take him to a vet, but that would have to wait until morning. Hopefully Mrs Hudson wouldn't mind having a dog under her roof for now.

'Poor boy,' he whispered, stroking the dog before starting the engine.

There were lights on in the lobby and his sitting room, but all was quiet as he put his latchkey in the lock and opened the front door. He was trying to make as little noise as he could, but he knew he would have to let Mrs Hudson know he had returned, so really there was little point in worrying too much about it. He opened the door to his sitting room and saw his landlady on the sofa, where she had been lying with a blanket over her. She sat up and looked at the clock on the mantelshelf.

'Just gone midnight,' she whispered. 'Time I was in bed. There hasn't been a peep out of Jerry. Did you sort out everything you were wanted for?'

'As much as I could. I had to bring my dog home. The garage was broken into and he was injured.'

'Poor doggie. He can stay here as long as he keeps off the furniture and doesn't go making messes. You'll need to brush the carpet every day, otherwise you'll never get rid of the dog hairs. I'll find you a cardboard box for him to sleep in.'

'Will do,' said Tim, understanding that the old woman had to think about the future when he and Jerry moved out and she would want to let the apartment to another tenant. He was relieved that she hadn't said the dog couldn't stay.

'Was much taken?' she asked on returning with the box.

'No, they wrecked the place and poured fuel everywhere, but the worst thing was that they knocked Michael out. He was only saved by the bobby on the beat turning up and frightening them off before they could start a fire.'

'That's terrible. Will Michael be all right?'

'Yes, I'm sure he will. He has been taken to hospital, though, just to make sure all is OK.'

'Well, I'll say a prayer for him,' said Mrs Hudson. 'It'll come as a shock to the family next door.'

Tim agreed, thinking he would let Lucia know what had happened first thing tomorrow. What he needed now was a good night's sleep, although it would be a miracle if he was able to nod off with all that was going on in his head. But first he had to tend Fang's wound. While he did so, uppermost in his mind was who could have informed those released from prison that he was still involved with the garage business. Maybe it could have been one of the two men in the car that had almost hit them on Boxing Day?

When he did finally fall asleep, it was to dream of masked dark dancing figures silhouetted against leaping flames, and through all this he could hear barking and Michael shouting for help. Only Tim couldn't reach him, and he woke in a sweat, but within minutes he remembered that Michael was alive, and so was Fang, whose yelping he could now hear.

Tim felt something land on his bed and a voice in his ear said, 'Dad, what's Fang doing here? He's wearing a bandage. How did he get hurt?'

'Get off the bed!' ordered Tim. 'Let me get up! I've a lot to see to today.'

'But you haven't answered my question – and I'm going to have to go to school.'

'As soon as you're dressed, go next door and tell Lucia I need to speak to her.'

'OK, is it about Fang?'

'You'll know soon enough.'

'I'll put more water in his bowl,' said Jerry.

'Good lad! But he'll need to be put outside for a piddle.'

'But he's hurt,' Jerry said. 'And he's too heavy for me to lift.'

'I'll do it.' Tim dived into his clothes and carried Fang out to the garden in his bare feet. He stood watching the dog and, as soon as he had relieved himself, Tim cleaned up after Fang and flushed the mess down the outside lavatory. He removed the bandage and was inspecting the dog's wound and telling him he was a good dog when a head popped over the fence and a feminine voice asked, 'Is that you, Tim?'

He gazed in Lucia's direction. 'Who else? I have something to tell you that you're not going to like.'

'It can't be about the dog because I like dogs.'

'Perhaps I should come round and tell you,' Tim said.

'Why, is it that bad you think I might faint? Is it to do with Jerry?'

'No, it's Michael.'

Lucia's fingers clenched on the picket fence. 'What's happened? Have you sacked him?'

'No, just be quiet and listen.' Tim told her everything that had happened last evening in a voice that quivered slightly.

'You swear that he's all right?' said Lucia in a tight voice, her arms wrapped round her as if she was feeling cold.

'I swear. I'm confident he'll be sent home today. There's nothing stopping you phoning the hospital, though. You're family, so they're bound to tell you how he is. Or you could phone Marjorie; no doubt she'll have already been in touch with the hospital.'

'I'll do that,' Lucia said.

'Lucia!' he called her back. 'Don't take this amiss, but I'm thinking that perhaps we should keep some distance between us. It seems I'm a dangerous person to get too close to.'

She almost burst out that she was prepared to take the risk, but instead said, 'If that's what you want, but what about Jerry? Won't he still want to go to school with Joseph and to play with him?'

'There's a thought – but I should think they'll be all right. Those responsible must have sussed out that I was still involved with the garage and decided to get at me there. Anyway, I've been in touch with Detective Inspector Walker, so he's working on the case.'

'I'm relieved to hear it,' Lucia said. 'Now I'll have to get a move on.' She was about to say 'see you later' when she remembered he wouldn't be calling round. She went indoors quickly, feeling near to tears.

Lucia phoned the hospital after all and was reassured as to her brother's wellbeing. She was feeling more herself by the time she arrived at the coffee bar but, as she explained to Maggie and Josh what had happened the previous day, she could see that they were as shocked as she had been.

'Crime certainly doesn't pay,' said Maggie.

'No, but Tim is doing his best to put the past behind him and go straight,' Lucia retorted. 'And he was really upset about Michael.'

'Understandable,' said Josh. 'Remember me getting coshed by

Monica's uncle as a way of getting back at me for my throwing him out of here for slapping her?'

'I'll never forget it,' said Maggie. 'I thought you might die.'

'I've a hard skull. Anyway Sam Walker was soon on the case and put him behind bars.'

'Tim told me that DI Walker is involved in this one too,' Lucia said.

'Well, he'll catch them and they'll get their just deserts,' said Josh.

Lucia found comfort in those words. She put her worries behind her and got on with her work, looking forward to summer and the arrival of Aunt Babs.

During the weeks that followed she saw little of Tim, despite Chris informing her via Nick that those responsible for wrecking the garage and injuring Michael and Fang had been caught. If he had not told her first, she would have had it from Michael who was a witness at the trial. She was hurt that Tim had not been in touch, but came to the conclusion that he had decided to carry on keeping his distance. It was from Jerry that she learned that his father had finished his book, but that the publisher wanted some rewrites. She presumed that they were not happy with the ending.

Whit weekend arrived. Nellie handed two bags over to Lucia containing several frocks for Gabrielle, which had once fitted Nellie's daughters. They showed little wear, despite being second-hand, and Lucia was extremely grateful. When she was a girl, her mother had always seen to it that Lucia and Theresa had new frocks for Easter, Whit and Christmas. Lucia longed to be able to do the same for her sisters, but it was beyond her pocket. Decent hand-me-downs were the next best thing.

One bright morning, towards the end of June, when Lucia arrived at Nellie's house, the front door was opened by her aunt Babs. Lucia had not expected to see her so early in the day and, although she knew that she could not linger as she did not want to be late for work, she stayed long enough to meet Babs's mother-in-law, who had blue-rinsed hair and was smartly dressed. Lucia felt slightly in awe of her and, having little time to get better acquainted with her at that moment, carried away with her an image of a haughty rich American matron, as seen in many a film on the silver screen.

Lucia arrived at the coffee bar to be greeted by a smiling Maggie with the words, 'What's wrong with your face?'

'Aunt Babs has arrived from America, I saw her at Aunt Nellie's.'

'I thought you couldn't wait for her to come,' Maggie said.

'I couldn't. But don't you remember me telling you that she was bringing her mother-in-law with her? Well, she did, and I'm thinking already that she's not going to approve of me or the kids.'

'Why?'

'Just the way she looks and her manner.'

'How does she look?'

'Posh! She looked down her nose at me.'

'Maybe she can't help that – she's probably nervous. After all, she's come all the way from America and is having to cope with meeting Babs's kinsfolk, who are all strangers to her.'

'She comes over as being standoffish, but I bet she's used to meeting all kinds of people without it bothering her.'

'I bet she won't have met many Liverpudlians, and there are those who think we're a rough lot. She may be a bit shy. And she's had sadness in her life, hasn't she? Babs is a widow, which means her mother-in-law has lost her son. It could be that she hasn't yet got over her loss and coming here is a big deal for her.'

'I hadn't thought of that,' said Lucia.

'If she's had boys and has grandsons, then I'm sure she'll soon get accustomed to your brothers. By the way, I've something to tell you that means I'll probably need you to come in a bit earlier mornings,' said Maggie, with an air of suppressed excitement.

Lucia stared at her. 'You're having a baby.'

'How did you guess?'

'I've been wondering when it would happen – and it's the only thing I could imagine you getting excited about. I suppose you're suffering from morning sickness and that's why you'd like me here earlier?'

'It would help, and you could knock off earlier unless we're really busy.'

'No problem,' said Lucia.

Twelve

Lucia was pleased when Irene, Tim's sister-in-law, turned up an hour later with her little boy. Lucia asked after her husband, Tim's brother, Marty, and his little girl, Josie, and also whether they had seen anything of Tim.

'I'm surprised at you asking about Tim when you live right next door to him,' said Irene.

'We don't meet often,' Lucia said, remembering how – not so long ago – Tim's plan had been for them to see more of each other. 'After what happened at the garage, he thought it best if he kept his distance. He didn't want any more of my family getting hurt.'

'Thoughtful of him,' mused Irene. 'Shame, though, because Marty thinks you and your family are good for him and Jerry.'

'Jerry still comes round to play with Joseph. We didn't think it fair to interfere with their friendship.'

'Too right! Anyway, sorry to disappoint you, but we have seen hardly anything of Tim. Maybe he's busy rewriting his book. I did hear that the publisher wasn't completely happy with it.'

Lucia was in the middle of saying she knew that when Maggie came over, so she took Irene's order and left the two older women to catch up on each other's news.

When Lucia dropped in on Nellie later that day, it was to discover her siblings in the back garden, having afternoon tea.

'What are you all doing here?' Lucia asked.

'Tony dropped by and told us Aunt Babs was here,' said Theresa. 'Gabrielle immediately nagged me to come and see her straightaway.'

Lucia looked to where Gabrielle was sitting cross-legged on the grass by Babs's mother-in-law's deckchair, holding up her Barbie doll to her. She wondered if she should go over and tell her sister not to be bothering her. Then she saw the middle-aged woman smile and speak to Gabrielle, so Lucia stayed where she was, thinking that perhaps Gabrielle might be good for her.

Nellie beckoned Lucia over and asked her to come into the kitchen as she had something to tell her, so Lucia followed her aunt indoors. She was thinking surely it couldn't be anything upsetting because Nellie was looking pleased.

'What's this about?' asked Lucia, as her aunt put the kettle on.

Nellie said, 'I thought I'd better prepare you for when Babs approaches you with a scheme she has.'

'What kind of scheme?' Lucia asked, looking puzzled.

'Perhaps I'd better explain: Babs has always wanted to give you a helping hand with the children since she first heard about our Lottie and David's accident.'

'I never expected her help,' said Lucia. 'What with her being a widow and living in America.'

'Well, her mind remained fixed on helping you, and it just needs you and me to agree to her plan.'

'What is it?'

'You won't find it easy, but you've got to think about whether it would turn out best for the children.'

'Aunt Nellie, will you stop keeping me in suspense? Cut the cackle and get to the point?'

'She wants to take two of the children to live with her in America.'

Lucia could only stare at Nellie, her breath completely taken away.

'Well, what do you think?'

'I . . . I don't know. It's so unexpected and we're a family. I don't think Mam would approve of them living with Aunt Babs.'

'They'd have a good life and it would take some pressure off you,' said Nellie.

'I'm sure you're right,' Lucia murmured. 'But it's a big decision to make, splitting up the family – I couldn't possibly give you an answer right away. It would take a lot of consideration – not least, which two children?'

'I was thinking James and Gabrielle,' said Nellie.

Lucia gazed wide-eyed at Nellie. 'They're close and I can only see there being ructions if I tried to take Joseph away from Jerry. As for Theresa, I don't think she'd want to go.'

'You don't have to decide anything right now,' said Nellie. 'Speak to Babs and the children and see what they have to say.'

Lucia thought she really didn't need to be told that, as she wouldn't make a decision without consulting Babs and her brothers and sisters anyway. She was appreciative of Babs's offer, although Lucia had no illusions about how painful it would be being parted from Gabrielle and James. But most likely they would enjoy the benefits of living with Babs and her family in America. She had noticed already how well Gabrielle seemed to be getting on with Babs's mother-in-law. Even so, she decided that she would visit Michael to get his opinion before speaking with anyone else.

It had been almost a fortnight since Lucia had seen her brother, so she wasted no time arranging to meet him and Marjorie at the coffee bar, not wanting to make the journey all the way to the other side of Liverpool. Besides, they needed to make arrangements, too, for them to see Babs while she was over here.

So, two days later, Michael and Marjorie turned up at the coffee bar just after two o'clock. Lucia had spoken to Maggie about it, and she had told her that – as long as the lunchtime rush was pretty well over – she could eat with them. Maggie had expressed the opinion that she thought it was an extremely generous offer from Babs, and that families more often than not went their own separate ways once they were free to do their own thing.

Lucia could not argue with that, as she only had to think of Babs having married and gone to live in America. Then Inspector Walker's sister had emigrated to Canada with her husband in search of a better life. Of course, the situation Lucia had to make a decision about was a bit different, but it was not as if Gabrielle and James were going to live with strangers as so many children had done during the Blitz; and what about the orphans who had been shipped off to different parts of the Empire in the belief they would have a better life; they had been sent to strangers. No, Babs was their aunt and was warm-hearted and generous.

Michael was not as flabbergasted as Lucia had thought he might be when she told him of their aunt's plan; he thought Lucia should jump at the offer as soon as Babs mentioned it to her. He also agreed with her that Gabrielle and James were the two who would benefit most from living with Babs. So, with that subject out of the way, Lucia felt free to ask him and Marjorie how they were doing.

'I'm starting another job next week,' said Michael. 'Mr Murphy gave me the names of a few garages I should apply to that might agree to accept me as an apprentice. One tried me out and has said they'll take me on. The money isn't as good as what Mr Murphy paid me, but he's given me a leaving bonus which will tide me over for a while.'

'That's decent of him, considering all he's lost.'

'He sold the firm's car and the insurance also paid out some money, but he's not sure about the viability of starting up in business again. He'd want to find somewhere else but at the moment he doesn't have enough money. He can't even sell the plot because he didn't own the land; he'd been paying ground rent and the bloke who owns it expects him to clear up the site, which still looks a mess and stinks of oil despite all the firemen did.'

'So what's he doing now for a living?'

'He's gone back to writing.'

'And in the meantime, what's he and Jerry to live on?'

'I don't know why you're worrying about him. He's a resourceful bloke and, besides, he'll still have some money left over from the insurance. He has tools he can sell, and if the worst comes to worst, he can sell the van, although I've a feeling he wants to hang on to it.'

'What on earth for?'

'To get about easier now he's got his confidence back and is driving again.'

She wondered why Tim wanted to get out and about when he needed to be writing at home. Suddenly she became aware that Marjorie was staring at her.

'What is it?' Lucia asked. 'Did you say something, Marjorie?'

'I asked whether your aunt Babs would like to come and have a meal with us and Mum in West Derby?'

'I'm sure she would love to meet your mother, but she does have her mother-in-law with her – does the invitation extend to her?'

'Of course. Ask them will four o'clock on Sunday be all

right? You can give them instructions on how to get to ours,' said Marjorie. 'You know which buses they'll have to catch.'

'All right,' said Lucia.

But when she arrived at Nellie's that evening, it was to discover that Babs had hired a car for the duration of her visit and she offered her a lift home.

On drawing up outside the house, Lucia climbed out of the car first and was waiting on the pavement for Babs to lock the vehicle when Tim came out of next door. Lucia and Tim stared at each other hungrily but did not speak. She expected him to go back indoors but he stood in the doorway, watching her. As Babs caught up with Lucia, Tim nodded in her direction.

Babs said, 'Hello!'

So Lucia decided there was nothing for it but to introduce her aunt to Tim. Otherwise it would seem unfriendly. Besides which, she would like to know what Babs thought of him, as Lucia had no doubts about Nellie having mentioned him to her sister.

Soon Babs and Tim were chatting away like old friends about cars and how they were essential in big countries such as America and Australia. Lucia shouted up the lobby for Jerry as it was time for him to go home, but she stayed on the step listening to Babs and Tim's conversation until Jerry appeared with Joseph.

'Couldn't I stay a bit longer, Dad?' asked Jerry.

Tim shook his head. 'Lucia has a visitor, and besides, I'd enjoy your company before you go to bed.'

'OK,' said Jerry, glancing curiously at Babs. 'Are you the lady from America?'

'I am,' answered Babs, smiling down at him.

'Have you ever seen any Indians?' he asked eagerly.

'Yes, but they weren't on the warpath so I didn't lose my scalp. There's no more fighting between cowboys and Indians because they've made peace.'

'But we like playing cowboys and Indians,' said Joseph.

'That's boys for you,' said Babs, glancing at Lucia.

'It's odd that it's popular again,' Lucia responded. 'A few years back it was cops and robbers and war games with pretend guns, tanks and grenades.'

'Next it'll be space games,' said Tim. 'Flash Gordon and aliens from outer space. It's down to what they see at the pictures. Although I suppose now real-life spaceman Yuri Gagarin launched into space, boys will be wanting to copy him.'

'Flash Gordon was before the young ones' time – and besides they watch telly more now,' said Babs.

'*Wagon Train*,' murmured Lucia. 'We'd better get inside, the kids'll be hungry.'

'I remember your mam once giving me a Chinese burn so I bit her. Mam belted us both for whingeing.'

'That seems a bit unfair,' said Lucia.

'It was stupid because it only made us whinge all the more.'

'So what did she do then?'

'Threatened to tell Dad on us when he came home, which again was stupid because he was away at sea. By the time his ship docked a fortnight later, we knew she'd have forgotten about it and, besides, her moaning about us would put him in a mood,' Babs said. 'And him in a mood was something to be avoided.'

Lucia shivered. 'I just about remember him. Mam used to make me hide when he was around. Fortunately that wasn't often.'

'Yes, it was our luck that he spent more time at sea than at home. So how often is the bloke next door's son here?'

'You mean Jerry!' Lucia lifted the frying pan down from a shelf and took eggs from the old fridge and potatoes from a cardboard box on the floor. 'He spends part of most days here. He and Joseph are best mates. Tim's writing a book so I don't mind Jerry being here. I bet Nellie told you that I'm in love with the unsuitable man from next door.'

'Well, on the face of it he doesn't exactly sound a catch. Widowed, ex-jailbird with a young son, and he's a decade older than you are; equally, I told her she was one to talk, as she fell in love with an escaped Italian POW during the war, who turned out to be a widower with a son.'

'What did she say to that?' Lucia's voice ended on a squeak as she began to peel and slice potatoes.

'That it was different. I told her that everyone says that when it's their own situation. To which she replied, she'd been older, with far less responsibility than you.' Babs paused. 'Here, let me help you.'

'OK! I'll peel and you can slice,' Lucia said. 'I'm making scallops to have with egg.'

'I love potato scallops with fried egg. Any vegetables?'

'That old standby, baked beans.'

'Delicious. Any pud?'

'Josh gave me some ends of cakes that were left over from yesterday. I've a tin of Bird's custard powder in the cupboard. It'll be a treat for the kids because we hardly ever have pud on a weekday.'

'Is it all right for me to talk to you now about my proposal? Nellie said that she'd mentioned it to you?'

'Sure. I've already spoken to Michael about it and, after some intense discussion, we agreed that the two children most suitable are Gabrielle and James. I haven't sounded them out yet because I wanted to hear your thoughts about our choice.'

'I think they'd be perfect.'

'So we're agreed then,' said Lucia. 'Gabrielle and James are both at a sensible age and they also get on well, so shouldn't give you much trouble when it comes to settling down. I know it'll be a wrench for us all being parted, but I think they'll gain so much living with you in America – and it's not as if it's the other side of the world.'

'No, just the Pond,' said Babs. 'I'm so glad to have this opportunity to help you out, Lucia. I know having them living with me will also enrich my life.'

'So a good decision all round,' said Lucia. 'After dinner you can speak to Gabrielle and James. Later no doubt they'll come and tell me how they feel about it.'

Babs nodded. Lucia noticed that there were tears in her aunt's eyes and thought it was going to be good for Babs to have some of her English family living with her in America. Tears sprang to her own eyes, knowing her aunt's gain would be her loss.

Lucia was washing the dishes while Babs was talking to Gabrielle and James. She prayed for all involved and wondered what Tim would say when Jerry told him, as Joseph was bound to let the news slip out.

As soon as she entered the room, Gabrielle came rushing

over to Lucia. 'Aunty Babs wants me to go to America with her. I'll be her special little girl, she said. I can go, can't I, Lucia?'

'Of course you can if that will make you happy, and it will be lovely for Aunty Babs to have a little girl to make a fuss of and to keep her company,' said Lucia, smiling as she thought they weren't going to have any trouble with Gabrielle. It could be different, though, when it came to James, who was gazing about the room as if he had never seen it before. His eyes came to rest on Lucia and she gazed back at him.

Then he stood up and came over to her. He rested his arm along the back of her chair and said, 'Do you want me to go to America with Gabrielle and Aunty Babs?'

'I want what's best for you,' Lucia replied. 'Of course, I'll miss you, but you could have an exciting, good life in America. Gabrielle wants to go. I'm sure there'll be times when she'll feel homesick, but you being there will mean she won't feel as bad as she would if you weren't there. And it doesn't mean you have to stay there forever or can't come and visit us.'

'Or you come and visit us in America,' said James, his face lighting up.

'There is that, of course,' Lucia said. 'I'll start saving my pennies straightaway. There's lots of places we've seen on the films that would be good to visit. I'm sure Aunty Babs will take you to some and her sons will take you to watch baseball games and American football.'

'They mightn't want me tagging along with them.'

'Why shouldn't they? The youngest one isn't much older than you. You just have to show enthusiasm for their sports. From what I've heard, Americans are friendly and welcoming, you just have to be friendly back.'

James nodded. 'I'm really going to miss you and the others, but perhaps they'll envy me because it's an adventure, isn't it? I'll be sailing on a big ship and Aunty Babs said she'll take me up the Empire State Building and to Arizona to see the Grand Canyon.'

Lucia felt almost envious of her brother for having been promised such treats, and grateful to Babs for providing him with something so special to look forward to. 'You'll have to make sure you ask her to take lots of photographs and send some to us.'

He nodded and said wistfully, 'I wish I had my own camera.'

Lucia remained silent, but was thinking that perhaps she could have a whip round the family and collect enough to buy a Box Brownie and several rolls of film. She spoke to Michael about it and he promised five shillings, and told her that he'd write to Tony and see what he could spare, while she spoke to Nellie.

To Lucia's delight, her aunt and uncle were willing to chip in with two pounds and Tony with five shillings. Nellie promised to have a word with Francis, and he handed over enough money to enable her to purchase the camera and one roll of film. When Jerry heard about it from Joseph, he mentioned it to his father, so Tim gave his son a ten-shilling note to give to James to buy more film.

Lucia was never to forget James's expression when she presented the camera to him the evening before he, Gabrielle and Babs and her mother-in-law were due to leave for America.

After receiving some instructions from Michael, James immediately got the family to group together and took a photo of them. Lucia did not need her brother to voice his thanks as his appreciation of the gift was plain to all. Even so, he thanked everyone effusively and she knew that the camera had eased the pain of parting for him.

She was also grateful that Gabrielle seemed just as pleased as James with the camera, especially as he took a photo of her posing with her Barbie doll. Lucia was also delighted by Tim's contribution. It proved to her that his heart was in the right place and she wished that they could resume the relationship they had once shared.

Thirteen

After Gabrielle and James had left with their aunt for America, Tim decided Lucia needed cheering up and made up his mind to take her to Llandudno for a day out. He knew she had time off work because Jerry had mentioned it. He placed the cover over his typewriter and went out to the van and set about tidying the cab.

Lucia gazed out of the parlour window at Tim's van. Having seen him climb into the cab about ten minutes ago, she wondered where he was going. Curiosity got the better of her and she went outside and waved to him. A moment later the cab door opened and he called to her. She approached him. 'Hi!' she said. 'Are you going somewhere?'

'I was thinking of going to Llandudno. D'you fancy coming?'

'Just the two of us?'

'Yeah, I think it would do us both good, and we need to have a talk. We can take the boys and Theresa out another time.'

'I'll just make sure that Theresa is OK with keeping an eye on Joseph and Jerry – and grab a jacket. Oh, do I need to make a picnic?'

'No, we can grab a bite at a café.'

Lucia wasted no time, and five minutes later they were on their way.

'I suppose it was Jerry who told you I was off work?'

'Yeah, but he didn't say why.'

'The cafe is being renovated so is closed until the work's finished.'

Tim was tempted to ask what she was doing for money. Here was one of those incidents when the unexpected happened and there was nothing she could do to prevent it. He wondered whether she had a rainy-day fund. 'That must be inconvenient,' he murmured.

'Yes, but Josh is paying me something; and, although I miss James, Gabrielle and Michael, my household bills are less.'

'I suppose there's always a positive side to everything in life,' Tim said.

'Talking about life – how's your book getting on now you're no longer involved with the garage? Has Isabella called lately?'

'I wondered when that would come up,' said Tim.

'Would you rather not talk about it?'

'No, it's fine and, oddly enough, she hasn't. I thought she would have because Chris knew about the ransacking of the garage and I'm sure he would have mentioned it to her at the *Echo* offices.'

'Definitely odd when she was forever going on at you about writing an exciting ending. Have you written about the incident and what happened to Michael and Fang?' She choked on the words.

'I've made a start, but it isn't easy because I get choked up like you.' Tim dug into a pocket and produced a handkerchief and passed it to her.

She dabbed at her eyes. 'You had such dreams for that garage, and Michael was so pleased about having an apprenticeship.'

'I know. He's a quick learner and worked hard. I felt terrible about what happened.'

'You couldn't have foreseen it.'

'I certainly didn't, but I was aware that I could still be a target for my enemies.'

'Shall we change the subject?' suggested Lucia. 'We don't want such talk to spoil our day out.'

Tim agreed and asked if she had heard anything from Gabrielle and James.

'Not yet, but I'm looking forward to hearing how they're getting on, and hopefully there'll be photographs, too.'

At last they arrived at the Mersey tunnel, and fortunately they were soon on the other side in Birkenhead. It was not long before they reached the turn-off for Queensferry and North Wales. Although there was a fair amount of traffic on the road, Tim did not expect there to be much of a hold up at Queensferry, which was known to be a bottleneck during the summer months for those heading for the north Welsh coast and the isle of Anglesey.

'It's beautiful countryside here, isn't it?' said Lucia. 'The trees might be beginning to turn and some fields have been harvested, but there's still a lot of green to be seen.'

'You haven't mentioned the mountains in the distance,' Tim said. 'That's Snowdonia if I'm not mistaken.'

'Keep your eyes on the road,' said Lucia.

'I am, but I'm also keeping my eyes on that van behind me. He's a bit close.'

'What are you going to do? Go faster and get away from him?'

'No, I'm going to signal to him to overtake me. I'd rather he was away in front.'

Tim signalled and watched through the mirror as the van made a move, only to realize the driver was not giving himself enough room and was going to veer into him. Surely the fool was not trying to run him off the road? But Tim soon realized that was exactly what the driver was attempting. His vehicle scraped along the side of the van with a horrible shrieking noise. The van shook so violently that Tim thought it was going to topple over.

'What's happening?' cried Lucia, gripping her seat.

Tim did not reply as it was taking all his concentration and strength to escape the road hog without speeding up and hitting the car a few yards ahead. He glanced towards the passenger window to see what was on that side. He could see trees and had spotted a narrow pavement earlier. He eased his foot slowly down on the brake and prayed. His van shuddered to a halt. He glanced out of his side window and saw and heard his mirror being ripped off. Then their attacker drove past and had soon overtaken the car in front.

Tim had done his best to note the van's licence-plate number but had trouble seeing clearly. He looked at Lucia. 'You all right?'

'I've banged my head. What about you?'

Tim held out his hands which trembled. 'As Elvis said "I'm all shook up". Although, really, this isn't the time for jokes.'

'No, but if we didn't laugh we'd cry.' Lucia covered his hands with hers and added, 'This has given me a dreadful fright. We could have been killed.'

'It's going to be all right. We're both alive, but I can't see us getting to Llandudno today. I could murder that swine for putting the kibosh on our day.' He drew her close and kissed her. She kissed him back.

At that moment there was a sound at the passenger window

and they both looked in that direction. A man was there and he signalled to them to open the window. Lucia did so.

The man said, 'I thought you were going to go over. I've never seen such crazy driving in my life. The side of your van is in a right mess, but it could have been worse. There's a phone box a couple of miles back, I'll go and phone the police and explain what's happened. That idiot might just go and hit someone else, the way he's driving. He needs catching.' He added, 'That's a nasty cut on your head, luv.'

Lucia touched her head where it hurt, 'It could be worse,' she said.

Left alone Tim said, 'It *is* a nasty cut. I bet your head aches.'

'It does.' Lucia decided to take a look at herself in the driving mirror. 'It shouldn't spoil my good looks,' she joked before turning to Tim. 'Now where were we? I'd like to get a few things sorted out before the police arrive.'

He drew her close. 'I love you, Lucia.'

'I love you, too.' She gazed at him expectantly from moist eyes and, taking out a handkerchief, blew her nose. 'Perhaps we can go to Llandudno for our honeymoon.'

'It's a thought,' he said. 'We'll discuss it later. I can hear a siren.'

A few minutes later, the police arrived and took statements from Tim and the driver who had phoned them. Shortly after, an ambulance arrived, as well as a breakdown truck, although Tim was more concerned about Lucia's head injury than the van at that moment. He noted the name of the garage to which the van was being taken, and hoped the insurance company would fork out for the repairs. Then he went in the ambulance with Lucia to the nearest hospital, where they did various tests before deciding to do an X-ray as an added precaution. It showed no fracture or bleeding, and she was given the all-clear to go home. Tim was given a check-over and prescribed tranquillizers because his nerves were in a state. He rang Marty from the hospital and his brother volunteered to come and pick them up.

Marty arrived just after a policeman had informed Tim that the road hog had been caught. He had been spotted further along the A55 near Conway and been arrested for dangerous driving. Fortunately Tim and Lucia's Good Samaritan had been able to supply the police with a description of the van and the driver's licence-plate number. The driver did not have a driving licence on him and was keeping quiet about his name and address, but had a definite Scouse accent. This caused Tim to wonder if there could be more to the incident than appeared on the face of it. All Tim could do was to wait and see what the police came up with.

Despite the doctor's reassurances that Lucia would be fine, Tim could not help worrying about her, and decided to stay with her once they arrived back at her house. She was willing, saying she would get comfort from him being under the same roof as her and she didn't care what people thought. Marty did not hold back from saying what he thought of Tim's plan to stay at Lucia's house before he drove off home.

'You'll have all the tongues wagging,' he said. 'I know what that's like, and Irene and I didn't spend even one night alone together in the house before we were married.'

'Lucia and I aren't going to be alone,' said Tim. 'There's the boys and Theresa.'

'That won't make any difference to the neighbours. Spend the night under the same roof without a grown-up to act as chaperone, and they'll believe the pair of you have slept together.'

'Well, time will prove them wrong. I've no intention of ruining Lucia's reputation.'

'Then think again about what you're planning,' Marty said.

'No, I want to be on hand if she needs anything,' said Tim, his mouth setting stubbornly.

Marty said mildly, 'Well, that says something about how much you've changed.'

'Yeah, I'm not as selfish as I used to be. And thanks, our kid, for everything,' said Tim, waving his brother off.

He went indoors and found Lucia sitting on the sofa in front of the fire, Jerry and Joseph sitting either side of her and Theresa and Chris gazing down at her.

'So tell us again what happened?' asked Chris.

'Don't you be bothering Lucia,' ordered Tim. 'You can ask me any questions you want answers to – and, you boys, it's time you were in bed.'

'Am I sleeping here?' asked Jerry.

'Tonight you are,' replied Tim. 'And so am I.'

Theresa and Chris shot him a glance but neither commented.

Lucia stood up, as if intending to see the boys to bed. Tim immediately told her to sit down and rest. 'You've had a bit of a day of it, so you've got to take it easy.'

She did not argue with him but sank on to the sofa and patted the seat next to her. 'That goes for you too. You've had a day of it as well.'

Theresa said, 'I suppose that means I've got to get the boys to bed.'

'No, it doesn't. We can put ourselves to bed,' said Joseph. 'Come on, Jerry. Up the apples and pears.'

'What does up the apples and pears mean?' asked Theresa.

'It's Cockney rhyming slang,' said Jerry. 'I learnt some when I lived in London. They say that instead of saying up the stairs.'

Theresa looked confused. As well she might, thought Lucia. A few minutes later, she heard the boys chanting, 'Up the apples and pears', as they went up to bed.

'Anyone for a cocoa?' asked Theresa.

She received a resounding 'yes'.

While they waited for their drinks, Chris sat the other side of Tim and asked him about the accident.

'It was no accident,' Tim answered, 'but a deliberate attempt to run us off the road.'

'But who would want to do that? Your old enemies are in prison, aren't they?'

'Perhaps not quite all.' Tim ran a weary hand over his face. 'But how he happened to be on the A55 at the same time as us mystifies me.'

'The van has a name on the side,' said Chris.

'I'm going to have to change that,' Tim muttered.

'By the way, does this crazy person have a name?'

'He wasn't giving it to the police, but they're going to get back to me tomorrow. I'll let you know then if my suspicions are correct.'

Chris was on his way out of the front door when a car pulled up at the kerb. Nellie climbed out and hurried up the step. 'Hold that door!' she called. 'Goodnight, Chris,' she added, brushing past him.

Theresa stared at her aunt. 'Who told you?'

'Irene phoned a few minutes ago, so I came without even combing my hair.'

'Or changing your slippers by the look of it,' Theresa said, glancing at her aunt's feet.

Nellie swore beneath her breath. 'What does it matter? Where are they?'

'On the sofa. There was no need for you to come, though. I'd made up my mind to sleep with our Lucia.'

'That's the spirit,' said Nellie.

'So you've had a wasted journey.' Theresa slammed the door shut behind her aunt and shouted, 'We've another visitor.'

'Hang on,' said Nellie, opening the front door and descending the steps hastily, only to lose a slipper. She called out, 'Michel, don't drive off. Come in a moment.'

Her husband got out of the car and came up the step, picking up her slipper on the way. 'I knew we should have stayed home.'

'Don't be like that,' Nellie said. 'You'd like to see that Lucia and Tim are all right, wouldn't you?'

'It could have waited until morning. We've gone and left the kids in the house on their own. Tony's away, remember.'

'All right! We'll only be here five minutes.'

'They'll guess why you've come.'

'So what? Lottie and David trusted me to keep my eye on their children.'

'Well, you took your eye off the ball with Michael,' said Michelangelo.

'I can't be everywhere. Besides, Marjorie was her mother's responsibility.'

Theresa smiled to herself, wishing her sister could hear this conversation. Although they both appreciated all that their aunt did for them, times had changed since their mother and aunt were young. This was the sixties and it was a much freer age. She could not wait to see Lucia and Tim's faces when her aunt and uncle entered the kitchen.

As it was, Lucia and Tim concealed their feelings well and instead just showed surprised pleasure at their arrival.

Lucia said, 'Who told you?'

'Marty told Irene and she phoned me. I wanted to see for

myself that you were all right, otherwise I wouldn't have slept a wink.'

'We're fine,' said Lucia. 'Just a bit shaken.'

'What about that plaster on your forehead?' Nellie asked.

'Nothing to worry about.'

'I believe they caught the fellow who did it,' Michelangelo said.

'Yeah, but he still wasn't giving his name or address last time I spoke with the police. Daft when you think about it. They've the number plate of the van and they'll get his name and address from the government department where it's registered.'

'Unless the van was stolen,' Nellie said.

'Why should it have been?' Lucia asked.

Nellie was conscious that her husband was slanting her a look that seemed to say *now get yourself out of that*. 'Because, by the sound of it, he appeared to be in a helluva rush.'

'Well, we'll know soon,' said Tim, who had been wondering if the police had thought of taking the driver's fingerprints. If he was one of the gang, they would be in the police records. 'I suggested to the Welsh police that they might like to get in touch with Inspector Sam Walker, as apparently the driver had a Scouse accent. He would recognize the name if they found a match for his fingerprints in the criminal files.'

'Are you thinking it's someone who knows you who could be responsible?' asked Michelangelo.

'It's possible.'

'Well, Tim, if he turns out to be connected with that gang you were involved with,' said Nellie, 'then I would like you to stay out of Lucia's life. You're not good for her.'

Lucia said, 'I know you care for me, Aunt Nellie, and I appreciate all the help you give me, but it's me who decides what is and what isn't good for me.'

'She's right, Nellie,' said Michelangelo. 'Lucia isn't a child. I'm sure Tim will do what's best for her and Theresa and Joseph.'

'You can trust me on that,' Tim said.

'I'm sure we can,' said the older man. 'I remember when you were warned not to have anything to do with me, Nellie, simply because I was Italian.'

'Would that have been because of the war?' Tim asked.

The other man nodded, adding to his wife, 'Come on, Nellie, time we were home.'

She accepted his hand and rose from the sofa. 'Goodnight. I'm sorry if my advice wasn't welcome. I only want what's best for you, Lucia.'

'Enough said.' Her husband pinched her arm. 'There's no need for you to have the last word.'

Theresa saw them out and then returned to the kitchen. 'Now who'd have thought they would have turned up like that?' she said. 'What are you going to do, Lucia?'

'About what?' Lucia asked sharply.

'Any favours you want from Aunt Nellie.'

'You mean I'll find it difficult asking a favour of her in the circumstances?'

'Exactly!'

Later, after he had returned to his apartment, Tim received a phone call from Sam, who told him that the name of the driver who was guilty of dangerous driving had been traced in criminal records and was one of the gang who had it in for Tim. The news was enough for Tim to put into motion plans to move away from Lucia in the hope there was no risk of her being hurt again because of her involvement with him. He knew it was not going to be easy – either telling her that he was going away, or being parted from her.

It proved to be even more difficult and upsetting than he'd thought, as Lucia reminded him that he had told her that he loved her and they had even agreed that they would go to Llandudno for their honeymoon.

'And now you're telling me that you and Jerry are moving,' she cried, folding her arms across her chest. 'The lovely future I foresaw for us and the boys has evaporated into thin air. Is it that you've changed your mind about loving me?'

'Of course not! I'll never stop loving you.'

'Then how can you possibly want to go away from me?'

'I want you safe. I've caused you and yours enough pain. Your aunt Nellie was right. I have to get out of your life.'

'I don't care what she thinks. It'll break my heart to see you go,' said Lucia on a sob.

'Please don't cry, love,' said Tim, attempting to put his arms round her.

She ducked beneath his arms and stepped back. 'Don't touch me. You've relinquished that right. If you're leaving me, go now. I hope you'll be happy on your own. I don't suppose you've given any thought as to how this will hurt Jerry and Joseph.'

He rubbed a hand across his eyes. 'Of course I have. And I don't see why they can't carry on seeing each other. Jerry will have to change schools, but there's no reason why they can't meet up either here or Joseph can go to the kids' matinee in Crosby. He can meet Jerry outside and I'll pay for their tickets. And this doesn't have to be goodbye forever. If there's no more trouble we can meet up again – say around Christmas.'

Lucia's heart lifted. 'All right, we'll see how things go.'

Tim forced a smile. 'You do believe I love you, Lucia, and I'm only going away for that reason?'

'I want to believe it,' she said. 'What about Isabella? Does she know you're moving?'

'No, I'll write and tell her I don't need to see her for a while and that I'll get in touch when I'm ready for her to see the completed manuscript.'

'That sounds sensible,' Lucia said. 'I'd much rather you didn't see her.' She took a deep breath. 'So when are you leaving?'

Not wanting a long-drawn-out farewell, Tim said, 'As soon as I've loaded my and Jerry's few belongings in the van, we'll be off to Crosby to have a butcher's there for a likely place.'

'Right,' said Lucia. 'I'll go in and tidy the house. I'll be returning to work in a fortnight and I not only want to be on top of the housework, but I want to have a few days out with the kids before the end of the summer holidays.'

'I'll say ta-ra for now then,' Tim said.

'TTFN to you as well.' Lucia lifted a hand in farewell and ran into the house before she gave way to tears again.

During the aftermath of Tim and Jerry's departure, Lucia felt as if life would never feel the same again. She felt worse than after James and Gabrielle had left. Now Joseph moped around, completely bereft without Jerry, whom he was accustomed to seeing every day.

At least their spirits lifted when the letters arrived with

American stamps on them, which Joseph instantly purloined for his stamp album. There were also several photographs with James's letter, showing Babs and Gabrielle at the top of the Empire State Building and one of James on his own and another of him with Babs's two sons dressed in a baseball cap and shirt with a baseball bat beneath his arm.

Relieved that the two seemed to be settling down nicely, Lucia felt a little less on edge. She had several days out with Theresa and Joseph. One day they went with Nellie and her youngsters to Southport, picnicking on the beach and spending time at the fair. They also went blackberrying along the Leeds–Liverpool canal, as well as catching tiddlers with nets and carrying them home in jam jars. The time seemed to drag, though, and a few days before the last of the school holidays, Lucia had to return to work. Theresa kept her eye on Joseph and Jerry, the latter having cycled from Crosby on his bike and was sleeping over for a couple of nights. The two boys spent their time either playing cricket in the back garden or taking turns to ride Jerry's bicycle around the block.

It was during one such day that Theresa was set on finishing a library book that was due back soon, so for a while she forgot all about the boys. She had believed them to be in the back garden, but when she glanced out of the window there was no sign of them. Thinking that most likely they had decided to play in the street, she went to have a look, but they weren't there either. She told herself that they could have gone to call on one of their mates from school and that there was no sense in worrying as they would turn up when they were hungry. If only Theresa had checked the boys' whereabouts three-quarters of an hour earlier, she would have saved several people, including herself, a lot of anxiety.

Fourteen

A short time before, Joseph and Jerry had been taking turns cycling on Jerry's bicycle and it had been Jerry's turn to ride round the block while Joseph waited on the pavement for his return. While he stood there practising heading a ball, a black saloon car drew up at the kerb and a man got out. He was a stranger to the boy, so that when the man spoke to him, Joseph ignored him. The next moment the man seized him, pinning his arms to his sides and lifting him off his feet.

Joseph yelled at the man to let him go, but the man ignored his cries, telling him that if he didn't keep his gob shut and stop wriggling, it would be the worse for him. Joseph yelled all the more and received a clout across the side of his head for his efforts before being slung into the back of the car.

'Don't try and attract attention or I'll knock your block off,' said the man.

Jerry had just turned the corner into the street and spotted what was happening, and so he acted instinctively when the car began to move off and cycled on the pavement, keeping one eye on the car, memorizing the licence-plate number in case he lost sight of the vehicle, because he knew he'd have a job keeping up with it, especially as it appeared to be heading for the dock road where there were few – if any – traffic lights to slow the car down. He narrowly avoided hitting a dog, and an old woman shouted at him that he shouldn't be riding on the pavement. Nevertheless he rode on, aware of the ache in his calves but determined to keep going. That man had his best mate and he wasn't going to get away with kidnapping him. He knew there were bad men who were enemies of his father who had destroyed his garage business; was it possible this man was part of the same gang? But why take Joseph, unless he might have thought he was Jerry, with them both being fair-haired and about the same build and height? It was just like a film on the matinee! Jerry groaned as he saw the car pass the

Caradoc pub and turn on to the dock road in the direction of Liverpool.

He knew it would take a miracle for him to keep the car in sight, so he prayed and then remembered it was a weekday; he knew the dock road would be busy with vehicles going back and forth to the various dockyards, so they would slow the car down. He continued to remain on the pavement, riding past various warehouses, timber yards and pubs. He was tiring but was determined not to give up, and was pleased with his efforts when he realized he was approaching the strengthened part of the road that crossed the Leeds–Liverpool canal that emptied into the basin of one of the docks. He did not know where he was exactly, but guessed he must be in Liverpool and had been pedalling for what seemed ages. On his left-hand side were streets of houses; he gave them only a brief glance before returning his gaze to the road just in time to see the car turn into one of the streets ahead.

It was then Jerry's luck ran out, because he got a puncture. He dismounted and, pushing his bike, ran with it to where the car had turned. It was not a long street but there was no sign of the vehicle. He repeated to himself the licence number, hoping to fix it in his brain so he would not forget it and, as he leaned his bike against a wall, he glanced at the street name. How much help that might be he was unsure, but at least it could pinpoint the area where the car had turned. He knew that Stanley Road and Scotland Road ran almost parallel with the dock road, and that there were other main roads that ran parallel in between, with streets running off them up to Scotland Road. It could be that the car had crossed Scotland Road to a destination in one of the streets on the other side. But thinking about that wasn't getting him anywhere. He needed help.

Unfortunately he did not have his bicycle repair kit with him, so could not fix the puncture. Digging his hand into his jacket pocket he found some coins and drew out several pennies and a couple of halfpennies. He needed to find a phone box, but had no idea where the nearest one was; then he noticed a woman coming towards him and hailed her.

'Excuse me, missus. Could you tell me where the nearest telephone box is, please?'

The middle-aged woman, wearing a headscarf wrapped in turban fashion over her hair, gazed down at him. 'I like a polite lad,' she said. 'There isn't one near, but Mrs McGuire who keeps the corner shop might let you use hers for thrupence.'

'Thank you, can you show me where that is, please?' Jerry asked.

'I'll take you there, lad,' she said.

He reached for his bike. 'I've a puncture and I want to phone me dad to come and pick me up in his van.'

'Has he far to come?'

'Crosby.'

'Well, it shouldn't take him long in a van,' she said.

Jerry hoped so, lifting his bike into the shop with the aid of his Good Samaritan, and thanked her again for her help before she left. It was she who had warned him not to leave his bike outside as it might be nicked. Fortunately there were no customers waiting in the shop so there was room for it.

'So, chuck,' said Mrs McGuire, resting her elbows on the counter and gazing down at him. 'You'd like to use my telephone?'

'Yes, please. I need to phone me dad.'

'Come on then, this way, and push your bike through into the back.'

He did as told, following her through a door into a back room cluttered with cardboard boxes and crates. The telephone was fixed to a wall.

'Would you like me to get the number for you?' she asked.

'Yes, please.' He gave the number and added, 'My daddy's name is Tim Murphy. Mine is Jerry Murphy.'

He watched her dial and then heard her ask for Mr Murphy before handing the receiver to Jerry.

He was so relieved to hear his father's voice that he had to blink back tears and take a deep breath before telling him where he was and that he had a puncture and needed a lift. Tim asked what he was doing there.

Lowering his voice, Jerry said, 'I'll explain later, Dad, and it's important that you get here as quick as you can.'

'Well, stay where you are. I'll come for you at the shop.'

Jerry had no intention of moving. His legs were feeling shaky and he was glad to sit down. He gazed at his bike, thinking of

Joseph, hoping the man would not hurt him further and that he and his dad could find him soon.

Joseph's feelings were running along the same lines as Jerry's. At least his abductor couldn't hit him right then, because he was driving and had to keep his eyes on the road. In no time at all they stopped in front of a block of flats. He thought that if he managed to escape he should be able to find his way home. He would have to find a bobby. When the car came to a halt near some new buildings, he fumbled with the door to try and open it and get away before the man could get out and catch him. Only he could not open it and he was filled with despair. He wished Lucia and Jerry's dad were there. Tears rolled down his cheeks and he attempted to scrub them away with the side of his hand.

The door opened and the man dragged him out by the shoulder of his pullover. He led him to the nearest building and, once inside, forced him up a flight of stairs and along a corridor. He stopped at a door and rang the bell. A few moments later it was opened by a smartly dressed, good-looking woman, who stared at him before throwing her head back and looking up into the man's face.

'Who's the boy, Will?' she asked.

'Ask no questions and yer'll get told no lies,' he said in a thick, rough voice. 'But if you must know, Bella, he's Tommy McGrath's brat. I'd have thought you'd have recognized him. I want you to keep your eye on him while I take the car back. I also want you to write a ransom note. See if we can get some of the dosh he got away with.'

Isabella had been about to say that she had only seen the boy once or twice, but she felt certain this one was not Jerry. Instead she said, 'Will, as much as I care for you and was willing to help you with other stuff to avenge yourself on Tommy, or Tim as he calls himself now, I didn't sign up for kidnapping kids.'

'Don't go turning soft on me now, Bella! Get out of the way and let us in. You just do as you're told or you'll regret it.'

She was shocked by his threatening her, and for a moment was frozen to the spot. He shoved her aside, thrusting the boy in front of him. 'Yer're not to let him out of yer sight and don't be talking to him. Yer'll probably get a load of lies out of him. No doubt he's another like his bloody father.' Will opened the door and pulled it shut behind him.

Joseph stared at the woman, who appeared vaguely familiar, but he could not remember where he had seen her. At least she wasn't in favour of what his abductor had done. He wondered what Jerry was doing at that moment. Hopefully he had spotted what happened and had gone for help. In the meantime he must try and escape somehow. At that moment his tummy rumbled and he said, 'Pardon me!'

'You hungry, boy?' she asked.

Joseph nodded wordlessly.

'Well, come into the kitchen and I'll make you a jam sandwich.'

'Thanks,' said Joseph. 'Can I have a drink of water, as well, please?'

She turned and looked at him. 'I'll say this for you. You've got good manners.'

'I was brought up to say please and thank you. Dad always said it pays to be polite to people.'

'Did he now? And who is your dad?'

Joseph thought about the question. If he told the truth, where would that leave him if that man came back any minute and she mentioned his father's name to him? He had to get out of here before that happened. Of course he could give her Jerry's father's name, but that would be a lie and a sin. 'I know your name,' he said. 'It's Bella.

'And if I'm not mistaken, yours *isn't* Jerry. Am I right in thinking that fool has got the wrong boy?'

Joseph nodded. 'What are you going to do about it?'

She did not answer immediately, but took a loaf from the bread bin and cut a slice from it before reaching for a pot of damson jam from a cupboard. 'Me ma would be turning in her grave if she knew I'd got mixed up with William again. I was a good sensible girl before she went and died, but that's love for you. You take note, boy, and don't get mixed up with the wrong crowd.'

Joseph did not know what she was talking about, so acted dumb and began sidling towards the doorway that led into the sitting room. He was through the doorway and across the other room before she turned round with the jam bread in her hand. He heard her call, 'Where are you? I'm not going to hurt you.'

Her words caused Joseph to slowly turn and stare at her. 'Will you let me go, please?'

'If I do that, my life won't be worth living. Sit on that sofa and eat your sandwich.'

'Can I go to the lavatory first, please?'

'You can, but I'll be watching out for you.'

Joseph nodded and followed her to the bathroom. Once inside he locked the door and glanced towards the window. At a push he could probably squeeze through it, but how far was it from the ground? He went and had a wee first and then washed his hands, leaving the tap running while he climbed on the bath, unlatched a window and pushed it open. He gazed out and realized he was too high up to risk climbing out and dropping down. At the very least he might break a leg, at the worst he could break his neck. He closed the window and listened and could hear the kettle whistling. It occurred to him that she would go to the kitchen to turn it off, so he left the bathroom. There was no sign of Bella, so he wasted no time creeping up the passage to the front door and nipping outside and running for his life along a corridor and downstairs.

Only to be caught at the building's entrance by his kidnapper, who seized him by the scruff of the neck and forced him back inside and upstairs to the apartment. Joseph was flung into a bedroom and, near to tears, he kicked the closed door, only to be told to stop that racket or he'd know about it. The boy went and lay on the bed and listened to the raised voices coming from the other side of the door. It was obvious to him that the man was tearing a strip off the woman for allowing him to escape. He heard her telling the man he was a fool and then came the sound of a slap and then silence. Joseph started to pray.

Tim wasted no time climbing in the van and checking his fuel before setting off to fetch Jerry, wondering what had caused him to cycle so far. Maybe he'd done it for a dare? One never knew what boys would take into their head to do if they got bored. Well, it was no use racking his brains, he would find out soon enough. Twenty minutes later, he drew up outside Mrs McGuire's shop and went inside. He was taken into a back room where he found Jerry sitting, eating broken biscuits from a tin and drinking a cup of water. The lad stood up almost straightaway and went over to Tim, whose arms immediately went round him. Jerry began to snuffle.

'Hey, there's no need to be upset,' said Tim. 'I'm here now and we can go home.'

Jerry threw back his head and gazed up at Tim through a mist of tears. 'I'm not upset for meself, Dad. It's Joseph. He's been kidnapped.'

'Kidnapped!' Tim's heart seemed to descend into his stomach. 'Tell me everything.'

Words poured out of Jerry so fast that Tim had difficulty making sense of what his son was saying. 'Slow down,' said Tim. 'Take your time and don't miss anything out. Have another drink of water first,' he added, handing the cup to Jerry.

The boy drank most of the water, waited a few moments and began to tell his story over again, ending with the words that he thought Joseph might have been mistaken for him. By the time he had finished, Tim had experienced a whole load of emotions, including admiration for his son's determination and bravery, as well as bewilderment and anxiety. If a member of the gang was behind the kidnap, this could mean he and Lucia might never be able to be together.

'You said you remember the licence-plate number?'

'Yes! It's one of the ways I managed to keep recognizing the car, because it was black like so many other cars but it helped that it also had a roof rack.'

'Good lad,' Tim hugged his son to him. 'Next move is to get in touch with Inspector Walker. He might have some ideas as to who might be responsible.' Tim was remembering that the ringleader of the gang could now be out of prison and be hell-bent on punishing Tim further by kidnapping his son, only to have mistaken his identity.

But it was no use thinking about that now; he was wasting valuable time. Lucia had been angry with him for what had happened to Michael. Tim guessed he would really be in her bad books if they didn't get Joseph back unharmed. He asked to use the telephone, handing over a half-crown to the shop-keeper to cover the cost of the calls he had made. She returned Jerry's thrupence to him.

Tim was in luck, being able to speak to Sam Walker straight-away, and he told him what had happened. He was glad to be able to give him the licence-plate number, as well as a descrip-tion of the car. Sam was able to confirm that the ringleader had been released from prison recently but, as far as they knew, he had not returned to his previous address as he had parted from his wife. Still, he would get a man on tracing the owner of the vehicle, although it could take some time and it was possible that it had been stolen. He would also put out a call for the bobbies on the beat in the area where Jerry had seen the car vanish to look out for it and report back if they had any luck.

For the moment Tim had to be satisfied that the police would do all that could be done to find Joseph. Although he did not have much hope of tracing the car himself, he decided to drive up to Scotland Road so Jerry could have a lookout to see if he could spot the vehicle. As they headed in that direction, he could hear Jerry praying under his breath and thought, *Why not?* They needed all the help they could get. They went up and down backstreets running off Great Howard Street and Commercial Road, and then across Scotland Road and up as far as Netherfield Road without spotting the vehicle, then, just when Tim was about to give up, Jerry spotted the car in the grounds of St Anthony's Church on Scotland Road. Tim parked the van in Newsham Street close by, and he and Jerry made their way swiftly to the church. Tim was convinced the car had been stolen and there was little hope of linking it to William Donahue.

Nevertheless, he and Jerry slipped inside the church, but Tim could see no sign of Donahue, so they went outside again where he and Jerry took up a position where they could watch the car. Tim thought how unusual it was to see a car in such good condition in this area.

Ten minutes later, he and Jerry saw a smartly dressed middle-aged woman approach the car, unlock it and climb into the driving seat. She sat there for a few minutes, having opened a compact and taken out a lipstick, she applied it. There was something about the way the woman performed that act that reminded Tim of someone, although he would have sworn he had never seen the woman before. But then it was some time since he had visited the area, and people he had known years ago would have changed, just as he had done. He decided to follow the car and see where it went. As it was, the chase took him all the way to an area of new housing close to West Derby village.

He could only think that the woman had once lived in St Anthony's parish but had since moved away. She must have returned to visit family or friends and her car had been *borrowed* for a short while without her knowledge. He decided to inform Inspector Walker immediately and, having remembered passing a telephone booth a short while ago, he drove back and phoned from there.

Sam was impressed with what Tim told him, and sent a constable to visit the woman. 'Leave this to us now, and go home, Tim,' he said. 'I'll keep you informed if we find out anything.'

'I'll be at Lucia's,' said Tim.

Fifteen

So, feeling dejected, father and son made their way to Lucia's. Tim felt even worse when he confronted her with his suspicion that Joseph had been mistaken for Jerry and abducted.

He watched with pity and guilt as her face crumpled, thinking her family was right and that she should never have got involved with a man like him, but when she appeared to be about to faint, he could not resist reaching out and putting his arms around her. 'There, there,' he murmured. 'All isn't lost,' and, as he told her what was being done to find Joseph, he felt her body start to relax.

She lifted her head and gazed up at him through tear-drenched eyelashes. 'He must be so frightened.'

'I doubt they'll hurt him,' said Tim. 'If Donahue is after a ransom, that would be stupid.'

'I bet he's heard about the book and thinks it's going to make a fortune and they want a share. You'll have the perfect ending for the book if Joseph is rescued, and you won't have to give the swine a penny in that case.' Lucia's head drooped against Tim's chest again. 'I wonder if Uncle Francis could help us? His parish is not far from St Anthony's and he knows a lot of the families in the area.'

Tim decided to mention this to Inspector Walker when he telephoned with news that evening. As it happened, the inspector sent his son Nick to call on Tim and Lucia. Apparently fingerprints had been discovered on the car door and steering wheel and elsewhere, which the car owner told them most likely belonged to her brother. Nevertheless, the police checked their files and found that they matched William Donahue's. When the police informed her that the car had been used in a kidnapping, she was furious, saying her brother had borrowed it while she was in church. She wasted no time providing them with an address on Everton Brow where he was most likely staying.

A few hours later, the tense and anxious Tim, Lucia, Jerry

and Theresa heard the doorbell ring. Rushing to get to the
front door first, they managed to block the kitchen door in
their haste. Eventually Tim held his son and Theresa back so
Lucia could get through and open the door.

Sam and Joseph stood on the step. Lucia swiftly drew her
brother into the house and hugged him fiercely. Then she
thanked Sam who had followed them inside.

Having reassured herself that Joseph appeared unharmed but
for a slightly swollen face, she asked him was he hungry. He
nodded and said, 'I've lots to tell you. Is Jerry here?'

She nodded. 'And his dad.'

'Good. Inspector Walker told me that Jerry saw me being
kidnapped and it was thanks to him and his dad that I was found
so quickly. I nearly managed to escape but the inspector said it
was best that I didn't.'

'Why is that?' asked Lucia.

'Because it was better my being found in the apartment with
that horrible man,' said Joseph. 'It meant he was caught red-
handed. The lady who was there was told she was an accessory
after the fact.' Joseph glanced up at Sam, as if he wanted reas-
surance that he had the words right, and received a nod.

Then Sam said, 'As it was, she told us she knew nothing
about it, and Joseph backed her up because he heard them
arguing. Donahue also hit her for allowing Joseph to almost
escape.'

'Her name is Bella,' said Joseph, 'and she was kind to me.'

'Well, all's well that ends well,' said Lucia, sitting next to Tim
on the sofa.

'I can't help feeling partly to blame,' said Theresa. 'If I'd kept
a closer eye on the boys it might not have happened.'

'You can't watch boys all the time,' said Sam. 'They have a
way of going off looking for an adventure in the normal way
of things.'

'I want to know what's to happen to Will Donahue,' growled
Tim.

'He'll be charged with kidnap,' said Sam. 'Which means a
long prison sentence if found guilty. It's not going to be too
difficult to prove he did kidnap Joseph, and had it in mind to
demand a ransom for his release, believing him to be Jerry. I'm

pretty sure that this woman, Bella, will turn Queen's evidence, as it will go easier for her, so hopefully the boys won't have to appear in court.'

Tim nodded, wondering aloud if the Bella in question could possibly be the journalist, Isabella.

Sam provided him with a positive answer. 'Yes, I recognized her from the times she asked questions for the *Echo* at police press conferences.'

'Her involvement with Donahue explains a lot,' Tim said in a tight voice.

'It proves what a devious woman she is,' Lucia could not resist saying.

'But how did she get to know Donahue?' asked Tim, glancing at Sam.

'She knows him from way back, found him attractive and exciting, then lost touch, but when he was arrested after the robbery, she went to the trial. She later visited him in prison and her youthful feelings for him were rekindled, apparently. When you reappeared on the scene, Tim, he told her that he wanted revenge. He came up with the idea that she approach you and find out what was behind you and Sid making a getaway. Apparently he had never quite trusted the cousin.'

By that time Joseph and Jerry were drooping with weariness, and Lucia went up to the bedroom with them.

'So what next, Tim?' asked Sam.

'I finish my book and take some time out to decide what steps to take to keep us all safe. My moving away obviously didn't solve the problem. Even though I didn't let Isabella know I'd moved. She must have been keeping Donahue informed of my movements until then. I remembered too late that I told her about my plans for the garage.'

'She used to go and visit Donahue in Walton jail monthly,' said Sam.

'Obviously she enjoyed flirting with danger,' said Tim, standing up and stretching. 'I'd better make a move.'

'You going back to Crosby?' asked Lucia.

'Not right now. My landlady wouldn't care to be disturbed at this hour. But you need to get some sleep. I thought I'd sleep in the van outside. Keep Fang company and my eye on this house and think things over.'

Lucia recalled the night after the car incident when he had slept under her roof, but she kept silent. Too much had happened that day for her to be thinking clearly about her feelings towards Tim.

The following morning Jerry and Joseph could be heard discussing their adventures of yesterday. As Lucia listened to them, she thought that – on the face of it – it seemed that they had come through the kidnapping unscathed, regarding it as a big adventure. Yet in the days that followed she came to realize that she was mistaken. They stuck to playing in the back garden, and during that time Joseph would often come inside to see where she was and Jerry would go out to the van that was still parked in front of Lucia's house. It had moved several times and she had thought Tim was returning to Crosby, but so far he kept coming back, as if he felt the need to keep his eye on the house, despite it being highly unlikely they would be bothered by Donahue and his gang ever again.

Deciding that both boys needed to be taken out of themselves, Tim made up his mind to ask for their assistance in renovating the van. He had already enlisted Marty and Michael's help in making the interior more comfortable. Now Tim wanted a completely new look outside, and for that purpose he had bought several tins of paint in a variety of colours and asked the boys to come up with a design that was bright and cheerful. They decided on a scene with animals and birds and lots of bright green grass and blue skies, so after removing a couple of side panels and putting in windows, Tim and the boys set to work painting the outside of the van. He talked to them and Lucia about going out on trips in the van. She welcomed the idea but was not overly keen to his face. After all, she had not been invited to see the interior of the van yet, although she had found pleasure in watching its outer transformation take place. Besides, he had said nothing more about them getting married.

As the leaves on the trees changed to russet, gold and red, floating to the ground and forming rustling carpets for hurrying feet, and the geese flew in from the Mersey estuary on their way to the bird sanctuary at Marten Mere, not only was the van finished to Tim's satisfaction, but Michael's eighteenth birthday approached and so did Donahue's day in court. He had already admitted his guilt, though, so it was only a matter of sentencing.

So that morning Tim knocked on Lucia's front door and asked if she would like to come and see what he had done to the inside of the van.

She accepted his helping hand to climb into the back via the rear doors where there was a space for baggage. She gasped in amazement when she saw the seating and how light the interior was. 'You and Marty and Michael did all this yourselves?'

'Yes, I thought we needed plenty of seating if we wanted to take the kids out before winter sets in, and if anyone else wanted to come as well.'

She stared at him, speechlessly.

His face fell. 'Don't you like the idea? Is it that you're still annoyed with me over what happened to you, Michael and Joseph and feel you can't trust me?'

'It's none of those things,' Lucia said. 'It's just that I'm amazed that you've gone to all this trouble.' She almost added *for me*, but he hadn't said anything anew that would cause her to believe that was the case. She guessed he was doing his best to make up for what had happened to Michael and Joseph and she liked him for that. But surely if he had anything intimate to say to her, then he would have suggested them having a day out, just the two of them, again? 'When did you have in mind to take the children out?' she asked.

He suggested that they check out the weather forecast before making a decision. Once this was done, they decided on the coming Saturday if she could get time off again. Tim suggested going to Thurstaston on the Wirral. 'It's years since I've been there but I remember having fun. There's a beach, but it's not the least bit like Seaforth or even Formby. There are sandstone cliffs where the boys can look for fossils, and there's plenty of grassy places and rocks and gorse bushes where they can play hide and seek and we can picnic.'

'It sounds great and I'm really looking forward to it and so will the boys,' Lucia said.

'But first I'd like to know that Will Donahue is going to be put away for a long time,' she added in a tight voice.

Nick came to give them the news that Donahue would be an old man by the time he came out of prison. Nick also handed Tim an envelope. After reading the contents he handed it to Lucia. She saw that the letter was typewritten and was from Isabella. Lucia soon realized it was an apology of sorts to Tim concerning the journalist's involvement in Donahue's scheme to bring down Tim. After reading it, Lucia handed the letter back to Tim. 'The things a woman will do for love,' she said.

It was on the tip of his tongue to tell her that there was a lot a man would do for the love of a good woman, but decided now was not the right time.

The day of the outing dawned and, although the sky was overcast and they moaned about the weather forecasters getting it wrong again, they decided to go out, knowing how disappointed the boys would be if they cancelled the trip. Fortunately, by the time they left the Mersey tunnel behind in Birkenhead, the clouds were starting to disperse and shafts of sunlight brightened the road ahead. Lucia glanced sidelong at Tim and thought he looked pleased and her happiness soared.

She began to sing the counting song, 'Ten Green Bottles'. Within minutes Tim and the boys had joined in, and following on from that she sang 'The Teddy Bear's Picnic'. It was Joseph and Jerry who piped up with 'We're off, we're off, we're off in a motor car.' Even Fang – curled up at the boys' feet – woofed.

Lucia shot Tim a questioning glance to see how he felt about this song, of which the following lines were: 'sixty coppers are after us and we don't know where we are'.

But he joined in, saying, 'I remember singing this when I was a kid and the mothers in the street collected money weekly so as to hire a charabanc to take us to Blackpool to see the illuminations.'

'Happy days,' said Lucia. 'I remember that as well. I don't think it happens as often these days.'

'Most likely because more people have their own transport, and maybe because a lot of those kids who are adults now aren't so keen on giving up their time and money to see the illuminations. They seemed magical to those of us who lived in houses lit by gas.'

'I've never thought of that being a reason for the magic,' Lucia said. 'Do you remember when electricity came to your old street?'

'Yeah, everybody was dead excited. I remember there was a cocky watchman who stayed in the street overnight keeping his eye on the trenches where the cables were laid and the like. He had a sort of tent and a brazier to keep him warm. Us kids loved that brazier; we'd go and warm ourselves by it when we were playing out in the dark.'

'I like it that we both have similar memories to share despite the age difference between us,' she said.

'Does the age gap still bother you?'

'It never has that much, except for knowing it bothered other people.'

'Then let's set it aside and make memories together that will bring a sparkle to your eyes,' said Tim.

She blushed, remembering that evening on the shore after visiting Nellie's. Unexpectedly Michael and Marjorie popped into her head. 'I wonder whether Marjorie will have a boy or a girl.'

'I doubt they'll care with it being their first.'

'I remember Dad saying "as long as it's healthy and you're all right, love", to Mam after each baby was born,' Lucia said.

'I think my dad preferred the girls to Marty and me.' There was a tension about Tim's mouth that caused Lucia to say, 'But your mam, I bet she loved the bones of you and Marty?'

'Oh yeah, I was her darling boy and Dad hated that. Thinking about it now, it wouldn't surprise me if that was the reason why he was so hard on me.'

'He was jealous of the attention your mother gave you?'

'I suppose there could have been that, but I was thinking more that he thought she was making a sissy out of me and he believed that to make a man of me he had to beat me to toughen me up.'

'That's ridiculous! He sounds a right bully, and you could have ended up like him – a child-beater.'

'He wasn't a child-beater altogether, though. I was the only one he hit.'

'How was your mam with your sisters?'

'She loved the girls; enjoyed going shopping with them and talking about clothes and cooking, as well as churchy things. Of course, she likes babies and is made up because our Lil, her husband and the baby still live with her. Lil hates me and thinks I'm a disgrace to the family. She told me so to my face.'

'So no sense of family loyalty then?' Lucia thought how his sister's actions must have really hurt him, because he had mentioned that to her several times.

'She blames me for Dad's death; said if I hadn't gone to the bad he wouldn't have died. She just won't accept that Dad fell in the canal because he was blind drunk. There was no way Dad would have committed suicide: he loved himself too much. Can we change the subject now?'

'That's fine with me.' Lucia gazed out of the window at the hedgerows.

'Where are we?'

Tim peered through the windscreen at the road ahead. 'I think we're near Irby, so we shouldn't be long now. I've never driven to Thurstaston before; it's on the opposite side of the Wirral from New Brighton, near the river Dee, below Hoylake and West Kirby.'

'I see,' said Lucia, although she didn't. Living in Seaforth in Lancashire meant that, unlike Tim, who had grown up in Liverpool, she had seldom crossed the Mersey on the ferry to visit places in the Wirral, but rather had been taken to Formby, Ainsdale or Southport and Ormskirk as a child. 'Have you been further afield locally in Lancashire?'

'Yeah! Us kids used to go on the tram on our own to the bluebell wood in Kirkby, and then if Mam couldn't afford the fare we'd walk to Stanley Park near Anfield football ground, or to the Pierhead to watch the boats coming and going.'

It was not until they arrived at Thurstaston that Lucia realized just how wide the Dee was at that point because the distant coast seemed miles away. She asked Tim if he knew how far away the Welsh coast was.

'About five miles, but the Dee gets narrower and narrower the further upstream you go. It's tidal, just like the Mersey. Chester was once a more important port than Liverpool, then the Dee silted up, most likely due to the monks – who lived in the abbey in Chester where the cathedral is now – building a weir. In fact the river used to come up as far as the walls of Chester Castle in medieval times, but now you can cross the Dee by bridge at several points in Chester. It was due to the Dee silting up that Liverpool grew as a port and King John gave it a charter, using the port to transfer troops to Ireland when necessary.'

'How do you know all this?' asked Lucia, impressed.

'Our Marty asked a bloke at Chester museum and I listened in. He told us about the Romans being at Chester too.'

'I didn't realize you were interested in history.'

'Only the local stuff. Liverpool used to have a castle, you know, just like Chester. Only Chester still has its castle.'

'I suppose if I'd given thought to it I'd have realized that Liverpool once had a castle because there's a Castle Street.' Lucia paused, and looked about her for the boys, but they had already disappeared. 'Where have the boys and Fang gone?' she asked.

'Down to the beach, no doubt,' said Tim. 'There's a path of sorts just over there,' he pointed. 'Come on,' he added, holding out a hand to Lucia. 'You'll want to check Joseph is all right and I want to show them how to look for fossils.'

Lucia said, 'I did ask Theresa if she wanted to come, but she said that she was going to Michael and Marjorie's, hoping to see Marjorie's cousin, Janice, there. They met at the wedding and hit it off but have seen little of each other since. She said she'd take Michael's cards and birthday presents with her. I'm glad she's gone as I think she's been a bit depressed lately.'

Tim said, 'I wondered if she had a pash on Chris but was hoping she didn't, because chatting with him I got the impression there was something between him and Nick's stepsister, Bobby.'

'She'll get over it,' said Lucia. 'It'll do her good to have a girlfriend to go around with, so I hope she and Janice do meet up today.'

Tim nodded as he led the way to the narrow footpath that went down to the beach. Lucia followed him and was glad to accept his hand to help her descend.

Jerry and Joseph had already removed shoes and socks and were paddling in the water. Lucia stood watching them for a few minutes and then she turned round to see what Tim was doing. He was chipping away at the cliff face with his penknife. As if sensing her eyes on him, he glanced over his shoulder at her. 'I'm looking for fossils,' he said in answer to her unspoken question.

'You'll need a bucket for if you find any,' she said.

'I'll go and fetch one,' he said.

He was off up the path between tussocks of grass and coconut-scented yellow flowering gorse before she had a chance to say, 'I'll go.' She thought back to how limited in mobility he'd been in the early days of their relationship, and was so pleased that he was so much improved. After they had stopped going to the baths regularly, he had taken Jerry and Joseph on several occasions when she was occupied with Babs. Maybe she should suggest them going dancing in the near future and see how he coped with that?

When he returned with the pail, she took it from him and clutched it to her while he continued chipping away at the cliff face. Within minutes he turned towards her and held out a fossil to her. She gazed at it and held out the bucket and he dropped the fossil into it. He called to the boys and they left the water and came running towards them. The fossil was shown off and Tim said, 'Do you two want to have a go at finding some more?'

There was a resounding 'yes' from the two boys.

Tim dug into his trouser pocket and produced a Swiss Army knife and gave that to Jerry. He handed the penknife to Joseph. Then he explained to them what to look for and what to do before gazing around for Lucia.

He raised a hand to his lips and blew a kiss when he saw her standing ankle deep in the water, facing towards the shore, and was gratified when she blew one back. As he walked down to the water's edge, he was singing beneath his breath a Lonnie Donegan hit of 1957 'Puttin' on the Style'. Although the King of Skiffle was no longer as popular as he had once been, he would always be one of the best musical performers as far as Tim was concerned. There was something about Lonnie's bouncy style that could always bring a smile to his face, and right now he felt like smiling. So what if he was going to have to wait a while before he felt in a position to ask Lucia to be his wife.

Today he had no doubt that that day would come to pass. At least they were doing things together, and God willing there would be many such days to come. He held out his hand to her and she took it and went willingly into his arms when he drew her closer. He kissed her lightly. 'Are you glad you came?' he asked.

'Of course!'

'I'm glad to hear it. So let's just enjoy these moments and try and forget the bad days,' Tim whispered against her ear. 'I love you.'

She felt her heart flip over and, looking into his blue eyes, said, 'What did you say?'

'Do you want me to shout it?' he asked.

'The boys will hear.' Her fingers curled on the front of the plaid shirt he was wearing.

'Does that matter, as long as you hear me for certain this time?'

'I did hear you, I just wanted to make sure I wasn't mistaken.'

'What did you think I said?'

'I'm too shy to repeat it.'

Tim gave her a teasing look. 'I don't believe you, but I'll say it again. I love you.' His voice was loud and joyous and the boys' heads turned in their direction.

'Look what you've done now,' Lucia said, blushing. 'And there's a family coming along the beach.'

The two boys came running towards them and Lucia made to free herself, but Tim gripped her hand tightly. Joseph held his hand out towards them, on which was a weird-looking creature and said, 'Look what we've found.'

'What is it?' asked Lucia.

Joseph said, 'A fossil, of course, which is an ancient creature's impression that was left after the creature was trapped in the cliff face and remains long after the creature has perished. I read about it in an *Observer* book,' he added.

'Good for you,' said Tim.

'I know they can be millions of years old. This is a trilobite,' Jerry said.

'Well done.' Tim grinned. 'I've a couple of brain-boxes here.' Both boys looked pleased with themselves.

'I'd like a go at finding one,' said Lucia. 'I've never had a go at anything like that.'

The four made their way to the cliff face, and now Tim and Lucia searched for a fossil. At first they had no luck at all, only discovering ordinary pebbles or stones and even shells stuck in the cliff face.

At the sight of Lucia's disappointed face, Tim said, 'It's possible that some shells might have been here for hundreds and hundreds of years.'

'But there's loads of shells,' said Lucia. 'How do you tell the ancient ones from the newer ones?'

Tim did not have an answer to that, and so they carried on looking for fossils until eventually their luck changed and Tim managed – with the blade of his penknife – to prise out a couple of decent fossils. Only one was a trilobite; the other was a fern. 'It's beautiful,' Joseph said of the latter. 'You have it, Lucia.'

Lucia accepted the fossil of the fern, which perhaps was not a fern but maybe some ancient form of seaweed, she thought. Then she suggested that it was time for their picnic. The boys raced up the footpath.

Tim exchanged glances with Lucia and said, 'We'll continue our conversation another time.' He led the way up the path, pulling her up behind him.

They found the boys delving into the bags containing the picnic. In no time at all the bags were emptied. Lucia flopped on to the blanket and Tim lowered himself next to her and held his face up to the sun, breathing deeply of the fresh air. 'This is the life,' he said.

The boys brought food over to Lucia and Tim. She had made sandwiches filled with eggs mashed in butter and milk, and she had bought some chocolate-coated marshmallows too. Tim's contribution was boiled ham sandwiches, tomatoes, and digestive biscuits covered on one side with Dairylea cheese spread; he had also brought bottles of cream soda and dandelion and burdock.

They tucked in. Once Lucia and Tim were replete, the couple lay back on a towel on the grass, having declared that it was the best picnic they had ever had. The sun was pleasantly warm and there was little breeze, so it was only Jerry and Joseph who were in the mood to be active. The adults were content to lounge and let their meal digest. Half an hour later, though, the sky started to cloud over and Tim said they should start making a move homewards.

When they arrived back home, Lucia found Theresa reading in her bedroom. The sisters asked about the other's day and both admitted to having had a great day out. Theresa said she would be seeing more of Janice and had arranged to meet her in town next Saturday. Joseph and Jerry were ready for bed, so needed no persuading to retire upstairs. Lucia made cocoa for herself and Tim; he said it had been a great day out and mused over where they should go next. They were sharing the sofa with but a few inches between them.

Lucia wished Tim would sit closer still and put his arm around her. Surely, after what he had said on the beach, he wasn't thinking she still held what had happened to her and her brothers against him? After all, his enemies were back in prison, so the danger from them had passed. Maybe he just needed some encouragement to make him realize that she was ready and willing for a kiss and a cuddle? She shifted towards him, closing the gap between them, aware that her heart was beating ten to the dozen.

Sixteen

For several minutes Tim made no move towards Lucia, so that she began to consider getting up and sitting in one of the armchairs. In fact she rose to her feet and took a step away from him.

Immediately Tim reached up and tugged the hem of her skirt. 'Hey, where do you think you're going?'

'I thought you might think I was crowding you,' she said in a breathy voice.

'Not at all.' He drew her down beside him and put his arm around her shoulders and, cupping her face with his free hand, he lowered his head and lightly brushed her lips with his own. A sigh escaped her and she slipped an arm about his waist before pressing her mouth against his and keeping it there. She had no idea how long the kiss lasted, but it seemed ages before they drew apart and breathed deeply. Then they kissed again and again and those kisses were all that she desired.

But where do we go from here? Lucia wondered. She felt his hand on her skirt and drew in a quivery breath, wondering if he was going to put his hand up her skirt and go further. Into her head popped Nellie's warning about men who used innocent girls to satisfy their sexual urges without committing themselves to marriage. She didn't want to believe Tim was like that; besides, if he was, surely he would have tried it on with her before now? She was just considering slapping his hand away when she felt him smoothing her skirts down and moving his hand to her waist. She was so relieved that she put her all into their next kiss.

He responded passionately and then he moved away and said, 'I think that's enough for now.'

'Don't you want me?' she asked in a whisper.

'Of course! But I'm not going to rush you into doing something you have no experience of – and besides, I'd rather we waited until we were married.'

'And when will that be?' she asked, her spirits soaring.

'Once I'm in a position to support you – and the children.'

'I don't expect you to support my brother and sister. I do receive family allowance that helps towards their keep, and besides which, I have my job at the coffee bar.'

'Maybe I'd better put things a different way and be perfectly honest with you, Lucia love. I have some savings which I'm living off right now, so I can support Jerry and myself for approximately a year. I need to earn regular money to carry on supporting myself, Jerry and you.'

'What about your book, won't that bring money in?'

'Yeah, in the short run, but it won't go on and on. It'll tail off after a while.'

'Can't you write another book?'

'Not an autobiography. I've only had one life,' said Tim earnestly.

'What about the articles you write?'

'They only bring in a few pounds.'

'What about garage work?'

'I don't believe anyone would employ me and I can't afford to set up in business again just yet.'

'I've run out of ideas,' Lucia said, looking downcast.

Tim gazed at her and felt not only helpless but a failure.

Then she said, 'If we married soon, you wouldn't have to pay rent because you'd be living here.'

'I understand that, but I still need to get a job. I'm not going to sponge off you – and besides, I'd want you to give up work.'

'That doesn't make sense. Why can't I go out to work and earn the money while you stay at home and be here for me and the kids? You can cook a bit and iron, use the washing machine, clean up and the like.'

'It's not man's work.'

'Rubbish! You've done some of those things since your wife died.'

'Only in a small way. It's no use, Lucia love. I won't marry you unless I can support you.'

She stared at him from brimming eyes. 'It's just your male pride that is preventing us from marrying.'

'No, it isn't. I've regained some self-respect and I want to hang on to it. Surely you can understand that, love?'

'You call me love – surely it's love that matters?'

'Love soon goes out of the window if there isn't enough money coming in,' Tim said.

'Ohhh! You make me so mad!' she said, getting up and pacing the room.

'Don't you think I'm frustrated, too,' said Tim, removing himself from the sofa. 'I'd better be going,' he added, reaching for his jacket on the back of a chair.

'If we were married, you wouldn't have to go.'

'Enough! Goodnight. I'll see you tomorrow.'

She felt like saying, *No, you won't. I'm going to see the estate agent about putting the house up for sale and move somewhere else and not tell you where I'm going. I'll get over you.* Only she knew that she *wouldn't and, besides, it would upset Joseph never to see Jerry again.* So she let Tim go without a word and would have slammed the door after him if it hadn't occurred to her that it would likely wake the children. She felt so angry that she wondered how she could have ever loved him in the first place. She was at a loss about what to do, but deep inside she knew that they were going to have to discuss their future again, and soon.

The following morning she decided she needed to put on her best bib and tucker to face him, so after washing the breakfast dishes, she removed her apron, hung it up on a nail in the kitchen, then she put on her best dress and some make-up and went and knocked at the door of the van.

After a few minutes, Tim showed his face, looking as if he had not slept. His flaxen hair was unruly, he had dark rings beneath his eyes and his shirt was unbuttoned. 'Yes,' he said shortly. 'What can I do for you, Lucia?'

'You've already told me that you can do nothing for me but I'd like you to rethink what we discussed last night,' she said.

'I've done nothing else but think most of the night.' He stifled a yawn. 'Anyway, you're looking good. Going to church, are you?'

She put a hand to her mouth. 'I'd forgotten about church. Thanks for reminding me. I'd better get cracking and be on my way before I'm late.' She stepped down and flounced away with a twirl of skirts.

'Say one for me while you're there,' he called.

'I'll say one for both of us. We can't go on the way we are,' she said. 'So near, yet so far away.'

'There's a song with those last words,' he said inconsequentially. 'I know how you feel and I'll carry on thinking of a way we can be together.'

She turned away as Tim said, 'I've just remembered that song. It's one of Billy Fury's.'

'I know, it's "Halfway to Paradise",' said Lucia, turning to face him again. 'We were that close.' She held her thumb and forefinger an inch apart and then wiped her eyes with her sleeve. 'See you around, Tim,' she said on a sob.

'Please don't cry, love,' he pleaded. 'I can't bear it.'

'Then do something. If I was really your love, you'd marry me.'

Tim stepped out of the van and went down on one knee. 'Please, Lucia, promise me that you'll give me three months and then do me the honour of marrying me? I just need some time to work things out.'

Her tears dried almost magically. 'I will! But don't you go letting me down.'

'Am I allowed a kiss?'

A kiss! she thought, *which might have to last her three months. Christmas!*

She went into his arms and held up her face to his. His mouth covered hers in a kiss filled with a passionate yearning; when it eventually tailed off, their lips clung before they eventually released each other.

An exchange of glances and then she walked away in the direction of Our Lady, Star of the Sea Church.

Tim drove off in the direction of Crosby, and it was not until Fang came and poked his head through the space between the two seats and yelped, that Tim remembered he had left Jerry behind. Then he recalled his son had his bike with him so would be able to cycle home when he was ready. There was an ache in the region of his heart, but he was convinced he was doing the right thing in waiting a while before marrying Lucia. He had let too many people down in the past by rushing into things and not thinking over matters. He wanted a marriage between Lucia and himself to be as good as possible. Unlike his first wife, Bernie, Lucia didn't place overwhelming importance

on money, and nor did she seem to realize what a strain a
shortage of funds could put on a relationship, which seemed
strange to Tim when he considered what a struggle she'd had
over the past year managing to support her brothers and sisters.
She seemed to believe that love could conquer all – and maybe
true love could. Of course she had received help from her aunts
so that was something. But Tim wasn't taking any chances. He
had to find a job – not easy with his track record – while at
the same time considering whether he could perhaps write a
novel.

And so it proved: when he tried to apply for vacancies at
various garages, he couldn't get a job. He even tried going
freelance, offering his services to friends and family and his new
neighbours in Crosby, at a price cheaper than those who had
proper garage facilities, but it soon proved to be a no-no. Not
enough money coming in, and there were jobs he just couldn't
do without garage facilities, as aside from having to buy parts.
Some jobs he passed on to Michael at the garage where he now
worked, which he and his boss were grateful for. It seemed
hopeless, and Tim was starting to think he'd never find suitable
work when Nellie's husband, Michelangelo, offered him a job
in his marble tiling business. Unfortunately, Tim didn't possess
the knack either to cut marble or to actually put up the tiling,
which had to be perfect for Michelangelo's wealthy customers.
He saw nothing of Lucia but sent her a letter, telling her that
he missed her and the children. He was seeing more of his
brother Marty, his sister Peggy, and her husband, Pete, who had
given up his job in a shipping office to train to be a teacher.
They were sympathetic, but could not help with his search for
employment.

'What about your book?' asked Peggy. 'Surely you'll make
some money from that?'

'Yeah, but one book isn't going to provide me with an income
for years.'

'When is it due out?' she asked.

'February.'

'I thought it would be out before then,' said Marty.

'Excerpts are going to be serialized in the *Liverpool Echo* before
then,' Tim said.

'Couldn't you carry on writing something else while looking for another job?' Pete asked.

'I am, but there's no guarantee a publisher will take it.'

'Ask advice from your publisher,' Pete suggested.

Tim was reluctant to do that, preferring the idea to come from the publisher.

'Why don't you ask Chris for advice?' asked Peggy.

'Now there's an idea,' Pete said.

'I haven't seen Chris for a while.' Tim stroked his chin and looked pensive.

'I'll mention to Bobby that you'd like a visit from Chris, shall I?' asked Marty. 'She often pops in to have a chat with Irene.'

'Thanks,' said Tim. 'I'd like that.'

In the days that followed, Jerry and Joseph continued to see each other. Jerry cycled to Seaforth to see Joseph twice a week, and Lucia's brother walked to Crosby's Regal cinema and met Jerry there so they could go to the children's matinee together on a Saturday. Afterwards they went to Tim's apartment, not far from the cinema, to have something to eat and to play some indoor games. Then Tim and Jerry saw Joseph on to the bus, Tim telling him to give his love to Lucia and all the family.

One Saturday midway through October was slightly different, in that Joseph told Tim that Mrs Hudson's new lodger, Jack Jones, was in the habit of talking to Lucia over the back garden fence after he'd finished work and Joseph had overheard him asking her to the cinema.

This information was enough to cause Tim's spirits to plummet. 'What did she say?' he asked.

'That she'd think about it,' Joseph replied.

Tim breathed easier, thinking that at least Lucia hadn't jumped at the invitation. But what if this Jack Jones was persistent and asked her again? She had not replied to Tim's latest letter; hadn't even given Joseph a note for him as she had done in the past. Maybe she was completely fed up with him. Even if she did not see this Jones character as a future husband, perhaps she would decide to go out with him. Tim did not like that idea at all and wondered what he should do about it. Tim was glad that he only had to wait a couple of days before Chris's visit.

He really wanted his advice about what he was writing at the moment.

Chris arrived on a wet and windy day that held a hint of winter. Tim opened the front door and invited the young man inside. He led him into a rear room that was somewhat larger than his sitting room at Mrs Hudson's. A coal fire burned in the modern tiled fireplace and the sash window overlooked a paved area with a lawn beyond, with an apple tree at the foot of the garden and a few straggly chrysanthemums in a flowerbed.

'Nice,' said Chris, noticing the desk with the typewriter and a stack of paper to the left of the machine and several sheets of carbon paper. 'What are you writing? I thought you'd finished your autobiography.'

'I have. Now I'm having a go at something else and I'm stuck. I'm hoping you might be able to help me. I need to earn enough from writing to support a wife and several children.'

'You need to write at least a novel a year, and for them to appeal to a large readership.'

'But what kind of novels?' Tim was aware of a rising excitement. Perhaps he could make a success of writing fiction.

'Write about what you know, but make the story take place in a world you create that appeals to you,' Chris said. 'I suggest you visit some of the bookshops, and also W. H. Smith's in town, and take a look at what's doing well. Talk to those behind the counter about books – and don't forget the libraries. Have a talk to the librarians about books. Crime, romance and Westerns tend to be popular.'

'That's true,' said Tim. 'Romances are mainly Mills & Boon. They used to have red dust jackets with a couple in a clinch on the front. I remember my sisters used to read them secretly, knowing Dad wouldn't approve.'

'And crime novels tend to be black with a dagger or gun on the front, and sometimes a silhouette of a man in a trilby looking threatening,' Chris said. 'Westerns usually have a cowboy on the front.'

Tim smiled. 'I've read a few of them.'

'But you wouldn't want to write one?'

'Of course not! All I know about cowboys is what I've seen on the flicks,' said Tim. 'I thought crime would probably be best as I know something about it, but I need to be on the side of law and order now and think like a detective.'

'Read, read, read, and see what kind of detective appeals to you. Patricia Highsmith is good. And Agatha Christie— she's been writing for years and is still as popular as ever.'

'I like her books. I like Edgar Wallace as well. Although his books are very different from hers.'

'Well, study plots and think about doing a series of books with the same detective, amateur or professional, involved in solving a crime or mystery. Christie's a writer who's written about what she knows. She was a pharmacist in a hospital during the First World War so knows about drugs and poisons. But there are also crime magazines such as *True Crime*, but I reckon that some of the cases they include are purely made up. You need several people with a motive for murder and you need to know all about them. You have to work out a few red herrings, and also you need to drop clues for the reader but keep enough back to keep them guessing. And no revealing the murderer's identity until almost the end.'

Tim was absorbing everything Chris was suggesting and feeling hopeful that with a good bit of research he could write a successful crime novel. He had already made a start and now he felt confident enough to be able to complete it. After all, he did know something about the subject. Why shouldn't his amateur 'tec be a reformed criminal who is assisted by his parish priest who visited him in prison?

'You seem to have gone off in a trance,' said Chris. 'So how did you finish your autobiography eventually?'

'With the kidnapping and Joseph being reunited with his family. Hopefully there'll be space for an Epilogue with Lucia and I getting married.'

'That sounds perfect,' said Chris. 'But not what Isabella had in mind.'

'No. Especially as she had been in cahoots with the kidnapper to bring me down. Although she had no knowledge of Donahue's plan to kidnap Jerry. But you've probably had all this from Nick.'

Chris hesitated. 'He swore me to secrecy. Apparently her name is being kept out of it. I believe it was she who persuaded Donahue to admit to his guilt.'

'I'll never understand her,' said Tim. 'Anyway, let's change the subject. I've heard that there's a new lodger next door to the Brookes family who appears to be taking an interest in Lucia. Have you caught sight of him?'

'Yes, and spoke to him. He seems an OK bloke. I come across Michael now and again and he told me that Theresa had mentioned him. She thinks him good looking and she told me that he's asked Lucia out and she's seriously thinking of accepting his invitation – apparently she's fed up of never going anywhere. Understandable! I can't understand why you decamped to this place if you love her.'

'It's *because* I love her. I want to marry her but I've nothing to offer her. I explained it all but she couldn't put herself in my shoes; she thought it acceptable for me to move in with her, jobless, and let her support me.' Tim stood up. 'I feel like a beer. What about you?'

Chris nodded. 'I am thirsty. Lucia's a much more modern person than you are,' he said, accepting a beer from Tim. 'The days of wives expecting to be kept by their man, staying home and doing all the household chores, have gone. The war gave them a taste for freedom and also their own earnings. They no longer have to go begging to their husbands for the money to buy a new frock, or even a set of new pans.'

'Of course, she shouldn't have to beg, but I want to be able to shower presents on her and share the responsibility and expense of bringing up the kids.'

'Theresa said that Lucia only wants to be first in someone's life and to share that life with them. She likes presents as much as the next person, but she's a sensible woman who has a realistic view on life. On the whole life hasn't been easy for her and her family; a lot was expected of them, so none of them expects the future to be a bed of roses.'

'But I don't want it to be a wilderness of weeds for her, either,' Tim said.

'Why don't you take her out in your snazzy van? Somewhere completely different. You're going to have to meet her halfway if you don't want to lose her.'

Seventeen

Tim gazed into the distance, thinking. In the past, seldom had faith or self-sacrifice played a part in his life, although it had been a sacrifice moving away and not seeing Lucia every day, enjoying their conversations and being close. But now he was going to have to sacrifice his own opinion of what was right for them, and have faith Lucia's way could work for them and that their love could be strengthened by them working together as a married couple. As he made his preparations to take Lucia out, he was glad that he'd had extra keys made for the front door and the apartment for Jerry in the eventuality that Tim was not at home. He had also had a word with his landlady. He thought how life had been less complicated when he'd had Lucia living next door. He wrote a note for Jerry and left it propped up against his typewriter before leaving. He sighed as he gazed at the sheet of paper in the machine, thinking he still had a fair way to go before the manuscript would be ready to send off for his editor's perusal, having decided to try it out with his present publisher. He called Fang and went out to the van, and by two thirty he was on his way to Seaforth.

To his relief, Lucia was delighted to see him. 'I've only been home from work a few minutes,' she said. 'To what do I owe this pleasure?'

'I couldn't stay away any longer. I wondered if you'd like to go out for a meal this evening so we can discuss our wedding?'

With her mouth half-open, she could only stare at him, and then she let out a whoop and did a little dance on the spot before saying, 'You are serious?'

'Don't I sound serious?' he asked.

'Yes, but the three months aren't up yet.'

'I know but, as I've just said, I couldn't stay away any longer.'

'Then I accept your proposal,' she said, throwing her arms around his neck.

They kissed. 'So where are you taking me?' she asked.

'A restaurant in town, not far from the Victoria monument. I remembered Pete mentioned going there when he was still working in the shipping office down by the docks.'

'OK. When have I got to be ready?'

'You've several hours, so plenty of time to dolly yourself up.'

'What about Jerry?'

'I left him a note. By the way, is it all right for me to leave Fang here? He's in the van at the moment.'

'Of course, but why don't you nip back to Crosby and bring Jerry here. He can stay with Joseph. I'll ask Theresa to stay in and look after them.'

'Fine, I'll do that.'

Tim wasted no time returning to Crosby and fetching his son, who was delighted to be going to Seaforth.

The evening was dry with a nip in the air when Tim and Lucia caught the train to Liverpool. Both of them were in a cheerful mood as they left Exchange Station and walked in the direction of Dale Street and the Mersey, only to turn left, well before they would have reached the river glistening beneath a setting sun. The restaurant was in North John Street and Tim had chosen it, not only because he had heard good reports of the food and the ambiance, but also because it had no memories of Maggie or Bernie. As they were shown to a table, he was aware of Lucia gazing about her. He thought how it was likely that most of the businessmen and workers from solicitors', insurance and shipping offices lunched here, unless they decided they needed fresh air and had brought sandwiches, and in that case they would walk down to the Pierhead to watch the ships coming and going.

'This is a bit classy,' Lucia whispered across the table to Tim.

'I hoped you'd like it. Pete recommended the food, so unless it's changed since his day, we should be in for a good meal.' He reached across the table and covered her hand with his. 'I've something important to discuss with you.'

'The date of our wedding?' she asked.

'We can discuss that after I say what I think needs saying,' Tim said.

'So you haven't changed your mind about us getting married then?'

'Of course not, but I've been wondering whether we should move away from the Liverpool area.'

'You don't think there could be someone else who has it in for you, do you?'

'I don't think so – but I want you and the kids safe.'

'I think you're worrying unnecessarily. Unless you think it possible that, when your book comes out, someone – other than the gang – who reads it might take offence?'

'The thought had occurred to me,' said Tim. 'If it wasn't too late to cancel, I might have withdrawn it, but I've spent most of the advance so I can't give it back. Besides which I'm hoping it'll be a lesson to any kids who think there's something glamorous about joining a gang and breaking the law. I want them to realize that crime really doesn't pay in the long run.'

'Then stay with it,' Lucia said. 'What I hate is the thought of you spending time with Isabella when the book is launched.'

'By then you and I should be married, so I'm hoping you'll be at my side at all the publicity events.'

Lucia gave a wriggle of pleasure. 'So, when will we get married?'

'I thought the beginning of December, so we can enjoy the run-up to Christmas as a married couple with the family.'

'Sounds good to me,' Lucia said.

'I'm glad. So how about if we order now and continue this conversation later?'

They reached for the menus the waiter had placed on the table in front of them and began to peruse the food on offer. Lucia chose a prawn cocktail for starters and Tim settled on the soup of the day, and for the main course both decided on medium-rare rib-eye steak, fried onions, French fries and seasonable vegetables. Dessert they decided to choose later.

Tim ordered a bottle of rosé and a pint of Guinness and having done that, they leaned back in their chairs and smiled at each other. 'I'll ask our Marty to be my best man. I was thinking that you'd probably want your Michael to give you away.'

Lucia agreed. 'I'll ask Theresa to be my chief bridesmaid. I doubt Joseph and Jerry will want to take part in the service.'

'They could help hand out service sheets. Would you mind asking Josie to be a bridesmaid? It would please Irene and Marty.'

'I'd be happy to do that. After all, she is your niece. Do you think Peggy will want her little girl to be a bridesmaid? It's just that I don't want there to be too many little ones for Theresa to have to keep her eye on.'

'Understandable, and besides, if you ask Peg's little one, you'd have to have our Lil's daughter as well. Too many!'

'I agree. Besides, we can't possibly afford that many bridesmaid frocks and posies. Although, if I could have our Gabrielle as a bridesmaid, I would. But I can't see her or James being at our wedding. Although it would be lovely if they could come over with Aunt Babs.'

'Do you think it'll be all right to have the reception at your house?' asked Tim.

'It'll save money on hiring a hall,' Lucia said. 'And it's not as if we're going to have loads of guests.'

'Mainly just family,' said Tim. 'Although, I'd like to invite Sam Walker and his wife, and Nick and Chris.'

'And Bobby . . . and I should invite Josh and Maggie – if you don't object?'

'Of course,' Tim said. 'And Monica – and what about Irene's brother, Jimmy, and his wife.'

'How many people is that now?' Lucia asked, beginning to count names on her fingers.

She was interrupted by the waiter bringing their starters.

As she began to eat her prawn cocktail, she said abruptly, 'You know who we've forgotten – your mother.'

'And we mustn't forget Mrs Hudson,' Tim said. 'And your aunt Nellie, Uncle Michelangelo—'

'And maybe Uncle Francis will help out at the service,' said Lucia.

'My head is starting to spin,' Tim said. 'Let's forget about the wedding for now and be quiet while we eat.'

Lucia agreed, thinking she was beginning to feel a bit dizzy herself. How she wished her father were alive to give her away.

By the time the crockery and cutlery from the first course had been removed and their main course placed in front of them, they were both feeling calmer.

'We need to book the church and have the banns read,' said Lucia.

'Our Lady, Star of the Sea?' asked Tim.

Lucia nodded. 'The first Saturday in December. We'd better speak to the priest when we go to church this week.'

Tim agreed.

'I hope Michael and Marjorie's baby doesn't decide to arrive too early,' Lucia said.

Shortly after, the dessert trolley arrived at their table. She stared at the various sweets on offer and finally chose the chocolate pudding with clotted cream. Tim decided to have sherry trifle and wasted no time digging in.

Tim finished first, but Lucia took her time, savouring every mouthful, thinking that it would be best to have a buffet meal for the wedding breakfast. She would ask Josh and Maggie to make her a couple of their special sherry trifles as well as a coffee and walnut cake. She mentioned this to Tim on their way out of the restaurant and he agreed that was an excellent idea.

'What about our honeymoon?' Lucia asked.

'Are you still of a mind to go to Llandudno?' said Tim.

'Yes, although the seaside in winter isn't the most appealing of places.'

'There are theatres and cinemas, so we'll be able to go and see some shows and films, and the scenery is lovely. We can walk in the hills away from the sea.'

'You've convinced me,' Lucia said.

'Then I'll book us a room.'

Having made several important decisions about their wedding, Tim and Lucia informed some of their nearest and dearest as soon as possible.

Theresa said, 'I'm glad you've made up your minds to go ahead and get married at last. But what are you going to say to Aunt Nellie?'

'I'll just remind her about what Aunt Babs told me about her and Uncle Michelangelo and her first husband.'

'I didn't know Aunt Nellie had been married before,' Theresa said. 'Tell me everything?'

So Lucia told her sister about their aunt having married a Proddie and having been cut off from her family, only returning to her grandfather's house after her mother was killed and sister

Lottie had been injured. She had then had to cope with the death of her soldier husband and miscarrying their baby. Fortunately she had met Michelangelo, but their relationship had been far from smooth because he was an escaped POW and could have been sent back to Italy if Francis had not got involved. Francis had informed the authorities that Michelangelo's mother had been English, and besides, by then he had officiated at Michelangelo's and Nellie's wedding, which meant Michelangelo could stay in England.

Theresa had been aware of some of this, because Tony was proud of his father risking entering Italy towards the end of the war in search of him and his mother after the Germans had invaded Italy. Tony had been placed in an orphanage after the death of his mother. 'Well, all I can say is, you stick to your guns if you want to marry Tim,' said Theresa.

When Lucia and Tim told his sister, Peggy, and her husband the news, she said, 'Let's hope it doesn't snow.' She gave Pete a dazzling smile.

'Of course, you two were married in December,' Lucia said.

'Yes, and it snowed a few days before the wedding and the roads were icy,' said Peggy.

'And we'd booked a week in the Lake District for our honeymoon,' recalled Pete. 'The weather forecasts put the wind up us with advising people not to travel.'

'As it was, everything worked out and the Lake District looked magical and we got there and back with little difficulty,' said Peggy.

'Well, I'm hoping nothing goes wrong for us,' Lucia said.

She was to wish that she had kept her mouth shut when, halfway through October, the newspapers were full of the news that the Russians planned to have a base on Cuba with nuclear weapons. Naturally the Americans objected and blockaded Cuba. Lucia feared that a Third World War was about to break out that would be even more devastating and destructive than the first two. It seemed that nobody could talk of anything other than the threat of nuclear war. Tim and Lucia discussed bringing the date of their wedding forward.

Then President Khrushchev and President Kennedy decided to talk, and an extremely tense situation relaxed as both countries stepped back from the brink and the whole world breathed the easier. Lucia and Tim continued with their wedding plans, extremely grateful for what they had. She stopped worrying about something else happening to prevent their wedding.

Even when Marjorie went into labour two weeks early, Lucia decided it should not affect her Big Day. Then the day after her nephew was born and all seemed well with mother and baby, Michael phoned to tell her that Marjorie's mother had had a minor heart attack, and naturally Marjorie was in a bit of a state. She and her mother had always been close and she had been depending on her help during the early weeks after the birth. Suddenly Lucia was waiting for something else to go wrong. Although she had always claimed not to be superstitious, she was remembering her mother saying things came in threes. With only a week to go to the wedding, Lucia was at a loss what to do. She and Tim cancelled a planned journey to see the comedian Ken Dodd switch on the Christmas lights in Liverpool city centre – the decorations were reputed to have cost just over five thousand pounds – in order to spend time with Marjorie, having accepted what her brother said about Marjorie needing help. For although the girl had recovered physically from the birth, she was suffering from what was called 'baby blues', and on top of that she naturally felt depressed over her mother's sudden heart attack. Of course Marjorie's aunt and cousin were willing to be of help, but neither was available during the daytime.

The next thing to happen was that Joseph came down with mumps. This complaint worried her more than if it had been chickenpox, or even measles again, because she was convinced that Jerry was bound to catch it, and that meant Tim was in danger of being infected. Lucia, Michael and Theresa had suffered from mumps as children, so she was not concerned for herself or them, but for an adult male to catch mumps was a serious matter. There was a danger that it could make a man sterile.

She wasted no time in visiting Tim and telling him this. She suggested that Jerry move in with Joseph, and then it was a matter of hoping for the best and that Tim did not catch it too. This also meant that Lucia was unable to give Marjorie a helping hand with the baby. It really seemed that she and Tim had no choice but to postpone the wedding. The first thing Tim did was to cancel the hotel in Llandudno, as they could see no way of them getting away, and the next act was to cancel the wedding. It almost broke Lucia's heart to do so, and she cried as she folded her wedding dress and placed it back in tissue paper in its box.

Then, three days before the wedding had been due to take place (it appeared that Tim had managed to avoid catching the mumps, despite Jerry and Joseph still having a slight appearance of hamsters with cheeks stuffed with food), Lucia had a visit from Nellie and Francis.

Lucia was pleased to see them, but one look from her aunt and uncle silenced her. She was told to leave off making cups of tea by Nellie, and to stay where she was, as Francis had something to say to her.

As her aunt left the room, Lucia gazed expectantly at her priestly uncle. 'Are you going to perform a miracle for me?' she asked.

'Not exactly! But I'm hoping what I'm planning will meet with yours and Tim's approval.'

'Should I go and phone Tim?' she asked, excited but not convinced that Francis could make everything right.

'No, you can tell him later. As I'm hoping he'll have something to tell you, too. My plan's not perfect but I'm hoping it'll do.'

Then Francis revealed his plan. Lucia and Tim's wedding would go ahead, but he would officiate and it would take place at his church near Scotland Road. Michelangelo would give Lucia away so Michael could stay with Marjorie and the baby. On top of that, Francis had hired one of his parishioners, who was a private nurse and who had also been a midwife in her younger days. She would be available to assist Marjorie with the baby and her mother. Nellie also suggested that the reception be held at her house, so that Lucia need not worry about anything but getting to the church on time.

Lucia jumped to her feet and kissed her uncle. 'I can't tell you how much this means to me,' she said.

'Nellie and I want you to have your wedding. You deserve it and so does Tim. He's really turned his life around and we admire him for that.'

She kissed him again and kissed her aunt as well. Then she drank her tea before excusing herself and going to phone Tim. Before she could say more than, 'Tim, is that you?'

He said, 'I'm leaving the apartment now and coming to see you.'

The phone went down at his end and she replaced the receiver and returned to her aunt and uncle. 'He's on his way,' she said brightly.

She did not have to wait long before seeing the van pull up at the kerb. Opening the door, she ran down the step to greet him. He did not climb out but told her to get in. As soon as she was seated, he drove off.

'Where are we going?' she asked.

'Formby, to see Maggie's sister-in-law, Emma.'

'Why?'

'I had a phone call from her and she asked could I take you to meet her.'

'What on earth for?' Lucia asked.

'She just said it would be to our advantage.'

'I suppose you know her through Maggie,' Lucia said.

'That's right.' He paused. 'So what have you got to tell me?'

Lucia proceeded to tell him what Francis had said, and watched with pleasure as his blue eyes widened in astonishment. 'It's incredible,' he said. 'It means a lot to me that Father Francis and the rest of your family and friends are prepared to help us get married on the day we planned.'

'Me, too. You don't think Emma is in on this as well, do you?'

'I can only think of one way she might be involved,' said Tim.

'Why do people have to be so secretive? I wish you'd told me over the phone about going to visit Emma. I'd have put on my best frock.'

'What's the point? We'll have a walk in the woods and on the beach later, so best you're not all dressed up,' he said.

She made no reply, wondering how he could be so dense. He just didn't seem to understand that she wanted to look her best when visiting Maggie's sister-in-law. Maggie had once been a model and dressed really stylishly, as well as being very pretty. Lucia had always felt drab in her company in the past. She could so easily imagine Emma comparing her to Maggie, and Lucia falling short.

Neither spoke for a while.

'What's the long face for?' Tim asked, glancing at her as they passed Formby Railway Station.

'I'm remembering how marvellous Maggie always used to look.'

'That was because it was her job to look like a fashion plate. It's no longer necessary, so she can wear what she likes and eat what she likes,' Tim said. 'She's happy now, isn't she?'

'I'm sure she is. Especially now there's a baby on the way. I sometimes wonder, though, if she has any regrets.'

'Why should you think that?'

'Well, when you think about it, she's gone down in the world, hasn't she? Once she had her face on the covers of magazines, and now she spends more time in the kitchen wearing an apron. But I suppose that at least she followed her dream for a while before giving it all up for love.'

'She didn't give it up for love but for her wellbeing,' Tim said. 'You should know that her health would have suffered if she had stayed in London chasing her dream. Love just came along at the right time in the shape of Josh.'

'But you went out with her first,' blurted out Lucia.

'Yeah, but I wasn't the right one for her, so fate stepped in, and I for one am glad it did. I'm sure Maggie is, too. Fame isn't everything, and Maggie has walked right back to happiness. It's what I want for us, Lucia,' he said. 'I might have some regrets but I've never regretted taking your advice and coming to look at the apartment next door to your house. Now, stop worrying, you look great. Unless you're regretting saying yes to my proposal of marriage, and wishing you were fancy-free to go off and do something that you've never told anyone about.'

'I've never been free to please just myself. I've always had to consider other people,' Lucia said. 'But I don't think I'm alone in that, and I just accept it's the way things are. I reckon it's better than having no one to care for or not being needed. A voice on the wireless is not enough to rid oneself of loneliness.'

'Point taken,' said Tim.

It was not long before he parked the car at the kerb in front of a detached house. The front door opened as Tim helped Lucia down from the van. Hand in hand they walked up the path to the house.

'How nice to see you again, Lucia,' said Emma. 'It's a while since we last met.'

Lucia agreed, remembering now waiting on the older woman at Josh and Maggie's engagement party.

'Come on in and have a coffee.' Emma stood aside and ushered the pair in.

They followed her into a large kitchen at the rear of the house, and sat at the kitchen table while Emma put the kettle on and spooned instant coffee into mugs. 'It won't be as good as what you serve at the coffee bar,' said Emma, 'but at least it will warm you up, and I can offer you a slice of homemade cake to go with it.' Emma produced a Victoria sponge cake.

'Lovely,' said Lucia.

Emma cut several slices and, placing them on plates, pushed two plates towards the couple. 'Now, I won't waste time getting to the point. I heard from Irene that Tim had to cancel your honeymoon hotel, and so I'd like to offer you my cottage in Whalley for a week, if you'd like to use it?'

Lucia had heard about the cottage from Maggie and Josh so she said, 'That would be lovely. It's very generous of you, isn't it, Tim?'

'Exceedingly so,' he replied, thinking the offer meant more to him than it did to Lucia, because it was a sign that not only had Irene forgiven him for his past failures by getting in touch with Emma, but also that Maggie's brother and sister-in-law had forgiven him as well for his past behaviour towards Maggie. He was touched by the kindness being shown to him and Lucia, and knew he would never forget it.

After they left Emma, Tim drove the van to the car park down by the beach, and he and Lucia walked hand in hand along the sand. There was no wind and all was still and silent, except for the lapping of waves on the beach and the occasional cry of an oystercatcher.

'This is lovely,' said Lucia.

He agreed, squeezing her gently about the waist. 'It'll be just as lovely at the cottage in Whalley because we won't have to go our separate ways at the end of the day or be disturbed by the kids. We'll have the cottage all to ourselves.'

'It'll be heavenly; just the two of us for a whole seven days before having to settle down to ordinary life.'

'Bliss,' Tim said. 'We'll have to make the most of our time alone together.'

'I can hardly believe we're going to be married at last.' Lucia sighed contentedly.

'Me neither. But if we'd have rushed in to it, I doubt we'd have had the families alongside us,' Tim said. 'So we did the right thing taking things slowly.'

The following week was far busier than they had expected, although it had little to do with their wedding. Christmas would be only a week away when they returned from their honeymoon, so they needed to do some shopping for the children, as well as to order food and drink in for the Christmas period. While in the city centre, they took the opportunity to go and see *Live Now, Pay Later*, starring Ian Hendry and John Gregson, at The Futurist cinema on Lime Street. They decided it was a film very much of its time, showing how life had changed from the austerity of post-war Britain to the consumerism of the late fifties. The Pathé News was interesting, covering among other items the engagement of Princess Alexandra to the Honourable Angus Ogilvy.

Tim and Lucia decided to leave buying a Christmas tree until their return, although Tim gave Theresa some money to buy balloons and the like to decorate downstairs. He also transferred the rest of his and Jerry's possessions to Lucia's house. The couple's only regret was that Joseph and Jerry could not attend the wedding because they had not completely recovered from the mumps, but then Francis arranged for the two boys to sit upstairs in the church out of the way, where they could watch the service without mingling with the other guests. Something they boasted about in the days to come, saying they'd had the best view of all of the ceremony.

Tim was not able to get on with his writing the way he would have liked, and was also concerned about the first three chapters and the synopsis of his crime novel, which he had posted to his existing publisher. He really needed to know if he had a fair chance of it being accepted if he was to support Lucia and the children in the future. But he waited in vain for a response during the days before the wedding. The weather was not what they would have wished for, either. But they reminded each other of the scare in October, when it appeared that the world had been on the brink of nuclear destruction. Tim and Lucia agreed that they could cope with ice, snow and a touch of fog in the circumstances.

When Tim rose on the morning of the wedding in Marty and Irene's home, he prayed that there wouldn't be any nasty surprises today, but that everything would go off smoothly. Then, to his surprise, his former landlady in Crosby phoned to say that what looked like an important letter had arrived in the post for him that morning. He decided to go and collect it. He restrained himself from opening it until he was alone in the van. It was the news he had been waiting for – the publisher had enjoyed what he had sent and would like to see the rest of the manuscript as soon as possible. He made several suggestions for Tim to bear in mind when he was working on the rest of the manuscript. There was also a wedding card, wishing him and Lucia every happiness. He decided to keep the news to himself until after the ceremony, wanting to hug it to himself for a short while.

'You're cutting things rather fine,' said Marty, emerging from the house as the van pulled up behind a shiny black wedding car. 'Was it worth the journey?'

'I'd say so, but I'll tell you later,' Tim said.

Marty said, 'Have you got everything you need?'

'I should be asking you that. You have got the rings?'

'Of course!' Marty patted his pocket. 'How times have changed. Once there was only one ring to worry about because men didn't wear wedding rings.'

'I think it's a change for the better,' murmured Tim, sliding into the back seat next to his brother. 'I wish Dad was here to see me getting married.'

Marty stared at him. 'You surprise me. You never had time for Dad.'

'That was because he never had time for me. He always

treated me like I was a disappointment to him, a failure. I'd have liked him to see me make good. He'd approve of Lucia.'

'Yes, and Irene,' said Marty. 'Say that about Dad to Mam. It'll give her pleasure.'

Their mother and sister Lil and her husband were going straight to the church, as it was close to where they lived, and so were Peggy and Pete.

Meanwhile, Lucia was being fussed over by Theresa and Nellie, and tears were near because they were wishing that members of the family who were absent could have been there. They thought about Lottie and David, as well as that branch of the family the other side of the Atlantic. A telegram had arrived from Babs and the children, which would be read out later by the best man.

Wiping away her tears, Lucia said, 'I suppose most weddings are a mixture of tears and smiles. I am happy, though.'

'Good for you,' said Michelangelo, offering Lucia his arm. 'Always look for the silver lining, and the pair of you will win through.'

Nellie nodded. 'Time me and the kids were going. The bridesmaids next. Then you two don't be late.'

'We won't,' said her husband.

Less than an hour later, Lucia and Michelangelo stood at the back of the church. Francis signalled to the organist, who launched into Purcell's 'Trumpet Tune in D', celebrating the entrance of the bride, with gusto. Lucia felt perfectly calm as she processed down the aisle, her hand resting lightly on her uncle's sleeve. She scarcely noticed those in the pews either side as her attention was on her future husband.

As she drew alongside Tim, he winked at her. She felt her smile widen and whispered, 'I love you.'

'I love you, too,' he mouthed. 'You look lovely.'

'So do you,' she responded.

'Dearly beloved . . .' began Francis.

Immediately he had their attention, and the wedding service proceeded. When he pronounced them husband and wife, a big cheer went up. Tim did not wait to be told he could kiss the bride, but took his wife in his arms and kissed her tenderly. Once on the way to Nellie's house, he told her about writing his crime novel, and the encouragement he had received from his publisher.

'What a clever husband I have,' said Lucia, kissing him.

'And what a lovely, kind, encouraging wife I have,' Tim responded. 'I just wish my father could have experienced this day with us.'

'I felt like my father was in church, and Mam too, smiling down on us,' said Lucia. 'And we have the honeymoon to look forward to, and after that Christmas.' She felt she might burst with happiness after the trials they had been through. If only the weather would improve, because she could not help feeling apprehensive about the journey up to the cottage, but did not want to say so to Tim.

The reception went off perfectly, with no disharmony at all. Nellie had prepared a wonderful buffet, which included Maggie and Josh's special sherry trifle, and coffee-and-walnut and chocolate cakes. Marty was the first to make a speech, pulling no punches about his brother and what a scamp he had been when younger, but how they had missed him when he had gone on the run, and been so relieved when he turned up again, and how Marty, in particular, had rejoiced when Tim had set his mind on turning over a new leaf. He praised his courage in saving a boy's life, which had resulted in Tim paying for his past sins and then being blessed by meeting Lucia.

Michelangelo's speech was heart-warming in his praise of his niece, saying that she had shown she was made of the right stuff, even as a child, when she had been her parents' little helper, willing to do any task they asked of her. In marrying Tim she had proved that she was up to any challenge presented to her, and he did not doubt that she and her new husband had an interesting and enjoyable life ahead of them, because they had both been through tough times and loved each other.

After the speech and the wedding cake – a surprise gift from Josh – had been cut, the tables and chairs were pushed back and Monica, Nick and Tony and the rest of the music group were there to entertain the wedding couple and their guests with old as well as new songs. Naturally there was some jazz for Tim and the romantic tunes of the fifties, as well as those in the new decade of the sixties, including Helen Shapiro's 'Walking Back to Happiness'.

Tim and Lucia had decided to leave at two o'clock, wanting to arrive at the cottage before dark. It was not only Nellie who voiced her concern about driving conditions as the newly married couple put on their outdoor clothes, but Marty as well, and then Theresa piped up with her worry, and when Lucia went into an upstairs bedroom to say her farewells to Joseph and Jerry, they clung to her and said they didn't want her and Tim to go. They were both remembering the car skidding on the icy road earlier in the year, and Joseph was thinking about the car crash in which his parents had died. She told them to stop worrying and decided she had to speak to Tim about the boys' fears.

Tim was waiting outside on the landing, looking tense. He raised a questioning eyebrow as she came out of the bedroom. She said, 'I've been thinking—'

'So have I – little as I like to suggest it, I think we should postpone our honeymoon.'

'I'm so glad you said that,' Lucia said. 'I didn't want it to be me saying it, in case you thought I didn't trust your driving.'

Tim took her hand and touched her shiny new wedding ring. 'I'm not completely stupid. As much as I was looking forward to us getting away on our own, I was aware that it was risky, us making the journey to Whalley. We have responsibilities, and if anything were to happen to us, it would upset the boys and be a great inconvenience to our relatives.'

'So, what are we going to do? I was hoping it would be just me and you alone tonight?' Lucia said.

'I've been thinking about it, and suggest asking Nellie if the children could stay here tonight and you and I will go back home and stay there.'

'Just the two of us,' she said, snuggling in to him.

'Yeah, just the two of us,' he reiterated, kissing the top of her head.

Eighteen

A few hours later, Lucia and Tim set out on foot for home, having discovered that, even if they had not already changed their mind about going to Whalley, they would have had no choice but to do so. Freezing conditions as the evening drew on meant they couldn't even get into the van, as the keyhole was frozen.

They huddled together as they walked carefully along the pavement in the direction of Seaforth, making just a couple of stops on the way. By the time they reached the house they were cold right through. Fortunately they had no trouble opening the front door, so all that was needed was to put a lighted match to the fire after clearing away the cinders and ashes and building a new pile of newspaper, wood and coal.

They both knelt in front of the fire, holding their hands out to it. Then Lucia stood up and went and put the kettle on the stove and collected some cutlery and plates. She returned to the fireplace and looked down at Tim. 'Do you know what I want?'

'Tell me?' he said.

'A bath. The back boiler should soon heat the water up but, just to speed it up, I'll switch the immersion heater on as well.'

He gazed up at her with a quizzical expression. 'You wouldn't rather go to bed? I don't know about you but I'm freezing after the walk, and we'll soon get warm in bed.'

'Humour me,' she said. 'Bed can wait. You'll soon warm up if you stay in front of the fire while I'm making us a hot drink. After all, it's not nine o'clock yet. It would be a good idea to put a couple of hot-water bottles in the bed. You could do that while I have my bath. Then we'll have food and go to bed.'

'All right, if that's really what you want,' he said, not moving. 'If you could get the hotties out.'

She felt a rush of love for him, pleased that he had fallen in with her wishes. She had bought a chicken from the cooked meat shop, so she only had to cook vegetables and make gravy.

For pudding she had some of the trifle in a small bowl. She prepared the vegetables and put them in water in pans, and also took the hotties from a cupboard. As the kettle was boiling she made a pot of tea, and then filled the kettle again and put it on for the hotties.

She told Tim what she had done and, after drinking a cup of tea, she said that she was going upstairs to run her bath. The water was hot enough for her so Lucia added bubble bath and wasted no time undressing and lowering herself into the scented, foaming bathwater after automatically locking the door. She freed a sigh of pleasure, thinking this was the life. No kids around wanting something from her which would entail her having to cut short her soak in the bath.

A few minutes later there came a rap of knuckles on the door and Tim's voice floated through, asking could he come in. For a moment, a flustered Lucia could not think what to say and then, remembering he was now her husband, realized he was entitled to come and talk to her while she was in the bath. There was no need for her to feel embarrassed by his seeing her naked as the bubbles covered most of her body. Besides, they would be sharing a bed later, so she called to him to come in.

'I can't, the door is locked,' he said. 'You'll have to unlock it.'

'That means I'll have to get out of the bath and I've only just got in. I'll catch cold.'

'It's not going to kill you to get out, is it? You can get back in again. It's me that's getting cold out here. Now open the door, please?'

She swore beneath her breath. This was not how she had imagined her wedding night. She remembered her dreams of marrying a rich man who would take all her cares from her shoulders. In those dreams, she had never thought much about what she would have to give up in return for such a life.

She thought about hurrying from the bath to the door and back in her bare skin. He would see her in her birthday suit and she would not look her best. She thought about the pretty pink and cream nightdress still packed in the suitcase in the van. She had planned to be wearing it when he came to bed; had pictured him staring at her and telling her how lovely she looked, before he climbed into bed, kissed her, and switched off the bedside lamp. Then they would snuggle up and that was as far as her imagination had gone. Nothing was going to plan.

She climbed out of the bath and scuttled over to the door. 'Now, promise you'll keep your eyes closed until I tell you to open them?' she said, drawing the small bolt.

'You are joking?' said Tim, gazing down at her.

She stared at him, wondering, why was he clad only in a towel, and that slung about his hips? She let out a shriek and turned and headed for the bath. She felt his arms go round her slippery body and he lifted her up before lowering her into the hot water. *Bliss!* she thought, before becoming aware he was climbing in the bath as well.

'What are you doing?' she asked, only catching a brief glimpse of him as he disposed of the towel.

'Having a bath? You don't mind sharing, do you?'

'I don't know. I haven't shared a bath since I was a toddler.'

She felt his foot rub against her thigh. 'D-don't crowd me,' she stammered.

'Crowd you? There's only the two of us. I used to dream of us sharing a bath together. I thought it would be heaven. This is married life, love. Sharing experiences.'

Lucia thought about how different men and women were and she remembered her past dreams, which quickly faded now she was faced with the reality of being married to a real man.

'Us two alone together,' said Tim, reaching out a hand to her. 'When I was growing up in a house with no bathroom, and having a bath entailed filling a tin bath with kettles of hot water, the thought of being in a bathroom where the hot water came from a tap was one of my dreams, so when I fell in love with you, I thought having the two together would be real happiness.'

She took his hand. 'I never had to fill a tin bath with kettles, but I do love a good soak, so I can understand where you're coming from. Mind you, I've always had to cut it short because of the kids. So, can we come to an agreement? We can, every now and again, share a bath, but I also want the bath to myself at times.'

'Sure! Shall we shake on it?' They shook hands and kissed.

'The trouble with having five beings under one roof is that there's little room for intimacy and privacy between us.'

'So what's your plan?'

'That we make space for ourselves by having time away at least every other month, if we can. It would be great if one day we could afford to buy a cottage in the country, or by the sea.'

Lucia said, 'How about buying a caravan in Wales that we could escape to?'

'That sounds like a great plan.' And Tim started singing, 'Walking Back to Happiness'.

Lucia threw a sponge at him. 'You never told me that you sang in the bath.'

'Well, now you know, am I banned?'

She looked as if she was giving that some thought before saying, 'No! I've always enjoyed a good singsong. Besides, this is our honeymoon and that means lots of loving.' She scooped up a handful of soapsuds and threw them at him.